# Zara

# Zara

## Melvin Sterne

INK
BRUSH
PRESS

This is a work of fiction set in real places, though the
characters—except for Zara—are entirely drawn from
imagination; otherwise any resemblance to people living or
dead is purely coincidental.

ISBN: 978-0-9835968-4-4
Library of Congress Control Number: 2011932619

Cover Design: Michael Sanchez
Manufactured in the United States of America

Ink Brush Press
Dallas and Singapore

# ACKNOWLEDGMENTS

I'd like to thank Jerry Craven, who is not only the director of Ink Brush Press, my publisher, but is also editor-in-chief of the magazine *Amarillo Bay*, and the first editor (outside of a student literary magazine) to ever publish my fiction ("The Couch," in 2001). I am eternally grateful for his support.

There are also a number of teachers and professionals who encouraged me along the way. These include: Marilyn Smith, Steven Quig, David Bosworth, Dick Dunn, Pam Houston, Daniel Lazar (of WriteHouse), Clarence Major, Robert Olen Butler, Julianna Baggott, Mark Winegardner, Dan Vitkus, and Deborah Coxwell-Teague.

I also owe several friends a debt of gratitude for their support, especially my friends in Bombay. These include: Bapsy Jain, Madhur Shroff, Jaideep Varma, Murzban Shroff, Sean Mahoney, and Saket Gokhale. I'd also like to thank the good folks at Café Basilica (in Colaba, Bombay) where I wrote most of Zara, and Zara herself (wherever she may be).

And last, but far from least, I want to thank my father, who instilled in me a love of writing by telling me not to do it—the surest way of getting me to do anything.

## Other Fiction from Ink Brush Press

Laurie Champion, editor, *Texas Told'em: Gambling Stories,* with an introduction by Doyle Brunson

Terry Dalrymple, *Fishing for Trouble*

Andrew Geyer, *Siren Songs from the Heart of Austin*

Andrew Geyer, *Dixie Fish*

H. Palmar Hall, *Into the Thicket*

Greenfield Jones, *Don't Lose This, It's My Only Copy*

Dave Kuhne, *The Road to Roma*

Myra McLarey, *The Last Will and Testament of Rosetta Sugars Tramble*

Jim Sanderson, *Faded Love*

Jim Sanderson, *Dolph's Team*

# For Zara

She lives.

# Chapter 1

An old black-and-yellow Fiat cab rattled to the curb in front of the Café Raj. The café was closed and dark, the front windows and door steel-shuttered and padlocked. The *peons* who worked there were sleeping in the entry alcove on piles of newspapers. The cab door creaked open and Paul climbed out. He spoke sharply to the driver before handing him a bill. Zara stepped out behind him. Paul and the driver argued in broken English. The time of night. The fare. Rides cost more after midnight. Paul checked his watch and grumbled. The peons stirred and woke, watched in sleepy disinterest.

Zara looked up and down the street, took in the scent of charcoal and tandoori permanently smudged into the air around the restaurant, saw the flickering of a candle in the overhanging window of a building across the street where an insomniac schoolgirl studied her lessons late, watched a furtive pair of dope peddlers or thieves lurking in the shadows behind a bus stand across the street. A block away, a boisterous knot of men crossed the road and disappeared into the gap between two buildings seeking an illegal country liquor bar, or a brothel, or a gambling house. The ghost of their laughter lingered in the air. A motorcycle zipped gears in the distance, fizzing and fuzzing up the steep bridge over the railroad tracks at the Grant Road flyover. The air was hot, wet and heavy. The monsoon was building. The intuition that it was too quiet flashed across Zara's consciousness, but her mind was whirling and the thought faded. Paul—she called him *English*—was leaving in the morning, and she was distracted, her heart suspended somewhere between sorrow and fear.

Paul took Zara by the hand and she fell into step beside him. They turned down an alley lit by a single watery yellow light. Some hundred steps in, Krishna the pimp appeared from the shadows, eyed Paul and Zara, nodded, and melted away. They stopped in front of a dark doorway. Paul took Zara in his arms, leaned her against the wall, and they kissed, a long, lingering embrace; hands knotting and binding, pulling one body to the other. Between kisses they whispered. When they parted Paul pressed a small parcel into Zara's hands. "A gift," he said. They kissed once more, quickly, on the lips. Then Paul turned and hurried down the alley.

Zara called after him, "I love you," but the words caught in her throat and came out hoarse, more like, "I leave you."

Paul turned and hesitated under the light. For the past six months their conversations had been double-edged with hope and misunderstanding—his paltry Hindi, her broken English. They locked eyes. He smiled, waved, and disappeared around the corner. A car door clicked open and chunked shut, an engine clawed to life, and the cab pulled away, drive shaft creaking, a brief flash of headlights stabbing the night.

And so it ends, Zara thought. But even as she considered this, she was filled with the certainty that endings and beginnings were not so clearly defined. When one door closed, another opened. Who could say what tomorrow might bring? Six months ago English walked into her life and now he had climbed into a cab and driven out of it. She raised a hand to the empty place where he had been and said, *"Inshalla."* If God wills. Perhaps they would meet again. There came no reply, only the river-like murmuring of the city; nonsense syllables, ten-thousand distant sounds blurring together. Bombay, she thought, an endless flood of people. She thought of her home—no small town, but she calls it her village. A trickle, a spring, a fresh, mountain stream compared to Bombay. Bombay, she thought, a swamp into which all rivers flow. A sewer. A sink. A trap.

Zara sighed, felt the parcel in her hands. A metal band wrapped in smooth, brown paper tied with a bit of coarse string. A gold bracelet? The parcel was the right size and weight. She would know in the morning when she unwrapped it. Until then she would savor it, sleep with it in her hand and anticipate. English would not leave her a parting gift of imitation jewelry. Not his way, she thought. But then again, you never know. Men. And jewelers—they call plated-brass gold and sell junk to fools, and the world is full of fools. They will never run out of fools. She traced the bracelet through the paper with her fingernail. I should have been with him when he bought it, she thought. No doubt it would look fine in the morning. Her friends will crowd around her and coo and try it on, tease Zara about her boyfriend.

A rat scurried in the heap of trash mounded in the alley and set off a cascade of rolling bottles. She started, the hackles on her neck raised. She looked up and down the alley, then turned and climbed the steps to her house.

The stairwell was unlighted, the steps worn, the building 200 years old, maybe more, and the miters and joints and grooves of the carpentry, once precise and tight, were now loose and dry and age-cracked and broken. She walked slowly. Three flights up, she paused at the landing and touched a door of iron bars. Behind the door and to her left was a short hallway leading to a room lit by the flickering blue glow of a television on without sound. She rattled the door gently and in a moment Malika, the house *maataa*, appeared with a small flashlight in one hand and a polished bamboo *lathee* stick in the other.

Malika was dark and mountainous fat, round-faced with bulging eyes that almost popped from their sockets. She unlocked the door. "Zara," she said. It was neither a question nor a greeting. A statement of fact.

Zara nodded, said, "Eh," and stepped inside.

"He's gone?"

"*Ap*," Zara said. Yes. Malika shut the door and they passed through the hall into the main room. A dozen women slept on the floor. Malika lay down on a wooden bench under an alcove sheltering a stone statue of Ganesh garlanded with wilted yellow carnations. The sleeping girls on the floor were shapeless lumps under their wraps. Only two were awake: Montaj and Gita, sitting close by the TV, holding hands. They turned as one, looked back, mouthed a silent "Hello." Zara nodded in return.

Zara opened a small drawer and, fumbling in the dark, removed a loose cotton nightgown. She stripped and pulled on the nightgown, slipped English's gift into her pocket, then folded her clothes indifferently and shut the drawer with her bare foot.

She looked back, saw Malika, sleepy-eyed, watching her.

They argue often about getting involved with customers. When they do, Malika always says, "It never works. They promise you the moon, and next week they promise someone younger and prettier the stars."

Malika was so fat and tough that it was hard for Zara to imagine her with a lover. Perhaps once, years ago. Now, Zara thought, Malika was envious, the bitter jealousy of a woman disappointed in love.

"He wants to marry me," Zara replies.

Malika laughs when Zara says this, a gaping, gluttonous, vulgar laugh.

"He loves me," Zara insists, and adds, with little less conviction, "and I love him."

"Right," Malika says. "You'll see."

The rest of the girls tease Zara like school children, "Your boyfriend called. How's your *boyfriend* today? When are you going to America with him?" Zara blushes and pushes them away. She is not the only girl with a lover on the side—some of the girls have two or three. But she is the only one with a foreigner, and that affords her a certain level of status.

Zara saw Malika watching, thought, She's nothing but an ugly old Nepali whore, and if she weren't so big and fat and bossy she would have been thrown out onto the streets years ago. What would she know about boyfriends? But then again, she thought, what do any of us know? Worse, in the back of her mind she worried, What if Malika was right?

English asked Zara to come with him. She could go but what would she do? How could she live among the *phorens*? Above all, she wonders, Can I trust him? Her mother married and her father was no good. One of her sisters married, and her husband was no good either. A drunkard. What would English be like, really?

Malika says you can trust nothing but the money in your mattress. "Life," she says, "is simple. Trust no one and you won't be disappointed."

But everyone trusts something. You make *pujas* to your Gods, offer them garlands and incense and pray that they bless you. You pay *hafta* —protection—to the cops and the gangsters, trusting that they will leave you alone, even though you know they won't. You trust the manufacturers of condoms to ward off diseases, and doctors when the condoms fail. You trust the pharmacists who dispense the pills the doctors prescribe, and the crooked corporations who invent and distribute the medications, and the crooks who counterfeit them. You trust the men who climb on top of you that they won't beat you or strangle you, and you trust that when they do, the pimps will stop them.

Even Malika trusts. She reads the horoscope every day in the *Express of India*. She knows the birthdays of all the girls and keeps a running commentary on their fortunes: what to hope for, what to avoid. This last morning Malika shook her head and told Zara that in the coming week she would have to make an important decision regarding her future—that the week would be calamitous. Your intuition is going to be tested, it read. Take your problems one at a time. Put off an important decision until you have gathered all of the facts. Confusion can be your enemy or your friend. It all depends on your point-of-view.

English says you can forget about fortune tellers—the *fakirs*—even the fancy-mouthed ones spouting big words in the newspapers. They prey on stupid peoples' superstitions. Once, when they were traveling together, English paid a swami to tell her fortune. Zara was not supposed to take trips with customers, so the whole thing was on the sly. They were killing time in Goa, waiting for a bus to Bombay. It was early evening. A bony man with mottled brown and white skin wearing nothing but a dirty orange loin cloth and an orange turban materialized out of the crowd like a carp floating to the surface of a pond. His beard was long and gray, braided into forks and strung with dull red and blue stone beads. His eyes were unnaturally glassy, almost entirely black, save a blood-red ring around the outer rim. *A hashishan*, Zara thought.

The *fakir* beckoned English to sit on a rock bench while he squatted on the ground in front of him. He traced the lines on English's right hand and smiled. "You have made a lot of money," he said. The *fakir*'s twisted mouth missed half its teeth. He stroked his beard lightly with his left hand. "But you have not yet found what you wanted. This up and down in the fate line. You seek peace, but it eludes you." He beamed at English, tapping the middle of English's palm. "You will make your peace, but first you will become like me, a holy man. You will wander. You will dwell—" he seemed to puzzle over his words, "you will live on the street."

English shrugged, his face impassive. He told Zara once, "I hold my cards close." She knew what it meant to hold something close. People held her close all the time. She asked, "What cards?" He explained that cards are a game. You don't let people know what you are thinking. This made sense. We all keep secrets.

The *fakir* pointed at the marks on English's hand, "Your heart line is strong, you have a powerful need for love, but it begins here, between the index and middle fingers." He sighed. "You give your heart away too easily. This will fix." The *fakir* took from around his neck a worn silver charm about the size of a ten paisa coin and handed it to English. The charm was hung on a thin black thread. English held the charm to the light—on one side it bore an image of Kali the Destroyer, on the other, Ganesh. He hung the charm around his neck and handed the *fakir* a 100 rupee note.

Zara rolled her eyes. When English gestured that the *fakir* should read her fortune, too, she tried to pull away, and only sat down under squabbling protest. The way foreigners throw money around, she thought. The *fakir* gazed at her hand while chanting a prayer in a faint sing-song voice, his lips barely moving. "Your head line begins here, under the index finger," he said. "This means you are very bright. And it is flat. You are practical, but not flexible. All business." He frowned. "But this, your fate line, which starts here," and he indicated a point on her wrist, "this means that your path was fixed long ago, another lifetime, perhaps, some old *karma* still to work out?" He searched her face. "Or maybe in this life, when you were a child. You would change your fate, but are you able?" He looked at her palm, transfixed, so still he did not seem to breathe. "And your heart line," he said. He shook his head and traced the line beneath her middle finger. He clicked his tongue.

"What?"

"Here it ends."

Zara leaned forward and frowned. "What you mean, 'It ends?'"

"It means—" he tapped her palm slowly. "Do you see, here? It means that the way is—" His eyes glazed over. "Uncertain."

Zara jerked her hand away so quickly that the *fakir* fell back on the ground. She jumped to her feet.

On his back the *fakir* pleaded, "For a few rupees I can purchase herbs. You can offer them at the temple."

English threw the *fakir* another hundred rupee note and he and Zara hurried away.

Behind them the *fakir* called, "There is still time!"

An hour later Zara and English were on the bus to Bombay, the farmland rolling past—houses clustered around stone wells, goats and chickens, dogs and cows and bullocks, and people in bright clothes, all drawn on a tapestry of rich green hills. Zara stared out the window, then down at her palm. The *fakir* had smudged it with red dye like dried blood. She wiped it on the seat, but the stain remained.

Zara crossed the room, stepped carefully over the sleeping girls, and passed through a long hallway to the back of the building. To the left and right were doors to rooms just big enough for a bed and a bucket of water. The girls were not allowed to sleep in these beds unless a customer paid. At the end of the hall was the kitchen and, just before it, another small stairway leading up and to the right. Abishek the cook slept on the floor, blocking the entry to the kitchen. The two houseboys, Rahim and Ravi, who cleaned and ran errands, were curled up together on the floor beyond him. A mouse scurried across the counter. Farther back in the dark room, something else stirred. A rat, perhaps, or a snake. It made a scraping sound in the dark.

Zara turned and climbed the narrow steps, crouching because the doorway at the top was low. Inside the room she stretched. She should have been sleepy, but the premonition she ignored outside returned. Who knew what triggered it? The face of a stranger lingering in the alley? A snippet of conversation overheard? Heightened awareness was born of many difficulties and much pain. In a game one cannot win, the best thing one can hope for is to put off losing. She crossed the room to the window and studied the alley below. It was dark and still. To the west, lit by faint starlight, floated the endless rooftops of Bombay; and beyond them, the deep cleft where the railroad tracks cut through the city; then the dark canyon of Nana Chowk, the market; and the spires of Al Noorani Mosque where the *muzzenin* would, in a few hours, shrill his high, sweet song, calling the faithful to dawn prayer. And beyond the roofs of the old city rose the glass-and- concrete towers of Malabar Hill, where Bombay's rich and famous lived. English stayed there.

Zara followed the lights of the scattered cars winding their way up the hill and wondered which of them was the cab carrying him to his apartment. Three times she had been inside that gleaming tower—*she*, a poor girl from a two-room stone hut with a clay-tile roof and a packed dirt floor; a girl who was in her teens and menstruating before she wore her first pair of shoes, walking a floor of polished marble and making love on a featherbed. How strange, she thought. She took the package from her pocket, tore off the paper, felt the cool weight of gold in her hand. She pressed the bracelet to her forehead, then to her lips and heart before she slipped it over her right wrist. She traced the engraved pattern with her left index finger and wondered how it would look in the light.

English told her a few things about America. He had a house and a cat. He showed her pictures. The cat was black with green eyes, the house small and white. Not a slum *chawl*, not a flat, but a cottage. There were trees and a grassy yard. "It is quiet," he said. He had no servants. He washed and cleaned and cooked and took care of the house by himself. I could help him, she thought. I can leave.

But to what? She did not speak much English and did not know American ways. They drove on the wrong side of the road. They used plastic cards instead of money. And in the back of her mind, there was always the question: What if? She has trusted men before. They have always let her down. Why should she believe he would be any different?

# Chapter 2

It was late Monday afternoon and the *peon* had just brought Inspector Godbodle his tea. The inspector shoved aside a stack of papers and rested his chin on his hands, stared at the tea while he waited for it to cool. The papers were routine stuff: duty rosters; equipment requisitions; mileage reports; a couple of commendations; a single, mild rebuke of a subordinate; a report about the increasing incidents of pick-pocketing in the markets; a gang targeting bank and jewelry couriers. Annoying, but the kind of thing that Godbodle was, for a Bombay cop, good at. It wasn't hard to stay on top of those things. File your reports. Tell your superiors what they want to hear. Keep the wolves, so to speak, from their doors. Do this and you could be optimistic about moving up the old ladder, perhaps all the way to the High Commissioner's office. That was how it worked. I scratch your back, you scratch my back—the man with most back-scratchers wins.

Like most Bombay cops, Godbodle was a Marathi; dark, compact, and stocky. He wore his hair close-cropped and sported a thick, black moustache that was the most prominent feature on his large, square face. But in some important ways Godbodle was not the typical Bombay cop. He was not fat with the paunch that was the source of so many cop jokes. He was proud of his workout routine, and lectured his charges weekly about the necessity of keeping fit. He lifted weights three times a week, and three times a week ran the length of the Worli Seaface and back. He even had a crash course in judo, the result of an impression made on him during a two-week exchange with the Baltimore police department, in the USA. The average Indian miscreant might be scrawny and thin, but there were plenty of Indians who didn't fit that mold—Punjabis and Bengalis—and there were foreigners, too, especially the Nigerians, the dope peddlers. Ordinarily foreigners didn't concern Godbodle, but from time to time they did, and when they did, he was confident he could take them, and that was, to Godbodle, a good thing. The affairs of the day had turned into one of those unusual times. Godbodle looked at his watch: 4:00 PM. In a couple of hours he would change into his civvies, drive to the gym, and work out his anxiety on a weight machine. It wouldn't make the problem go away, but it would give him time to consider his options.

It started with a group of prostitutes walking into the station demanding to file a First Information Report about cheating on the part of some employer or other. Not routine, but not earth-shattering, either. His men had handled the situation just like they'd been taught. They refused to take the report, thrashed one of the girls to frighten the rest, and chased them out of the station. That should have ended things, but it didn't. Two days later, one of the girls came back and demanded to see him personally. He'd refused to meet her, of course, and then the phone calls started. To one of them they attached a picture. Of him. Naked. God damn them, he thought, a picture. Not that he gave a goat's turd what pictures they took, but in a professional sense, it was not the kind of thing you wanted floating around the station.

It wasn't the threat that fazed Godbodle, but the brazenness with which it was made. Who was this damned girl who dared blackmail a police inspector? He didn't care if she went to his wife. Godbodle had had his share of women, and he would have more. Once he'd even gotten a disease from some girl or another, but he'd gone to the doctor in time —thank God—before he'd passed it on at home. The doctor had warned him about AIDS, and advised him to use condoms. After that, he'd resolved to be more careful, but he hadn't slowed down. He had a nice flat in Bandra and three kids in school, and a girlfriend (his wife knew about) in a studio in Gomdavi. Let the whore call. If his wife didn't like it she could pack up and move back to her village. She was getting fat and quarrelsome anyway.

The threat wasn't the point—the girl was less than a mosquito to him. But when a person had the audacity to challenge the system—that was what bothered him. Such a person might bear minding. What was it they called them in Baltimore—loose cannons? So he took her call, met the girl, was surprised to find that he knew her, remembered fucking her on this very desk a year earlier. A pretty girl from somewhere in the south. Andra Pradesh, maybe? And not a bad fuck. Nice tits. Nice ass. A little on the dark side, but not bad. Just another country whore in the city. Or was she? He sipped his tea and nibbled on a biscuit.

Her complaint was simple. The girls had done some sewing on the side. When the woman who was supposed to buy their goods found out who they were—or, rather—*what* they were, she had refused to pay them. And could blame her? Would you want to wear clothes sewn by whores? The girl wanted the inspector to pay the woman a visit. All they wanted, she said, was their wages.

9

The story differed from what his men reported. From what they said, there were some whores who were complaining about their wages—not something the police would want to muddle with unless there was the chance to pick up a stray bribe. But if the house was so poor that they couldn't pay the girls, the likelihood of picking up significant *hafta* was bleak. It seemed the kind of problem that you treated like a blister. Leave it alone and it went away on its own—mess with it, and it got infected. But it hadn't gone away.

It would have been easy to fix. Godbodle could have visited the shop and told the woman to pay up. It was on a main road. Hell, he passed it at least three times a week. But he hesitated. Who knew who the shop owner knew? If she had money to piss away on one of those little artsy specialty shops, she might have connections. She could be the cousin of a cousin of a cousin who had married into some big-shot's family. She was a business-woman, the kind of person he was supposed to protect. As for the whore— "Forget it," he told her. "You'll never get your money."

And then the High Commissioner called. "I don't know what's going on in your district," he said, "but there's a girl trying to blackmail some local politicians, something about their wages not being paid. Take care of this *today*. Bring me the phone with the photos. I don't want to hear about this again."

"I have no idea what you're talking about," Godbodle said.

"Yes, you do," the commissioner replied. "She mentioned you by *name*. She's talked to your men. She's been in your office. She can describe the pictures on your desk. She said she can describe the birthmark on your ass in court if needed. There's a cell phone," he said. "I want it. You know which one I mean. If I'm not mistaken, there are pictures of you in it, too. If you find the one with the birth mark, I'd like to see that."

That afternoon Godbodle returned to the brothel and collected the offending telephone. He didn't even have to beat the girl, though he could have. Perhaps, in retrospect, he should have. He walked in and she looked up like she'd been expecting him. He said, "Give me the phone," and she did. She didn't even ask why—just took the phone out of her purse and handed it to him. That should have been the end of it. He called the High Commissioner, said he had the phone, and the commissioner told him to bring it in as soon as possible. He didn't say, "Now" or "Right away," but, "As soon as possible." That meant, to Godbodle, whenever. With the phone in his pocket, the problem was solved. And at five minutes to four, just after the *peon* inquired if Godbodle wanted his tea, the phone on Godbodle's desk rang, and when he answered a voice said, "Drive to the tidal bridge in Worli. Park your car there and walk east, along the south bank of the slough. Be there in a half-hour. Come alone."

Godbodle was caught off guard. Maybe it was just that the call came at the time of day when his attention wandered. Or maybe it was all the other distractions eating at him. "Who is this?" he asked—the dumbest of questions, he knew—as if the man would actually give his name. The voice laughed in response. Godbodle checked caller ID. It was a land-line, probably a public pay phone. Out of habit, he wrote the number down.

"You don't expect me to answer that, do you?" the voice said.

"I guess not. But tell me, why should I come?"

"Trust me. We have a common problem, and a common solution."

"I have no problems," Godbodle said.

"There is a cell phone, and a small problem concerning photographs and the women who take them, and politics, and money. A great deal of money, perhaps. If you come, you'll stand in good graces with some very important people. If you don't, you'll be in the High Commissioner's office first thing in the morning and you can kiss your cushy job goodbye." The man hung up.

The *peon* came in with the tea and Godbodle pushed away the papers on his desk and rested his head in his hands. He checked his watch, sipped his tea, and called Rane, his most trusted sub-inspector. "I need you to go to Gomdavi right now. Take one man with you, someone you can trust in a fight. If you can change out of your uniform, do it. The less conspicuous, the better. Hurry. Park below the bridge over the tidal slough and walk west, one of you on the south side, one on the north. I'll be coming up the south bank from the west. Keep your distance and say nothing if you see me. You are there to back me up if I need you."

The inspector finished his tea, took a 9mm semi-automatic from the top drawer in his desk, inspected the clip, chambered a shell, checked that the safety was off, and replaced the revolver in his holster with the 9mm. Then he hesitated, put the revolver back in his holster and tucked the 9mm into his belt behind his back. Trust, my ass, he thought.

At 4:10 he left the Girgaon Police Station. At 4:25 Godbodle was parked at the south end of the bridge. He checked the revolver and left the snap of the holster unfastened, re-checked the 9mm and double-checked that the safety was off. He headed east along the south bank.

The water was still—it was mid-tide, and until the tide went out again the slough was little more than a stagnant sewer. The banks were filthy with trash: paper, bottles, plastic bags, human excrement; whatever could be thrown or flushed or dumped or blown by the wind. Godbodle had walked no more than fifty meters when he met a one-eyed ragpicker in a red shirt and with a red rag wrapped around his head. He was scratching the ears of a mangy white dog. The ragpicker pointed back towards the bridge. "Go that way," he said.

The inspector ignored him. Lunatics who talked to themselves were a dime a dozen in Bombay. But the man stood up and shouted, "Go that way, he's waiting there." He pointed back towards the bridge.

"Who's waiting?" Godbodle asked.

The old man shrugged his shoulders. "I don't know," he said. "He told me to tell you he's waiting by the sea, on the other side of the bridge. He is waiting."

Godbodle slapped the man and the man fell down. The dog slunk out of kicking range and turned to watch. The old man lay on his back in the garbage with his hands protecting his face. "I don't know, *Sahib*, he paid me to tell you."

"Who paid you?"

"He said to tell you, 'That way.' He is waiting."

The inspector spat at the ragpicker. He looked west. The bridge was wide and the opening underneath, where the slough flowed, formed a long culvert maybe five meters high and forty meters long. It was dark under the bridge, but the light from the other side was bright, and Godbodle could see the silhouette of a man standing at the far end. The man waved. Godbodle headed for the bridge. Behind him, the dog barked.

Godbodle paused at the opening. It was paved underneath but flood waters had eroded the concrete and left piles of gravelly debris. The footing was treacherous. The man on the far side was smoking a cigarette. He turned his back to Godbodle. Godbodle paused and loosened the revolver in his belt. He stepped into the darkness.

Three meters into the culvert a man with a steel bar stepped from behind a pillar and swung at his knees, dropping Godbodle to the concrete, screaming. The second blow found Godbodle's right shoulder and cracked the collarbone and patella. Godbodle dropped the revolver. The third blow broke ribs, driving one into Godbodle's left lung. The fourth blow crushed the back of Godbodle's head. It caved like a melon. Godbodle lay still.

The man at the far end of the culvert hurried away.

The figure under the bridge worked quickly. He secured Godbodle's hands behind his back with handcuffs and draped a loop of manila rope around Godbodle's neck. He took a small length of bamboo from his back pocket, slipped it into the loop, and twisted. In a moment, the rope had cinched the skin to cutting. Godbodle's windpipe was crushed, his legs and arms twitched. When he lay still, the man took the service revolver and the cell phone from Godbodle's belt, searching the body with his hands in the dark. He hesitated when he found the 9mm, but took it too, tucking it into his own belt. He emptied Godbodle's pants pockets and took his keys, and a roll of bills from the front pocket, his wallet from the back. He took Godbodle's shoes. When he was finished, he wrestled the body to the edge of the water and shoved it, face-down, into the slough, where it began to turn in slow circles. The man stood for a minute, watching the body, then exited the culvert from the west side, crossing the bridge and heading north along the beach.

A few minutes later Rane appeared on the north bank, with the other cop on the south. They were dressed in jeans and tee-shirts, walking slowly from the east. The cop on the south bank paused and eyed the rag-picker. "Have you seen a police inspector?" he asked.

The ragpicker shook his head.

The cops climbed to the roadway and met in the center of the bridge. "What now?" the cop asked. Rane shrugged. They crossed the road and looked out over the Arabian Sea, but seeing nothing of interest, they re-crossed the bridge. They found Godbodle's jeep and felt the engine. It was already cool. Fearing that somehow they had missed him on their first sweep, they doubled back along the slough. The ragpicker and his dog were gone.

# Chapter 3

Zara wondered how many insomniac nights she had climbed the stairs to this room and looked through the window, watching the lights of the city wink and dim as the morning light grew stronger. It was the only window in the house from which she could see anything but the walls and windows of the buildings across the alley. Somewhere on Malabar Hill she knew English was undressing to sleep. Funny, she thought, how doors open and close at the wrong times. That was what made choosing so difficult.

Against the wall was a narrow bed with a lumpy mattress stained grey with dirt and sweat and blood. Zara remembered the first time she came into this room and lay on that bed. The girls call it the 'room of blood' because it is the place they go to rest when they are menstruating and cannot service customers. But there was a more sinister connotation, too; one that everyone knew and nobody said. This is also the room to which the gangsters bring new girls to be broken. That's what they call it: *broken*. Trained to perform. Three or four times a year they come, chasing out the old, the ugly, or the sick, and replacing them with the young and pretty girls the customers want.

Zara arrived two years ago. Like most of the girls, she had been promised a job in the city. She arrived on a train, hopeful and frightened, riding into Bombay with three other girls and the agent who arranged her employment. By the time she reached the little alley, she knew something was wrong, but what could she do? There were four men waiting. They dragged her upstairs where she was beaten, stripped, tied to the bed, raped, sodomized, and made to do things so vile she would never tell another soul. They took Polaroids. "For your friends and family back home," they said, waving the pictures in her face. When they finished, they left her, naked and bleeding, locked in the little room. In the dark Zara prayed for death. The next day the men returned. And the day after that. And the day after that. And they brought customers who wanted the new girls; men whose pleasure fed on the forcing, the humiliation. They paid extra for that.

At first Zara fought. She bit and scratched and screamed. She begged the customers to tell someone, anyone, to send help. They all fight, she knew that now. She has seen it a half-dozen times since. She planned her escape, listening to sounds in the night, testing the bars over the windows, watching for a momentary slip: an unlocked door, an unguarded phone. She decided to play for time and escape. She would outlast them. After that, when the door opened and the pimps walked into the room, she lay down on the bed and spread her legs, waited for them to climb on top of her.

When they finished they smiled, pinched her cheek, and said, "There now, that wasn't so bad, was it?" They brought her food and clothes and a bit of makeup, and she ate and washed and dressed and went downstairs. The girls welcomed her with the love that only the damned know and have for one another.

The first chance Zara got, she took a knife from the kitchen and gouged deep slashes across her left wrist. The cuts were ugly and painful, but not deep enough. The gangsters carried her to a doctor who stitched her up. He would not meet Zara's eyes, he ignored her pleas. Only when he was done did he glance, momentarily, at her face. "Next time," he said, tracing a line with his finger down her arm, do it like this; lengthwise, not crosswise."

When they brought Zara back to the brothel, the bosses wrote down the cost of the doctor in the ledger where they kept track of her debt. An attractive, able-bodied girl, Zara would learn, sold for 20,000 rupees. About 500 US dollars. And she had to pay it back, every last *paisa*. And then there was the room again, and the beatings, and the fucking, and it went on for thirty days. In the end she learned that you cannot outlast them, and you cannot escape. If it is your fate to be a king, then you will be a king. And if your fate is to be a prostitute, you will be a prostitute. It was that or die.

When Zara surrendered, something changed. She did what she was told without question. The worst part—what shamed her and sickened her—was that after a while she wanted to please the pimps. It was involuntary. Her old beliefs—her former life—meant nothing. The body learned on its own that serving the gangsters meant an end to the beatings. She could eat and drink and wash. She could come downstairs and talk with the other girls, watch TV between customers. There is life even in the most inhospitable desert, on high mountains, in the depths of the sea. There is also life, of a kind, after the death of the spirit. The body does what it has to do for its own sake. When the instinct for self-preservation takes over, the spirit is but a hitchhiker, along for the ride.

Zara's days grew easier when she abandoned the struggle, but that ease came with a price. In her heart, in the place where hope and love and everything good and human grew, there was only emptiness. Which came first—the surrender or the hollow feeling—she could not say. At night, sleeping on the floor in the tangle of bodies, or staring out the window in the little upstairs room, Zara would try to remember a time when she was not saturated with the smell of strange men. She would try to remember what it was like to have dreams. Sometimes in the first year, she tried to piece together the events and make sense of it all. After a while, she stopped. Neither the questions nor the answers would change reality. Days passed, the hours marked by meals and men and conversations with the girls. Where are you from? Do you have family? Weeks melted into months which, in turn, folded into seasons. When one door closes, another opens. You arrive in hell, but at least you make new friends. And then something stirred in that hollow place.

# Chapter 4

The first call came while Anantharaman was meeting with a group of aggrieved transit workers in a grimy, pink-walled conference room of the Communist Party of India's Kerala Central Office. He ignored it. The second came ten minutes later, and the third five minutes after that. The calls were from Bombay, a number that didn't stir a blade in the pasture of Anantharaman's memory. Some party flunky trying to make an impression, he thought, or some irate citizen trying to raise a fuss. After the first call, he set his phone to mute. The transit workers he was meeting with were a real problem. They carried a lot of weight in Indian politics, and their complaint was legitimate—they weren't being paid for overtime and double-shifting. But the RTA—the Railroad Transit Authority—had a valid point, too, and they'd been hard-nosing the negotiations. The employees were creating their own difficulties by habitually showing up late for work. And this was true. If your *chai-wala* showed up late, you missed your tea. If the engineer showed up late, the train didn't run, and five or ten thousand irate commuters were late for work, and the shit, as they say, hit the fan.

To combat the problem, the Authority instituted a "no layover" policy, meaning that workers couldn't leave their shift until their replacement arrived. On paper it was a reasonable strategy. It kept manpower staffed at the essential level at all times, and the trains running as on-time as possible, given the state of India's rail system. But rather than having the intended effect—that peer-pressure would coerce workers into arriving on time—it did just the opposite. Workers knew that if they were a few minutes late, the trains would run without them. No big deal. Somebody else got a little overtime. So what? The whole thing would have amounted to nothing more than an employee circle jerk had it not been for the accounting department. The change threw them into a tailspin. Railway workers were paid by the run—by the kilometer, to be precise—and the mixing-up of shifts played havoc with the payroll. The accountants relied on knowing who was on what crew, and paid according to schedule. When the schedules went off, the payroll went out the window. And in typical business fashion, the cheapest and easiest solution (for the railroads) was that the routes in question weren't being paid at all; neither to the scheduled worker, nor to his or her replacement.

Anantharaman had already met with the Railway Ministry and heard their side of the story. That was a meeting in which he was truly in his element. Picture him: six-foot five inches tall; broad-shouldered and thickly muscled; his head shaved and waxed; a fat, black, down-turned moustache, the tips sweeping past his jaw-line; a heavy, silver hammer--and-sickle earring dangling from his left ear; wearing a rough, red, worker's shirt over a red cotton *lungee*; flanked on either side by a phalanx of party staffers, two of whom carried tridents. He was, literally, a giant in the party—a powerful man; well-liked, beloved of the faithful, feared by his enemies. That is how he looked in the photograph, too.

The picture made all the papers, even the rabidly anti-communist *Express of India*. And that, of course, was the point. In the end, the reading public would not remember the town of Cochin, or the Southern Railway Office that failed to pay its workers, or the threatened strike, or even if a satisfactory arrangement was negotiated and the strike averted. What the public would remember was the image of Anantharaman: Defender of the Worker. And when the elections rolled around, a picture was worth ten thousand words; especially in a country where 80% of the population was functionally illiterate.

The meeting with the railway officials did not take place in the outer lobby, where a specially-selected mob of party workers 'spontaneously' jostled with police and set some furniture and papers ablaze while journalists and photographers crowded around, strobes flashing through a smoky haze. The real meeting happened in a carpeted, well-appointed lounge upstairs where, over gin-and-lime coolers, a fat minister in a white suit pushed an envelope across the table. Anantharaman slipped the envelope into the inside pocket of his rough, red shirt. Every month of delay was money in the bank for the beleaguered railway, or—more likely—for some railway official; and timing was everything in the world of politics. They would come to a solution. In the mean time, even the Defender of the Worker had a bungalow to keep, tuitions to pay for his children, and a wife who liked diamonds.

Then, at the meeting with the transit workers, Anantharaman's phone began to vibrate, and a much less-flattering picture arrived via SMS. How did they get a picture? he wondered. In it, Anantharaman was staggering down a hallway, his arms draped around two very attractive young women, both naked, his hands filled with their large, firm breasts. He remembered the night. He'd been to a CPI convention in Bombay. After dinner he went

18

for drinks with friends. And after that, there was a friendly cab driver asking if he wanted a woman. There was an alley, a stairway, a room full of girls. So many to choose from. There were brothels in the south, too, but they were frowned upon, and not nearly as accessible as in the north. And in Bombay, there was less risk of his being caught. Girlfriends were okay, though a man in his position had to be discrete. That was one of the downsides of being a Communist: you were somehow expected to have higher standards. So he'd taken two girls to a back room, made them do things to each other while he watched—things he'd heard about, but had never seen—and then he'd fucked them both. He remembered the delicious feeling of pure *sex*haustion, like one felt after a spirited match of field hockey, only between his legs. And then his time was up and he was dancing down the hallway on shaky pins, not drunk, just well-fucked, flanked by the girls, and if there was a flash, he hadn't paid it any mind. The picture was bacchanalian. The message was blunt: *Call me.*

Anantharaman blanched at what he saw, then swallowed hard and gritted his teeth. Whoever did this would find out that he, also, meant business. He had friends—lots of friends—and some of them not very nice. You don't climb the ladder of labor politics by playing soft. "Excuse me," he told the railway workers, forcing a smile. "I have to make a quick call. Family, you know. I'll be right back." In his office he poured a glass of whiskey and walked to the window. He drained the drink, clinched his fists, and rapped the knuckles of his right hand against the concrete until they were red and pulpy. When he felt focused, he took out his phone and hit reply. To his surprise, a woman answered, her voice raspy and deep. "Hello," she said. Nothing dramatic, shady, or gangstery. Just, "hello." It was the voice, he thought, of a happy idiot; someone without a care in the world, or the brains to know that they ought to have care in the world.

Anantharaman paused. He was prepared to deal with a hardened criminal. He had envisioned a secret rendezvous, an exchange of money, and then an act of exacting vengeance. His mind worked quickly: a few broken limbs, a photo or two. "Like pictures?" he would ask. And then his *goombas* would finish them off. A bullet? Too quick. A knife? Too easy. Drowning? Too risky. Strangling? Perhaps. Yes, strangling would do. There was something on the order of poetic justice to silence by killing, and to kill by silencing. But the voice on the phone threw him off. It sounded like his little sister, not some hardened criminal. For a moment he lost his concentration. "What do you want?" he stammered.

"Oh," she said. She sounded unsure. "We want you to help us."

Anantharaman checked the number again. "Help you?" he asked. "You have a strange way of asking. Help with what?"

"Sorry," she said. Sorry? "We keep asking, but no one will help us."

Anantharaman ran his left hand over his bald head. He was sweating. He wiped his hand on his *lungee*. "Okay," he said, "You have my attention. Now I'm asking. What do you want?"

There was a long pause. The woman seemed to be arguing with someone. Then she said, "We want our wages."

Anantharaman laughed, a deep, rolling, belly laugh that rumbled until he had to sit on the floor to keep from falling. He wiped the tears from his eyes as the solution unfolded. A phone call. A few workers. A warning painted on a wall. Wages were easy to extract. He was back in his element. "Who are you?" he asked.

Anantharaman expected an evasive reply, but the voice said, quite simply, "My name is Zara."

Zara, he thought. Okay. "So tell me, Zara, how did you get this forgery and how many people have seen it?" The forgery part was bluff, and Anantharaman knew it, but appearances were often more important than reality. Especially in negotiations. But negotiations, he also knew, were a minefield of unpleasant surprises.

"I took it," she said. "So far no one has seen it but you. But if you won't help us, I have friends at the *Express of India* who would be very interested."

Anantharaman scrambled to his feet and leaned, knuckles-down, against his desk. "Let's not be hasty," he said, his voice lowered to a growl. "I am willing to help you, okay? Wages are easy to recover. Reputations are not. No one else needs to know about this picture."

"Of course."

"We are clear about that? That is the first thing, right?"

"Okay."

"And once you have your wages, we'll meet and you'll give me the phone. There must be no copies of this."

"That is fine. Like I said, this was the last thing for us. No one else would help."

"All right. But if I am going to help you, you need to tell me a few things. First of all, I take it you and your friends are prostitutes."

"Yes."

"But I am not clear who has not paid you."

"We wanted to start a business to purchase our freedom. We started sewing. We found a woman who said she would buy our things, but after we gave them to her she refused to pay."

"Who else knows about this?" Anantharaman asked.

"No one."

Anantharaman frowned. It didn't seem likely that no one else knew. She said they'd asked others. He walked to his desk and sat down. "I'll need names and addresses," he said.

On the train to Bombay he stared out the window, his mind churning over the details. He watched the sun set over the green palms of Kerala, and watched it rise over the dry, basalt foothills of central Maharashtra. In the dim light of dawn, at a station in the middle of nowhere, he bought *samosas* from a platform vendor. He bought an *Express of India,* too; a day old, but better than nothing. A story on the front page caught his eye: how thieves struck every monsoon season, cutting down trees and selling the wood. The cutting was illegal, but the thieves thrived by claiming that the trees fell in the storm. Storms were like that. The perfect cover. The thought that kept coming to him was this: that a storm was about to break, a storm no forecaster could predict. It began with a small cloud on the horizon, a breath of wind, a rise in the temperature and the humidity. Innocuous at first, until the rain and the wind struck in earnest. Small pebbles start great avalanches. No one knew, she said, but he doubted that. There was more here than met the eye. A boy came down the aisle selling *chai.* Anantharaman bought a cup. A plan formed in his mind. This girl might have friends at the *Express of India,* but Anantharaman had friends, too. First, he would help the girl. Then he will get the phone. And after that—well, that depended on how the second thing went.

# Chapter 5

Zara looked around the room, remembered that first night, and all that followed. If the pimps thought they could break her, they were wrong. She was strong—stronger than even she had realized. All the women in her family were strong: her grandmother, her mother, and her sisters. It was the men who were weak: her father the cripple; her brother--in-law, the drunkard; her brothers, lazy and unemployed. The pimps who tried to break her did not know how strong Zara was. They came close, but sitting alone in the dark, Zara knew that she had taken all they had to give. She knew, too, that she could not be broken.

Three things gave Zara strength to endure. Her understanding of this came gradually, in unexpected ways. The first was the love she felt for her sisters. In the beginning, Zara was terribly homesick for her family, and during the days following her failed suicide attempt, she decided that she would do at least one good thing before she killed herself. She would send dowry money home so her little sisters could find husbands. She would be certain that they did not share her fate. She figured it would take two years to save enough money. That was the first thing. And that saw her through to the second.

The second thing was Rachel. Rachel was pretty, with a thin face, long black hair, and very light skin. She was from Goa and proud of her Portuguese blood. And Rachel was a Christian—the first Christian Zara ever knew. Rachel said she was twenty-three, though she looked older. She had worked in the brothel for six years.

When Zara first came downstairs, Rachel took her under her wing and introduced her to the other girls. Rachel taught Zara the secrets of their sisterhood: how to fake an orgasm, how to put a condom in her mouth and roll it onto a penis with her tongue, to intuit what men wanted and act out their script. Rachel was adamant about condoms—Zara was to insist on them no matter what customers said. "There is a disease," she said, "that kills you."

Zara was Muslim. At her home in the south, she wore the caftan and burqa; never left home without the company of a male relative. To Zara, Sharia law was God's gift to protect her. It was the Hindus and Christians whose beliefs, even if sincere, were misguided. But once she lost her virginity, she began to think a little differently about religion. She could not marry, for if her husband discovered her impurity, he could burn her. The penalty for losing one's virginity was death—and it did not matter how it was lost. Rape and seduction were the same. And the gangsters—even if she fled—had the proof.

Rachel talked about Jesus and the miracles he performed. Zara thought Rachel and her religion were strange, but Rachel, Zara would learn, was too simple to tell lies, and she—Zara—was too frightened to be alone. Strange company was better than none, and in this crowded little room there was no place for divisions between the girls, even along religious lines. They needed all the help the gods could offer. One night, Rachel told Zara about Mary, the Mother of God, and Mary Magdalene, a prostitute, and how they were the only ones who did not run away when the soldiers came to kill Jesus. This made sense to Zara. Women, even bad women, didn't run. After Jesus was dead, Rachel explained, it was the two Marys who prepared his body for burial. Imagine that, Zara thought. A prostitute washed God's body. Why not? No one else would do it. We must count for something with God, she thought. After that, she bought a small silver image of Mary and wore it on a silver chain.

Her hand strayed to the chain and she lifted the image of Mary. Mary did not fear death, she thought. Why should I? She unhooked the chain and, holding Mary on her fingertip, rose and crossed the room to the window.

Rachel said Mary loved Jesus, and Jesus loved God, and God loved men so much he sent his son to die for them. Zara found all this talk about love and death unsettling. They should not, she thought, be spoken in the same breath. But when the sores appeared on Rachel's breasts, and the pimps took her to the clinic, the doctor said that love and death *were* the same. After that, Rachel threw herself under a train. Though she grieved for Rachel, their friendship kept Zara going until the third thing came along.

The third thing was English.

Zara looked at the image of Mary and wondered, What is love?

In her mind Zara heard a woman's voice, calm and clear: Love speaks without words, knows without proof, gives without exhaustion, and comes without asking.

She looked at the lights of Malabar Hill and thought about lying with English in his bed earlier that night. They made love, and afterwards, they talked. "Come to America," he said.

"How much is the ticket?"

"Sixty thousand rupees."

Her family could live on that for years. "Too expensive," she said.

"I have money."

"Next time," she said. "Next time I go."

Zara told English about her family. He knew she was their main support. But she did not tell him about her friends and their plan. They'd been taking pictures for weeks and they had just started sending them to certain people politicians, businessmen. The message was simple: *Help*. It shouldn't be difficult. But then there were complications. The police had gotten involved. An inspector came to their house and took her phone. Now what? She couldn't abandon her friends, not at the crucial moment. In a few weeks, or a few months, things would be different. She could go with him, live in America, eat strange foods, improve her English, maybe even get a job. She could send money home. Lots of Indians did it. She just needed a little more time to help her friends get on their feet. Timing was everything. Women don't run. She thought, I can't leave my friends.

She asked Mary, "What would you do if you had to choose between your family and your lover?"

The voice replied, I already made that choice.

Zara shook her head. "I can't see the way."

The voice said, It is not on our strength that we do great things. Go forward. You are not alone. Help will come from where your least expect it.

Zara fastened the pendant around her neck, and Mary slipped to the hollow between her breasts. What do I know? she thought. I'm just a poor girl from Andra Pradesh. Most days she was happy that something worse did not happen.

Zara ran her hand from the image of Mary down to her belly and then back over her breasts. She brought her hand to her face and breathed in English's scent, the dry sweat and cum that clung to her skin, an aroma dark and exciting. She pictured him as he pumped into her, the light blazing in his eyes, his jaw set, his neck taut, sweat streaming down his face. And when they finished they lay knotted, belly on belly, happy, exhausted, and "the two," as Rachel used to say, talking about how sex was meant to be, "were one."

How many men have climbed on top of me? Zara wondered. A thousand? Five? Ten? His was the only touch she craved.

English showed her a globe, once, in a bookstore. India, here. America, there. Imagine that—the other side of the world. All that she knew about America was what she saw on TV—that it was a rich place with women who were not modest. People ate with forks instead of their hands. And their houses—if the programs were to be believed—were all big and clean and bright. And she knew so little about him. His real name, for instance. The first time the pimps brought him to her house they shouted: "English! English!" because he was a foreigner, and that's what they've called him ever since. He said he was divorced. Maybe so, maybe not. He lived in America and had grown children. So he said. But what city? And what did he do?

Men. Malika said if their lips were moving, they were lying. But then again. . . .

Zara looked out the window and wondered what tomorrow would bring. And as she watched, three jeeps turned down the alley followed by a truck with a wire cage on the back. They screeched to a halt below the window, and a dozen cops piled out and rushed the stairs.

# Chapter 6

Ashok never rose before noon, and seldom went to bed before dawn. He was five foot nine and weighed two hundred pounds—big for an Indian—and most of that was muscle. He was toned and hardened, first from life on the streets, but later on, after he scraped his way out of the muck and into the *moola*, he worked out in a gym, though in the last few years he had slacked off from his routine. Two reasons for this: the first was the girlfriend he always said he didn't want. She arrived in the form of an aspiring actress named Ranjani, and he gave up some of his workout routine because of the demands she made on his time: shopping, dining out, and socializing with their friends. So many parties, so little time. The other reason was that he didn't feel the urgency to be in top form, now that he had a dozen or so underlings doing his dirty work for him.

It was noon and he lay in bed—one of his beds—for he had flats in Colaba, Worli, Malabar Hill, Bandra, and Navi Mumbai. They were useful acquisitions, these flats, and practical. An occupational necessity. He was never more than a few minutes from shelter if he needed to duck into the shadows and lay low for a while. And it was a nice perk, too, if he had a hot, horny woman hanging all over him, which happened often enough to make his life *very* interesting. None of the flats were in Ashok's name, of course, but in the names of various builders with whom he'd struck deals. Him, a kid who crawled out of the slime in Dharavi—the world's largest slum—rubbing shoulders with millionaire capitalists. He liked that.

He rolled over and fumbled on the nightstand for a pack of cigarettes, disturbing the sheets covering Ranjani and the girl they picked up last night at some discotheque. Ranjani and the other girl wrestled sleepily for a corner of the sheet. Ranjani came away with it and covered her bare breasts. The other girl's breasts were now exposed. They were fine and firm, a nice pair, with hard, pointed nipples. Ashok looked stupidly at the girl, tried to remember her name—Monika? Milisha?—who cared? He couldn't keep track. He shook a cigarette from the pack and lit it, lay down beside Ranjani, and stared at the ceiling.

He remembered staring at the ceiling as a boy, the first light of dawn filtering through the door of his hut. The monsoon rains had saturated the ceiling. It was practically tiled with tiny beads of water. It looked like it had been embroidered with gemstones. It was one of those odd moments of indescribable beauty that come upon the poor who can't afford store-bought art. And he remembered, too, lying in traction in the hospital with two broken legs, staring for weeks at the piss-yellow stains in the ceiling of the charity ward while one sick child after another died in the beds on either side of him, their grieving parents sometimes showing up to claim the bodies, and just as often, not. He exhaled, flicked the cigarette at the open window, missed, got out of bed and retrieved the butt, and leaning on the window ledge, aimed it at an orange-turbaned *saddhu* begging on the street below. Filthy beggar, Ashok thought. Get a job.

He remembered how, with his legs still in casts, he tracked down the man who broke them and cut his throat. And why not? When you live in a world where life is worth nothing, then, well, it is worth nothing. He shrugged. Not profound philosophy, but the best he could come up with on short notice. Funny how it worked. The rumors spread, the legend grew. After a while, it was easy. He looked around the room, the designer jeans and imported boots strewn on the floor, the jewelry—rings and chains and watches—piled in a tray on the dresser. All stolen, or given in payoffs for protection, or paid for with the money earned from his numerous interests. The clocks on the wall, the paintings, the furniture, the sound system, the flat-screen entertainment center, the big black BMW SUV parked on the street below, the driver sleeping on the front seat, all of it. Now he had a life worth living. A life, as they say, to die for. And all he had to do to get it was kill.

The girls moaned and Ashok turned. They were still sleeping, but cuddled. It was not so strange, watching others in the act of love. His parents did it. Ashok's father even did it to Ashok's sister, Nirupa. And the neighbors did it, and the homeless beggars on the street did it. The polite thing was not to look. In a world without personal space, privacy was a luxury. If you had it, you had it; if not, you did without. It struck Ashok as odd that only the rich were titillated by voyeurism. It was the invasion of privacy, he thought, that thrilled. It was the rich who patronized the bars where the girls danced near-naked, who bought the pornographic movies, and CDs and magazines, and who visited the websites. The poor—they were surrounded by sex and tried not to look.

Some people had no privacy, while others had too much. The ones with none had nothing to hide, and the ones with all the privacy in the world were driven to fill that space with dirty little secrets. And that space between—that blink between privacy and no-privacy—that was Ashok's window of opportunity.

At first, Ashok delivered porno magazines on his bicycle from the illegal little fourth floor print shop in Byculla to the street touts who hawked them surreptitiously in various bazaars. Later, when Ashok's father died, Ashok began running errands for the slumlord. And as Ashok grew older—and larger—more opportunities appeared. There was a racket for everyone and everything in Bombay: illegal electric, water, and cable hook-ups; phony medicine schemes; loan sharking; country liquor bars; the occasional turf rivalry that needed a little a muscle to resolve; the dance bars and brothels that needed girls. It was in this that Ashok excelled. There were always girls—agents brought them from the country by the hundreds every day. And there were migrants, too, who came on their own fleeing poverty in Bangladesh or Nepal or the backwards states of Bihar and Andra Pradesh. For a while, his specialty had been breaking girls, a task he took to with relish. But in time, his ambition outgrew that. You can only fuck so many girls in the ass before it gets old.

When the slumlord died, Ashok tried to take over his operation, but the Don—the big boss—had his own man in mind for the job. The rivalry made things dangerous for Ashok. That was how he got his legs broken. They might have killed him, but he had proven himself useful. Worth saving, even. That was their mistake. They broke his legs as a warning to keep him in line, but Ashok wasn't the kind of man who would remain in line.

Ashok began his revenge with the man who broke his legs, and didn't stop until he got to the top. He kept the Don's man alive for two weeks in the bottom of well. He got everything: names, phone numbers, addresses, habits, hobbies, vices, associates—all of it. And when he was done, he distributed the body parts to the higher-ups. And then he started down the list, killing them one at a time. The summons came, as expected. He struck a deal with the boss in the back seat of a black Mercedes. Afterwards, they had dinner at the Taj. So much talent, the Don said. A shame to see it go to waste. Let me offer you some direction.

Ashok had his territory, and the Don had a new right-hand man.

Ashok's phone rang. He looked at the caller ID: number not available. He frowned, thought about not answering. Ranjani groaned. Ashok answered, "Hello."

A voice said, "I need you to take care of something for me. Personally. This has to be done right."

"Where and when?"

"Meet me at the bridge over the tidal canal in Worli at 3:30. Don't be late."

Ashok hung up, heard a moan, and saw the girls awake, legs entwined, grinding rhythmically against one another beneath the sheets. He smiled. Life was good.

# Chapter 7

It only took Paul two days in Bombay to find someone whose divorce was worse than his. Some people Paul knew back home bragged about painless break-ups where the former couple remained friends. Maybe. More likely, Paul thought, those people either never loved to begin with, or had a Texas-sized dose of denial. His divorce nearly killed him. He loved Anne, and never in a million years expected her to leave. As far as he knew, their relationship was tip-top. Right until the moment she came downstairs with a suitcase and walked out. He was sitting in a chair reading the Sunday paper. "Annie?" he asked, as she tried to slip out the door. In the end, all drama aside, the divorce was fairly predictable. She'd taken a lover. She split and cleaned out the savings. Paul went all-but-crazy.

That summer, a freak waterskiing accident almost cost him his left eye. And that same weekend, he took a bad sunburn which broke out in shingles that went into a nerve condition called post-herpetic neuralgia. Paul was in physical pain 24/7. He couldn't sleep. He couldn't work. He soaked up his medical leave and drained his vacation time. He asked for a leave of absence. And then, sitting on his couch at 2:00 a.m. with a pistol in his lap and a suicide note on the table, he thought about taking leave from it all. He was fifty-one, divorced, bankrupt, in pain, and this close to dying. He had been in marketing for twenty-two years—since he had graduated from college. And where had that got him? In the dark he asked God one question: If this is what the rest of my life looks like, lonely, broke, and in pain, can I survive? The answer he got was, Yes, but things will get better.

He put down the pistol and called a counselor. They met twice a week for two months. "Think of all you have to live for," she said.

That was the problem, Paul replied. He couldn't think of anything to live for.

"Is there some place you always wanted to go?"

He had always wanted to go to India—sort of. But hadn't that just been a dope-induced teenager-in-the-60's fantasy?

"Maybe," she said, "and maybe not. Maybe there's something there for you."

Paul doubted that. Two tours in ' Nam had cured him of wanderlust. He'd seen enough of third world misery. And he had a very low opinion of people who went to India to get spiritual. Most of them, he thought, were psychos. But then again, what was he? As a stoned teenager in tie-dyed tee shirts and love beads, going to India had been all the rage, and he and his friends had, in an acid-induced euphoria, solemnly sworn that one day they would meet in Kathmandu. Late at night, staring out the window at a big, empty, full moon, Paul wondered, What happened to me? And then he thought, Sure. What the hell? What did he have to lose? The next day he called his boss, Frank, and quit his job.

Frank, listened patiently, then said, "Meet me for coffee first. If you still feel like quitting after that, go ahead."

They met later that afternoon. "If you hadn't been with Popular Imports for twenty years," Frank said, "I would have long since let you go. We've already hired your replacement. But for twenty years you gave us nothing but good work, and I'm not ready to give up on you. What you need," Frank said, "is a change of scene. A wake-up call. And maybe a nice piece of ass. What have you got in mind?"

Paul told Frank about India.

Frank thought about this for about two seconds and said, "We need another overseas buyer. Why don't you go to India and work for us while you're there? You have a good eye, and you know what kind of fabrics we want. We'll keep you on salary. Go see our suppliers. See the Taj. See the Red Fort. See how the other half lives. Take six months. Call it a working vacation. You'll feel better. And you'll be glad to come home when you do."

Frank's words leapt like fire across the table.

"Okay," Paul said.

Three days after he arrived, he had lunch with Sunil, who owned a fabric manufacturing conglomerate. Sunil had a great business card: WE ARE DYING FOR YOUR BUSINESS! But Sunil was not the chipper, happy man that Paul expected. He had the saddest eyes Paul had ever seen. In fact, Sunil looked like he was about to keel over dead right there in the lobby of the Taj Hotel. He couldn't eat. He had even less enthusiasm than Paul at the depth of his melancholy.

"What's going on?" Paul asked.

Sunil, it turned out, had a divorce story worse than Paul's. He had audio and video tape of his wife hiring a hit man to kill him. Amazingly, Sunil could not move out of his house. If he did, he would forfeit the property, and he could not legally throw his wife out before the divorce was granted. So they lived together, Sunil and the woman who wanted him dead, under the same roof, while the wheels of Indian justice crept along at less than a snail's pace. Five years they had lived like that. Sunil slept in a separate, locked bedroom, ate all his meals out, and never turned his back on his wife.

How did he manage? Paul asked.

Sunil took Paul to his first whorehouse. It wasn't the Honey Hotel in Bangkok, but it wasn't bad, either. After that, the party was on.

And so it was that one night Paul followed a pimp up the stairs of a rickety old building in an alley off Lamington Road. The girls lined up, and Paul looked them over. Taken as a whole, they were a good-looking bunch. As he looked from face-to-face, one girl caught his eye. He hesitated. She was not the prettiest of the group, but there was something about her that attracted him. He looked her in the eye and something passed between them. He felt it right away. Was it fear of that something that made him choose another girl? He picked Lakshmi, a slender girl with big breasts and a pretty face. He took her in the back room and fucked the hell out of her. But there was something in the eyes of this other girl that haunted Paul, and a week later he came back and took her instead. Her name, she said, was Zara. After a few weeks, he would not touch another.

Falling in love with a Bombay prostitute is not exactly something you write home about. Hi mom. Things are great. By the way, I fell in love with a nice-looking whore I met. No, it's not something you advertise. But he wasn't the first man in history struck that way, and he wouldn't be the last. How did it happen? There was no rational explanation. You made love and you lay in bed and she asked you a question, and maybe, for the first time in a long time, someone showed a little interest in you. And she was pretty, and vulnerable, and sad in a way that you couldn't explain. And you got the sense, cobbling a conversation, that there was something to this girl, that she was more than just a common whore. You traded stories in the dark. Slowly, you began to trust, to feel. And why not? Having married right once, and having your heart broken, this seemed neither better nor worse. Your rational mind told you it was just a game to her, that you were nothing but a customer. But there was something irrational about the whole thing, too. Something you couldn't explain. The way she wiped the sweat off your face with the inside of her blouse. The way she looked at you, cared for you. The way she called you, took you into her private life. The way she cried when you told her you were leaving. Tears, Paul thought, don't lie.

# Chapter 8

Zara touched her heart out of habit and watched as a police sub-inspector climbed out of the lead jeep and directed his men up the stairs. There were raids, and then there were *raids*. Visits by the cops were not unusual. The cops came for *hafta* and they came when rival brothels bribed them to harass the competition. Sometimes cops and NGOs raided to rescue minors, though more often the cops raided to take girls to the station and fuck them—especially the minors. English had been there once when the cops raided. That raid was about *hafta*—there were elections coming up—and everybody knew it was coming. Zara tried to warn English away, but he didn't understand. The more she tried to get him to go, the more he wanted to stay. Finally, she decided that the best thing to do was to fuck him and get him out before the cops came. But it didn't work out that way.

They had just sat down in the back bedroom. English perked up when he heard the commotion in the front room. "Police problem," Zara said. "No tension." But there was tension. How could there not be? A cop pounded on the door, and when she opened it, he jerked Zara into the hall. She looked back, and the cop grabbed English. But English shook the cop's hand off, and when the cop raised his *lathee* English said, "I wouldn't do that if I were you." For a moment, the cop and English glared at each other. Then the cop lowered his stick and pointed toward the front room.

English sat beside Zara on the bench while the cops ransacked the place. It was all an act—a put-on to exert their authority. In the end, the cops went in the back room with Malika, and she paid them off. But in the mean time, they had fun beating up Krishna the pimp, and showing off in front of the girls.

English held Zara's hand the whole time. After a while, one of the cops pointed at English and told him to go. Zara was stricken. She thought the cops were arresting him. She cringed at the thought of English rotting away in Arthur Road Jail. It wasn't his fault. She felt responsible for his being there. She wished that the cops had taken her instead, but what

33

could she do? She closed her eyes and prayed. After a while, the cops left and English reappeared. Zara threw her arms around him, smothered him with kisses, and then asked what happened. He said he was waiting downstairs in the alley the whole time. Zara burst into tears. She tried to explain what she felt when she thought the cops had taken him to jail. English said that, no, he had waited to make sure they didn't take her to jail. Looking back, she realized that it was at that moment she began to love him.

But this time, Zara knew, there would be no bribe and no rescue. English was on his way to America, and there was no money to make this raid go away.

The cops rushed up the stairs, boots pounding, dull vibrations echoing from the dark passage deep within the building. Zara sat on the cot and pulled her knees to her chin. There were no exits, not even unbarred windows. No way out, and no place to hide. Cops shouted in the rooms below. They began beating Krishna and Abishek. The girls shouted shrill obscenities in protest. Malika roared threats. The cops hit them, too. Footfalls drummed on the stairs to the loft. A cop smacked his head coming through the door. He swore, flipped on the light, and shouted, "Here's another one!" He crossed the room and slapped Zara, rolled her face down on the bed, and cinched her wrists behind her back with a plastic tie. He hefted her to her feet and shoved her towards the door where two more cops grabbed her by the elbows and dragged her down the steps to the main room. There she joined the line of girls being pushed and prodded down the stairs, and out of the house, and into the truck with the wire cage.

They sat quietly, bruised and bleeding, wrists bound, hands swelling. Shilpa licked blood from her lips and spit. Malika had a puffed eye and a gash on the bridge of her nose. Zara heard breaking glass upstairs. The cops were trashing the place. Not a light appeared in the surrounding buildings, not a face showed in the windows. Even the mongrel dogs had slunk away. At length the cops filed out and climbed into their jeeps.

The police station was only a few blocks down the road. The cops herded the girls inside and down another flight of stairs to a concrete-walled basement stinking of sewage and mildew. There were fluorescent lights, but most of the bulbs were out, and all but one fluttered. They shoved the girls against a wall, where they stood until the sub-inspector arrived. He was drinking from a fat brown mug. He looked the girls over and said, "We're looking for an American, a tall man with a beard. Who can tell me where he is?"

No one spoke.

Zara was stunned. She looked the sub-inspector over. He was thick-bodied and dark-skinned. She remembered him. His name was Rane. He was the cop who led the raid the time English was there. She closed her eyes and tried to remember everything about that night.

Rane started with Malika, slapped her three times and ripped the front of her gown, exposing her huge, floppy breasts. He said, "You know everything, cow. I know you know where he is, and if you don't know, then you know who knows."

Malika set her jaw. Zara might not like what Malika said about men, but Malika, for all her bad-mouthing, liked English, too. He brought the girls cakes on their birthdays, and mangos (when they were in season) for no reason at all, just to be nice. She was all business, and there is something to be said for loyalty to customers—at least, to a point. Malika was Nepali and mountain-tough, and when Rane tore her gown, she swore under her breath, and glared at him. She would tell him eventually, but on her terms, not his. She would make him pay, if only with annoyance and wasted time. And when she told him, her conscience would be clean. She shrugged her shoulders and said, "He never tells us anything. I don't know where he lives. Why would he tell us?"

Rane snapped his fingers. A cop left the room.

Sooner or later when the cops question you, you tell them what they want to know, or if you don't know, you tell them what you think they want to hear. It might be the truth or it might not. At first you don't want to tell them anything. You hold out to make it hard for them. You don't want to reward them for being pricks. But in the end, you talk. You sign the papers they put in front of you and hope—one way or another—for the pain to end.

The cop came back with a bucket of water and an electric cord with the socket cut off. He set the bucket in the middle of the floor and handed Rane the cord. Two bare wires hung like fangs from the end. Rane walked down the line of girls whistling softly, twirling the cord. He searched their eyes. He brushed Neera's face with the wire. She flinched. He blew her a kiss and moved down the line to Lakshmi, the pretty one. "Aren't you the American's girl?" he asked.

She shook her head.

He pulled her to the middle of the room by the hair and shook her head furiously. He shouted, "Where is he?" and without waiting for a reply, lashed her back with the bare wire. The wires tore her gown and left a welt and a splash of blood. Lakshmi screamed and writhed in Rane's grasp.

Rane let go of her hair and Lakshmi stood, trembling. Rane took a *lathee* from one of the cops and jabbed her in the stomach, doubling her over. He swung again at her kidney and dropped her to the floor. He tossed the cop the *lathee* and stuffed Lakshmi's face in the bucket of water. Five seconds, ten, fifteen. She twisted and kicked. He pulled her head out of the water and shouted, "Where is the American?"

She had barely time to grab a breath before Rane stuffed her face back into the bucket. Lakshmi's body wracked spasmodically. Ten. Twenty. Thirty seconds. He pulled her head from the bucket and dropped her, coughing and retching, onto the floor. He kicked her. "What is his name?"

Lakshmi sobbed, "I don't know."

He kicked her again.

Zara's eyes fixed on the bucket.

Rane pulled Neera from the line. She wilted without being hit, blubbering incoherently, and practically stuck her own head in the bucket. A fat cop sat on her back to hold her still, and rode her like a cowboy on a bucking horse. The cops laughed. They plugged in the electric cord.

Zara shut her eyes, but the darkness was almost as terrifying as the shrieks Neera made underwater, or her pleas in the precious seconds when she was allowed a gasp of air. The room smelled of burnt flesh. Neera passed out. The room fell silent, and Zara opened her eyes. Rane looked at her and smiled, a look of recognition crossing his face. "I know you," he said.

The cops can beat you or burn you, drown, shock, or rape you. They can hang you upside down until you have fits, chill you on ice until you cannot move, pile things on your chest until you cannot breathe, and if all of those fail, there are drugs: narco-analysis, they call it. They dope you out of your mind, and then you talk and talk and talk. When they are finished, they sometimes kill you anyway—inject you with things, and say you were dead when they found you, or take you somewhere secluded and shoot you in a fake encounter.

Zara heard the story from her mother—walking by the river, their backs turned only for a moment, the child floating face down, turning slowly in the current. Neither her mother nor father could swim, but a man in a passing rickshaw dove in and retrieved the child. They laid her on a flat rock and pounded her back like they were washing clothes. A moment of anguish, then a cough and a cry. Zara was too young to remember, but her body remembered. Sometimes in her nightmares she saw dark green water, the sparkle of light on the sand below, felt fluid in her throat and lungs, turned slow circles in the current.

Zara looked at the bucket.

Rane said. "When I look someone in the eyes and they look away, then I know they know." He nodded to his men.

# Chapter 9

No one was surprised when Sachin Bal was named the topper of his high school class, nor when he was voted Most Popular and Most Likely to Succeed, nor when, at the age of nineteen, he became the youngest graduate in the history of Wilson College. He was of medium build with long black hair and dark eyes; with thick lashes and graceful, arching, brows; full lips with cheeks that dimpled when he smiled, which was almost all the time. He was equally at home on the cricket field as in the physics lab, with the debate team as in the discotheque. But what to do with a boy this talented, too young to live on his own and hold down a steady professional position? His father and mother agonized. They were not rich. They deliberated with relatives who agreed to pool their resources. Sachin applied to graduate school in Los Angeles and was accepted, scholarshipped even. He would stay with cousins who could keep an eye on him. But in LA, Sachin fell under a cloud of suspicion. His cousins sent home cryptic letters. It was nothing that they said—they were far too tactful for that—but it became clear that Sachin would not be spending a second year in their house.

The troubles began even before Sachin left for LA, when it was dis-covered that he had applied to the College of Arts and Sciences, and was going to study Journalism, rather than prepare for Medical College as had been agreed. There was a big scene and a fight and a flurry of anger and excuse-making, tsk-tsking about the decline-of-youth and the state-of-the-nation, but there wasn't time to change direction. Nothing to do but proceed towards what everyone suddenly worried would be a disastrous ending. And they were right. The college adventure ended with an exor-bitant (by Indian standards) series of mysterious, undocumented medical bills, and a return ticket to Bombay.

Sachin's parents insisted that he withdraw from school, but once home, and in the face of Sachin's charm, the rumors faded like the memory of last year's monsoon floods. Sachin's fortunes turned when a former Wilson classmate helped him land a job with the *Express of India*. He wasn't getting page one stories—it might take a lifetime to climb the ladder that far—but he wrote competent prose, and made page twelve lively as he discussed oddball news from around the world: Gay Pride parades in Sydney, NRIs who were rewarded for volunteer work in Iceland, a town in Sri Lanka that voted to change its name to honor Gabriel Garcia Marquez. These stories came in over the wire, and for most of the day, Sachin surfed the internet for snippets that might prove entertaining, if not particularly newsworthy. He passed his time at the paper unrewarded and in virtual anonymity. The only attention he received was a mild rebuke, meted out by his boss, editor-in-chief, Kumar Singh.

That reproof was for writing an article about a promising oil exfoliation on the South Sea Island of Kontiki, where environmentalists were dismayed that the nesting habits of the Larry Bird might be disrupted by the drilling. The bird, according to the article, boasted the longest migratory path of any extinct seabird, riding the Gulf Stream from a rookery in the South Seas to a brewery along the coast of Scotland in a little over a month. The rebuke came, according to Kumar, because a reader had written to complain that Sachin misidentified British Petroleum as British Linoleum. Singh cast a doubtful eye as Sachin fidgeted.

Kumar had a habit of turning off the air conditioning when he called subordinates into his office. It was extremely hot that day, and humid, perhaps 40 Celsius. Kumar kept cool in the stream of air from a small fan on his desk. After calling Sachin's attention to the article's deficiencies he reclined in his plush, executive chair, folded his hands, and said nothing. Sachin squirmed in the hard, high-backed, wooden chair provided for visitors. At length Kumar cleared his throat and said, "I should probably have a word with our fact checker, as well, and don't you think?"

Sachin's throat was too dry to speak. The article had been written on a dare after a lunch break had turned into a long afternoon of piña coladas and shots of rum at a Colaba bar.

Kumar sighed and continued, "But when a promising young writer enjoys a reputation such as yours, no matter how undeserved, a harried editor might well pass along a story without proofing it thoroughly, don't you agree?"

Sachin nodded.

Kumar's secretary, a pretty girl in a green *salwar* suit, came in and placed a stack of papers on Kumar's desk. He took the top page off the stack and began to read. "If I were in your shoes," Kumar said, "I would never presume that editors are as diligent as you appear to be."

"It was a slow day," Sachin said, "one of those weird western holidays. I was sure I could make up something more interesting than what the wire had to offer."

Kumar looked up from his reading, his glasses far down his nose. "If you wish to write fiction, I'm sure you will be as successful at that as you are at journalism. Perhaps more so. Lord knows, there are enough hack writers cranking out trashy, highly-implausible stories these days." He gestured to a towering bookcase on the far wall. "Myself," he said, "I prefer the classics. And as long as you work for me you'll report the facts. Real facts, not made-up ones. Do I make myself clear?"

Sachin nodded and left. At the door he paused and looked back. Kumar had lowered the papers and was watching him, a bemused smile on his face.

Following that incident, from time to time, Sachin was dispatched to substitute for absent, more-senior reporters covering minor local stories —cars that fell into construction excavations, an elephant taken away from its *mahout* for neglecting it, a village woman who married a tree, an insignificant Bollywood "item girl" who had written a book of poems which received such scathing reviews that in tears at a press conference she threatened to kill herself.

So when the phone rang, it presented a real dilemma for Sachin, for the timing of the call was all wrong. It was nearly eleven at night, and he was in bed with that same item-girl-turned-would-be-poetess, a Bollywood starlet named Preity, whom he had been pursuing ever since her tearful interview. She was on her back, her clothes in rabid disarray, her dress up around her hips, her panties caught up on the ceiling fan, and Sachin, naked from the waist down, was inside her and pounding away for all he was worth. Then the phone rang.

And rang.

And rang.

It quit ringing.

He and Preity locked lips and knotted tongues like they were kneading bread. Preity had her eyes closed. She had lost her jeweled *bindi*—a genuine Andra star ruby set in 24-carat gold. The phone rang again. Sachin reached for it to shut it off, but only succeeded in knocking it behind the night-stand.

Preity had her legs cinched around his hips. It was their third time since dinner. She was soaking wet and moaning.

The phone quit ringing.

It began again.

He pushed himself off and fished around behind the nightstand, his hard-on throbbing. Preity grabbed for it and he turned away.

He missed the call. The number was not familiar. He threw the phone across the room into the trash bin. Preity sat up and begun to arrange her clothes. She felt around the sheets for her *bindi*. Sachin dove and pinned her, entered her again. She raked her fingernails like plows down the length of his back. "Bitch!" he shouted. He felt blood. The phone rang from the trash bin.

After they finished, Preity turned on her side and began to sing softly. Sachin had so praised her poems that she'd latched onto the hope that she had real talent and was setting all her poems to music. She sang them badly every chance she got despite the fact that she had no more gift for singing than she had for poetry or acting. There were reasons, Sachin knew, why Preity would never progress beyond being 'dancing friend number two' in B-grade comedy flicks. But as long as she kept her looks and entertained the directors in bed, she would find work. Sachin got up and found the phone. Nine calls and an SMS. He opened the message. "Mother of God!" he shouted. He called back.

A woman answered, "Hello."

"What do you want?" Sachin asked. "You know I don't make much money."

"I don't want money," she said, her voice raspy.

"What then?"

"I want you to write a story."

The demand was as simple as it was impossible, as perilous to carry out as it was to refuse. He was to write an article about a shop that didn't pay some girls for their work. If he didn't, his boss would see the picture. If he did, his boss would see the article. "I'll have to get authorization," he said. "I can try to talk my boss into it, but he might refuse."

"No," she said. "If you don't ask, he can't refuse. I'm sure you can find a way to slip it in." She hung up.

The next afternoon he asked anyway. Kumar stroked his beard and sat back in his chair while Sachin recounted what he knew of the story: A group of prostitutes had tried to start some sort of a garment factory to purchase their way out of bondage in the sex trade, but the woman who had contracted their goods sold the merchandise, and then wouldn't pay the girls. They wanted justice. It was the kind of story, Sachin said, that the *Express of India* thrived on. It had all the elements: fairness, the improving economy, changing ways of life, even a hint of scandal.

Kumar listened and said nothing. When Sachin finished, Kumar turned his back on Sachin and stared out the window. He rested his elbows on the armrests of his chair, folded his hands. He seemed to be praying. At length he swiveled around to face Sachin and said, "What the hell have you got yourself into?"

"Nothing, I—"

"How did you hear about this incident?"

"I got a phone call."

"A phone call?"

"Yes."

"From the girl?"

"What girl?"

"You know who I mean."

"Zara?"

"Right."

Sachin looked down at his shoes.

"Let me ask you a question, Sachin. Why did she call *you*?"

"Me sir?" Sachin was sweating. His shirt soaked through in the back. It peeled away from the wood as he leaned forward. "She reads my articles?"

Kumar burst out laughing. "I'd bet my beard and turban this piece of shit can't read a word in any language, much less English. Come on, boy, I've been in this business thirty-six years, you'll have to do better than that."

"Then I don't know, sir," Sachin said. "but if you'll let me write the story, I promise to find out."

Kumar scowled. "How long have you worked here?" he asked.

"Almost nine months, sir."

"And what have you learned?'

"Sir?"

"And what have you learned in nine months?"

"About what, sir? I've learned many things."

"About your job."

"That it requires integrity, sir?"

"Why?"

"It's a position of trust?"

"Yes. And how did you learn that?"

"I don't understand the question, sir?"

"Who taught you this?"

"You did, sir."

"And why did I teach you this?"

"Because you're a good editor, sir?"

"More than that."

"Because you're an honest editor, sir."

"More."

Sachin stared. His mouth hung open. No words came.

"Because I *am* honest," Kumar said, leaning forward in his chair.

"And because I am honest, it is very difficult to pass lies off on me. Now take the day off and come and see me in the morning."

The rest of the day Sachin alternated between terror and resignation. He considered his options. He could try to buy his way out of trouble, but the woman said money was not the issue, she wanted justice. Maybe he could talk to the shopkeeper—Mrs. Shetty—he had her address, a little shop on Warden Road. Nice upscale area. If all else failed, he could always go back to America. Even if his cousins wouldn't take him in, he could get his visa renewed, re-enroll in school. Leave all this India shit behind him.

Then another idea dawned. He could visit the girls, reason with them. If necessary, he could threaten them. All he needed was the phone. How difficult could it be to beat a phone out of a prostitute?

He took out his cell and looked at the picture, him and a girl naked in bed. The photo was from above, looking down. How had they done it? Through a vent? A hole in the wall? The bitches! It meant nothing, really, just him and a girl. Who would know? Who would care? He had friends in LA who passed around naked photos of each other all the time. But then he thought about his cousin in Los Angeles, or second cousin, or whatever she was. She was sixteen and in high school, and they do things differently in America. So he had fucked her. Why not? She wasn't a virgin, and she was practically begging him for it. Was it his fault she got pregnant? No way! But if new accusations surfaced—well, why wouldn't people believe them? His family would. His boss would. It could ruin him. He walked and he thought, and he thought and he walked. He waited for the phone to ring, he went to sleep that night long past midnight, and in the morning he woke up late for the meeting with Kumar Singh. But by the time he showered and changed and got down to the office, a police inspector had been found murdered, and the office was abuzz with the story, and everything else seemed to have been forgotten.

Then, that night, coincidentally, the second time Sachin bedded Preity, the phone began to ring again.

And ring.

And ring.

He lost his hard-on. With a sinking feeling he reached for the phone.

It was Kumar Singh. "Write the story," he said. "Page one, the day after tomorrow. Get on it. And while you're at it, I want you to find this man, Anantharaman. He's an agitator from Kerala. A fucking communist. He's come to town to stir up trouble. He's planning a *bundh*. He's mixed up in this too, somehow. I want to know how and why, everything. I'll SMS you his number. And one more thing—"

"Yes, sir."

"The *Express of India* is not now, never was, and never will be about fairness, or any of that other bullshit you were blathering about. We are in the business of selling papers, and what sells are sleaze and scandal, the curious and the morbid. Our readers don't give a shit about news, issues, or morality. They want to know who got caught doing what with who, and what weird, crazy, or perverse thing happened, so that when they put down the paper they can walk away feeling as though they have lived vicariously through our eyes. What sells is what people want to do, but won't do for fear of getting caught. The only rule we live by—and the sword on which you may perish—is that we never, *ever*, fall into that trap. When a newspaper man becomes the news, he's finished. We are above the news, and as such, above all else. Do you understand?"

# Chapter 10

The cops hustled Zara out of the room and down the hall to another room with a smooth concrete floor dark-stained in sticky patches with what looked liked blood but might have been anything from motor oil to battery acid. There was a rusting steel desk to one side with a straight-back wooden chair. Behind the desk, set in the wall, was a black glass that Zara knew from movies meant somebody might watch from another room. The cops dropped her there, in the middle of the floor, in the middle of the stain, under a single bright light. Zara tried to stand but Rane beat her down with his *lathee* and she waited on her knees, head bowed, her hands still firmly bound, trembling.

Rane smoked. The cops gossiped—cricket, movie starlets, past elections, the price of a flat. Someone fetched a bottle of whiskey and some small plastic cups and they drank.

Five minutes passed, then ten. Zara tried to track the time. It must be light by now, she thought. English should be in a taxi on his way to the airport. Zara has never been on a plane, never been to an airport, doesn't know about baggage and security. She knows if she were taking a noon train she could arrive at the station at 12:30 and have plenty of time to have a snack and some *chai* before boarding. But English was funny about time. Perhaps all *phorens* were that way. When they traveled he was so organized. She closed her eyes and imagined him speeding across town, the streets deserted at this hour.

After a while Rane's phone rang. He took the call, grunted, and hung up. He crushed out his cigarette, lifted Zara to her feet, and slapped her twice, fore and backhand. The second blow knocking her backwards over the desk. She struck her head on the floor and saw spots, tasted blood. She heard the chunk of metal on concrete. Rane jerked Zara to her feet again and stood her in the middle of the room. Before her, the bucket and the cord. She shut her eyes and prayed. When she opened them, Rane pointed his finger like a gun at Zara's head and made a click. Zara flinched. Rane chuckled and looked around to make sure the rest of the cops were watching. They looked bored. He pushed Zara to her knees, took her by the

44

back of the neck in an iron grip, and forced her face to the bucket. "What is your friend's name?" he asked.

In a panic she inhaled and choked. Rane kicked her in disgust. When she regained her breath he asked, "Where does he stay?"

"I don't know."

He pressed her face into the water. Ten seconds. Twenty. Thirty. "I said, 'Where is your friend?'"

She lay on her back, gasping. She tried to kick him.

He fended off her leg and his gaze ran to the spot between her legs. Rane plugged in the electrical cord and slipped on a pair of black rubber gloves.

The thin cotton nightgown was wet through and clung to Zara's breasts. Rane pinched the nipples through the gown. Wincing, Zara said, "He left town. I tell you he is gone."

"That's not good enough," Rane said. He pressed the wire to her thigh.

Zara gasped and arched in pain.

Five minutes passed, perhaps ten. Zara blinked away tears. Rane held her face in his gloved hand and squeezed her cheeks until she thought the bones would crush. The muscles in her arms and legs twitched spasmodically. The room smelled of burnt flesh.

"Where has he gone?" Rane asked.

"America."

"When?"

"He left" . . . she almost said it. . . *this morning*. If she could just hold out a few hours he would be beyond their reach. Just a few hours. How long would he need? ". . . last week."

"I don't believe you," Rane said. He fondled Zara's breasts. He had torn her gown from throat to navel exposing them. They were mottled with burns. He slipped his hand to the space between her thighs. She clinched her knees. He jerked her to her feet by her hair. The gown fell away. He shoved Zara to the desk, ripped her briefs off, forced her to her back, lifted her legs and placed them on his shoulders. He pulled her close, ground his cock against her through his trousers, then ran the tip of his finger slowly from her lips to the middle of her breastbone where he stopped at the pendant of Mary nestled between her breasts. He lifted it on his finger and looked at it.

# Chapter 11

You were six years old when your mother took you to a birthday party at your cousin's house. They lived in a fine old bungalow on a tree-shaded hill in what was, twenty years ago, a quiet village on the edge of town. Pali Naka, they called it. You have been there before and you like your cousins, Minisha and Nysa, shy, thin, mousy girls, one seven and the other, five. You like the big balcony that overlooks the back garden, and you like the swing affixed to the spreading banyan, and the sweets they made when they knew company was coming. Auntie Leesha made the best milk *peda* in the whole wide world, and you liked your auntie, a solid, round woman with a perpetual smile on her face—except when she was screaming at the servants. At the bottom of the hill there was a cave with a shrine in it. You and your cousins snuck out of the yard, and stood at the mouth of the cave daring each other to go in.

You took the dare. You were always the brave one. Still, there was something strange about that afternoon, standing outside the cave and facing your shapeless fear. Inside it was cool and dark. You walked from one dim passage into another, darker one. You walked all the way to the back wall without a lamp. You were proud to have ventured in, but a little bit disappointed. The cave wasn't near as scary as you thought. Just a dark, quiet place with a dank, wet smell. Still, you accomplished something you sensed was vaguely important. You were one person when you went in, and another when you came out. You walked home holding your head a little higher. You felt older.

You liked it—the cousins, the house, the cave, the sweets, your auntie —everything but your uncle, Kaka Gulshan, a short, thick-lipped, balding man with fat black eyebrows and watery eyes that followed you, even when he looked like he was looking elsewhere. The day of the party your mother left you for a sleepover, and you were glad when you snuggled down for the night with your cousins in a big, soft bed. But in the middle of the night Kaka Gulshan lifted you from the bed with wet hands and carried you to a small room in the back of the house. He sat you down on a narrow cot where, sleepy and confused, you undressed because he told you to. Then he undressed and sat beside you. What happened that night you will never tell another soul.

In the morning you were trembling and cold—you had not slept at all. You mother came and you clung to her sari and wouldn't pry loose. After that, you cried every time she suggested you visit your cousins. You grew thin and quiet, and you studied hard because when you said you had lessons—people left you alone. From time to time you saw your auntie, your cousins, and your uncle at family gatherings—when you could not escape them. When you had to see them, you stayed out of his sight, and when you couldn't avoid him you thought, One of these days I'm going to kill you. You thought about the cave. Nothing was as scary as you imagined before you tried. Even killing. But uncle wet-eyes died of a heart attack before you were old enough to kill him, and the first time you got into a fight with a girl at school, she beat you black and blue. You decided that you were not meant to be a killer after all, so you studied and you brooded, and you brooded and you studied, and when your parents talked about boys and finding you a husband, you said you wanted to go to college first. And when they asked what you want to be you said, "I want to be a policeman." The words rolled off your tongue.

"Isn't she cute?" they said. "Our daughter, the police-girl."

You went to the library to learn more about this and found out that until 1971, there was not a single policewoman in India. Not one. But the librarian showed you the biography of Kiran Bedi, India's first. In the face of opposition she rose through the ranks and became a district commander known for courage and honesty. Once, during the riots that preceded the Emergency, armed only with a *lathee* stick, she led a police charge against a mob of sword-wielding Sikhs. You took the book home and read it over and over and over again. At school, you drew pictures of Kiran Bedi in your sketchbook. Kiran Bedi with a *lathee*. Kiran Bede with a gun.

You went to college on scholarship, graduated at the top of your class, and applied to the All India Service. You got in. One day you woke to find that you had dreamed your dream into a reality. You were a policewoman. Then you drifted through a succession of mundane assignments. You guarded politicians' vacant bungalows. You typed reports in the  main office. You arrested a few female activists at a *bundh*—upper-class women who would have shrieked to high-heaven had they been so roughly handled by men. Then you wondered, now what? You accomplished something you sensed was vaguely important. But reality, like the cave, was a bit of a disappointment. Then they transferred you to street patrol and assigned you to the Girgaon station.

# Chapter 12

Behind Rane the door burst open and a tall woman in a green silk *salwar* suit rushed into the room. Panting behind her were two men in western-style clothes. The woman shouted, "Stop it, for God's sake! What are you going to do, rape her right here in the station?"

Rane looked at the intruders like they came through the wall and not the door. "Who the hell are you?" he shouted. "Get out!"

"My name is Sharmilla Oberoi," the woman said, pointing at Zara. "I'm her attorney." She smoothed her *salwar* suit and nodded to the man at her left, "This is my associate, Mr. Mistry." And to the man at her right, "Mr. Fernandez, from Congress Party headquarters."

Rane spit on the floor at their feet, but he let go of Zara. "Whores don't have attorneys."

"This one does," Sharmilla said.

Rane nodded at his men. "Throw her out."

The cops took two steps towards Sharmilla and the men in suits stepped between them. Sharmilla reached into her purse and pulled out a small, silver, digital camera. She snapped two photos, one of Zara, now crouching naked beside Rane, and one of the policemen hesitating halfway between Rane and the intruders. Sharmilla dropped the camera in her purse and said, "Take her upstairs." At the doorway Zara looked back just long enough to make eye contact with Rane. He scowled, his eyes expressing neither satisfaction nor disappointment. A cat from whom the bird has escaped, for now.

# Chapter 13

Down the hall and up the stairs to the ground floor, past a weary, middle-aged secretary slowly typing at her desk. Past grim-faced cops in starched khaki uniforms, drinking *chai*, smoking, chatting, falling silent as the group of officials with a near-naked girl rushed by. Down another hall, past the lobby where the duty officer fended off a jostling line of poor shouting Indians queuing up to file the morning's complaints; past a soft drink machine, humming. A chattering vendor pushing hot *vada pavs* and holding out his tray hopefully as they passed. An open door to an office where a sub-inspector slept in a chair behind a desk under the cool blast of an air conditioner. At the end of the hall another stairway up, and then another hall, where they almost knocked down an old man in a black suit creeping along the wall with a tall stack of papers. The old man cursed them in a high, thin voice—he had spilled his sheets and got them out of order. At last they reached a dusty room with a table and chairs, and rusting metal file cabinets piled with boxes of paper. The men deposited Zara in a chair and went out.

Through a grimy window with two cracked panes, Zara saw the morning sun turning the horizon a sickly, papaya-skin yellow. On the ledge outside the window a half-dozen bedraggled gray-and-white pigeons shuffled and cooed. Sharmilla appeared with scissors and cut the plastic ties from Zara's hands.

Zara covered herself with the torn remains of her nightgown as best she could. Rummaging in her purse, Sharmilla found a pair of safety pins and gave them to Zara, who fastened the gown, and then gazed at the woman standing on the other side of the table, looking back at her.

There are some people whose eyes you will always remember, Zara thought, your mother, your grandmother, your youngest sister, your first lover, your worst enemy, the woman who has just saved your life. They were both panting from the rush from the basement.

Sharmilla said, "Well, now what?"

Sharmilla was tall, maybe five foot seven, with long, thick, shining

49

black hair. Her cheekbones were high; her eyes bright, wide, and kohl—lined; her lips full, glossed a dark burgundy; her nails painted to match. Her neck was long and graceful, her body well-proportioned and thin at the waist. She wore a bright green silk *salwar* suit with gold trim and burgundy embroidery along the edge. She looked, to Zara, too young to be a lawyer. She could be twenty-four or five, but not much older. Around her neck hung a delicate gold chain with a gold image of Ganesh, a handful of bracelets around each wrist. On her forehead was painted a finger-width red stripe. A Brahman? Zara wondered. But her skin was not light like most Brahmans, though it was not too dark, either. Neither did she show signs of having applied lightener. Our color, Zara thought, is the same.

The men returned, one with a handful of wet paper napkins, the other with a bottle of water. Zara dabbed the blood from her face and, and seeing no place to discard the napkins, dropped them on the table in front of her. She drank the water.

The men took seats and Sharmilla said, again, "I'm Sharmilla Oberoi, and this is my associate, Romesh Mistry."

Mistry was fortyish, a little thick around the middle, but with a pleasant, boyish face. The small, gold-rimmed glasses he wore gave him a bookish appearance. He was fair-skinned and short, with a thin black moustache. His hair was fashionably long, falling to his eyebrows and hanging below his collar in the back. He wore a beige linen suit with a blue shirt and a pink tie. In the rush from the basement he had gotten blood on the sleeve of his jacket. He looked, to Zara, like a hot-shot banking executive or a sharp young jewelry trader; someone who wanted to look like a Bollywood star, but didn't have the fortitude for the job.

Sharmilla nodded towards the second man, who fished a cigarette from a silver case and searched his pockets for a lighter. "This is Gabi Fernandez," she said. "He's a CM from the Congress Party. He is also here to see that you receive fair treatment."

Fernandez took a stainless-steel lighter from his vest pocket and flicked the flint. He was tall and darker than Mistry or Sharmilla, dressed in a black, formal western suit with a red knitted vest over a white shirt and yellow tie. He looked ridiculous—shabby and careless. His facial expression suggested to Zara, that he did not want to be in the room, but was afraid to be elsewhere. A politician? she wondered. A CM? He was older than the others, bony and thin, with a pronounced, European nose, balding, with gray beginning to show in the dark hair around his ears. He looked more like a crank village dentist than a politician.

Lawyers? They might be, and then again, they might not. She didn't hire them, and nobody she knew could have hired them, except maybe

English. Certainly not the gangsters who ran the brothel, nor Malika, nor the girls. English would have the money, but how would he have known she was in trouble? And the lawyers hadn't mentioned his name.

Fernandez finally found enough fire to light his cigarette, and he inhaled greedily, then exhaled a thick cloud of smoke which filled the room instantly with the sharp odor of Turkish tobacco.

Sharmilla said, "They've charged you as an accessory in the murder of a police inspector named Godbodle. Did you know him?"

A murder? Zara thought. Not good. They hang people for that. "Yes," she said. "I know him." She looked over her shoulder out the window. "Knew him."

Sharmilla arched her eyebrows. "How did you know him?"

"I was in his office. A week ago."

"Why?"

"I filed a complaint."

"A complaint?"

"Yes."

"Why not file a complaint, like everyone else does—with the duty officer?"

"The duty officer wouldn't take it."

"What kind of complaint?"

"We did some work and were not paid."

"Not paid?"

"Our wages."

"Wages?" Sharmilla looked puzzled. "Do you mean the house did not pay your wages?"

"My house always pays my wages."

"What wages, then?"

"We did other work."

"We?"

"Yes, there were seven of us."

"What work?"

"We made lace."

The three looked at each other, then at Zara. "Lace?" Sharmilla asked. "For who? Why?"

"We had this idea that if we could start a business, a cooperative, that maybe we could do something else."

"Escape the brothel?"

Zara nodded.

Mistry and Fernandez spoke at the same time. "How did you get this idea?" "Who put this rubbish into your head?"

Zara sucked on her lower lip. It was pulpy and tender. There was a loose flap of skin and she worried it with her tongue. "One of the girls showed us how to make lace. She was—" Zara made a circle with her right hand in the air "—crazy. She used to sit for hours with her needles and thread. One night we watched a program on TV about rehabilitating sex workers. The idea just came to us. If girls in Calcutta could do it, why not us?"

Sharmilla nodded. "But when you did this. . . knitting. . . "

"The lady we did the work for refused to pay us." Zara shrugged. "What could we do? We went to the station to file a complaint, but they chased us out."

"And?"

"We came back. We went to Godbodle and asked him to help."

"And he said?"

" ' No.' So we told him if he didn't help we would make a scandal with his wife."

Mistry burst out laughing.

Fernandez flicked his ashes on the floor. "So you were blackmailing him."

"I guess you could say that."

He leaned forward in his chair. "How were you blackmailing him?"

"We had pictures."

"What kind of pictures?"

"You know what I mean."

"Pictures of him with women?"

"Yes."

Fernandez took a deep drag on his cigarette. When he exhaled he said, "Godbodle was fucking some of the girls."

"That's right."

"You are aware that blackmailing is a crime?"

"So is whoring, and not paying wages, and not accepting a complaint, taking bribes, and torturing prisoners. All we wanted was our wages. It didn't seem like much."

The three looked from one to the other.

Fernandez lit another cigarette from the one he was smoking and flicked the butt into the corner.

Mistry asked, "Who else have you called?"

"No one."

"Bullshit."

"No one."

"We know there are others. Why do you think we're here?"

"Then why did you ask?"

"Just tell us how many."

"There were a few," Zara said. "No one important."

Mistri said, "You showed him the pictures?"

"His."

"In his office?"

"We SMS'd them."

"But you went to his office?"

"Yes."

"And what did he do when you came?"

"He laughed and told me to get out."

"He wasn't worried?"

"He said he had better at home."

Sharmilla laid her hand on Zara's hand. "You called the others? You showed them the pictures?"

She nodded. "Yes."

"Who? Who else did you call? Who else do you have pictures of? How many pictures do you have?"

"I can't tell you."

Fernandez, who had been sitting on the edge of the table, stood up and ground his cigarette out on the table. He walked to the door and looked up and down the hall. He closed the door and crossed the room to stand behind Zara. He bent down close and whispered in her ear, "If you want us to help you, then you have to help us. Who else do you have pictures of? How many pictures do you have? And where is the camera?"

"I promised that if they helped us, we would not tell anyone. I have to keep my word."

"Right," Fernandez said. "A whore's promise isn't worth the air it floats in."

"What's the difference between a whore and a politician?" Zara asked.

Fernandez stared at her.

"A whore washes after she fucks you. You can make me a whore," Zara said. "But you can't make me a liar."

"Does your family know what you do?" Fernandez asked.

"No."

Fernandez smiled. "Maybe it's time they found out?"

"Now who's blackmailing who?"

"And why not? You're not cooperating with us."

"You know what will happen if you do," Zara said. "Why don't you just shoot me? It would be faster."

Fernandez sighed and sat down.

53

Sharmilla asked, "Whose idea was this—" she looked around the table at Mistry and Fernandez "—blackmailing?"

"Mine."

"The police are looking for an American. Do you know him?" Fernandez asked.

"No."

Sharmilla said, "The police say you do."

"So why did you ask?"

"They say you said he left town. If you didn't know him, how would you know that he left town?"

Zara shrugged.

"We are here to help you," Sharmilla said, "but you have to help us, too."

Zara looked from face to face. "I appreciate your help. Do you think you can help us get our wages? That's all we wanted."

Sharmilla laughed without humor. "You're stubborn, aren't you?"

"If I wasn't stubborn, I'd be dead by now."

Fernandez pulled another cigarette out of its case and began worrying the lighter again. After a moment he threw it against the wall and stood up. "The party knows your situation, and wants to help also."

"The Party? You mean Sonia Gandhi?"

"Yes, Congress, though Mrs. Gandhi is not personally involved. Yet." He sighed. "She may be, though, at the rate we're going."

Zara took this in. "How would Congress know about our. . . situation?"

"Word travels fast," Sharmilla said.

Zara shrugged and looked out the window. The pigeons took flight, leaving behind a few tattered feathers.

Sharmilla said, "Just tell us where the American is."

"If you answer one question for me, I will answer that question for you. Who sent you?"

The officials shifted nervously in their seats, but no one answered.

Zara asked, "Are you here to help me or the police?"

"We are here to help you, but you need to help us help you," Sharmilla said.

"I didn't kill anybody. I've told you all you need to know."

"But you haven't told us anything. If you have nothing to hide, then tell us how to find the American so we can talk to him. If he has nothing to hide, then we can clear this whole thing up in a few hours."

"May I use the toilet?"

Fernandez snorted.

Sharmilla looked at Mistry and he nodded.

Alone with Sharmilla in the hallway Zara asked, "How did Godbodle die?"

Sharmilla looked surprised. "Don't you know?"

"How would I?"

"Does it matter?"

"It does to me."

"Why?"

"He wasn't a bad fellow, for a cop. That's why I went to see him. I really thought he might help. Did you know him?"

"Yes," Sharmilla said, "I knew him."

A bent, bow-legged, white-haired old woman in a shabby blue cotton *sari* shuffled down the hall with a bucket of ammonia water and handful of wet red rags. After she passed Sharmilla said, "He was beaten and strangled. They found him in the river, but the coroner says he was dead before he was put in the water."

The lady's loo was narrow and cramped, with a yellow-tiled squat toilet on the left-hand wall. There was a dripping spigot and a plastic bucket on the floor for washing. One light, no windows, one door. Sharmilla went inside with Zara and looked around, then left Zara alone. When she was gone Zara bolted the door and leaned against it, pictured the inspector, tall, dark, muscular, with his thick, black moustache and handsome face. The first time they fucked was in the police station one night after the cops raided Zara's house. He was a big man, and strong. He would not be easy to strangle. Zara imagined a struggle. Godbodle was not the kind of man to go down without a fight. It would take a gang, or someone with a club. A blow from behind and then. . . She closed her eyes. Why didn't they just shoot him? she wondered. Why strangle him? Quieter?

She mused, remembering a story English told her about when he was young and in the American army, in Vietnam. He said that he was some kind of special soldier and that he and his friends wore black hats and traveled in small groups. He and another soldier were in a village, and they had been there for some time, but it was during the monsoon season and all it did was rain. He said that this village was important because it was on a river and surrounded by high mountains. He drew a little picture to make the story clear. He said that one morning the rain stopped, and he and his friend climbed the mountain to see what they could from the top. The mountains were wrapped in clouds. He said his friend didn't want to go, but they did. When they got to the top, English said they saw a camp crawling with enemy soldiers . He and his friend watched and counted, and then, before they left, English said he wanted to leave a card.

Zara thought that this was funny—a soldier leaving a card. In India, just about everyone carried business cards. Even her house had business cards and she gave them to good customers to pass on to their friends. But this wasn't what English meant. He and his friend crept up on two guards sitting at their post and killed them with knives. Then they cut off the ears of the dead soldiers. That was their card—the cutting off of the ears. It was about sending a message. English knew the inspector, Zara thought. He could have killed him. She shook her head. But why? That war was a long time ago. He'd changed. He could kill someone if he had to, but he would need a good reason. Godbodle, big as he was, could be killed. There were men around who could do it.

In the conference room, Mistry and Fernandez jabbered excitedly into their cell phones. They hung up as soon as Zara and Sharmilla returned.

Sharmilla said, "So, why did you want to leave your house?"

The question, on the surface, seemed really stupid. Zara wondered what Sharmilla was getting at. She looked her in the eye and held her gaze.

Sharmilla looked away.

Besides the expensive *salwar* suit, Sharmilla wore nice, soft, white leather shoes with a gold bangle on the top strap. Zara had never owned a pair of foreign-made shoes, though she had seen them in shop windows. They cost as much as she earned in a month. She wondered where shoes like that came from. America? China? Europe? Sharmilla had rings on three of the fingers on her right hand and two on the left, including one with a diamond that meant she was either married or engaged. She had ten or more gold bands on her wrists and a slim silver watch.

Zara had one gold band, one cheap ring, and a pendant of Mary.

Zara guessed that Sharmilla lived in one of those towers on Malabar Hill, or maybe in Bandra. She guessed that Sharmilla had a cook and a houseboy, a cleaning woman, a driver for her car. Her husband or boyfriend loved her right now, but after she had children and her breasts sagged and her hips spread, he would put up a younger, prettier girl in a nest somewhere. Or maybe he would come to Zara's house and whisper his complaints on stained sheets in a dark room. Zara thought, Maybe I've met him already. She looked at Sharmilla's ring again and then looked at Mistry looking at Sharmilla. He was absent-mindedly combing his moustache with his left hand. He, also, wore a ring. Sharmilla looked at Zara, but Mistry kept his eyes on Sharmilla.

Fernandez searched his vest pockets for a cigarette.

"I don't like whoring," Zara said.

And then Mistry asked what must be the dumbest question Zara ever heard, "Why not?"

She wondered what it was she liked the least about her life and decided it was the breath of the men who climbed on her. They were not all dirty, but many were. Some of the men were handsome and clean, but others had stinky gaping mouths full of crooked yellow teeth, bore the smell of their unwashed bodies, grease in their hair, sores on their lips. It was enough to make you cringe. There were abusers, too. Men with knives, or men who twisted her arms and hair, who only got aroused when they threw her across the bed and speared her from behind. She said, "I don't like men climbing all over me. I don't want to die of AIDS. I want to go home and be with my family: my mother, my sisters, my niece. I want a job like everybody else. I want to go to work in the morning, and come home in the evening, and eat my rice, and not have someone else's smell on my skin. And if I ever take a lover, I want it to be someone I want, not someone who wants—" she shrugged, "—whatever."

Sharmilla asked, "What would you do?"

"I don't know. Anything. Something that pays better than making lace for nothing."

"Blackmail?" Mistry asked. "Is that what you want to do now?"

"No."

Sharmilla said, "If we could find the phone, this whole thing might go away."

Zara shook her head. "If there's a dead police inspector, nothing will go away until that's settled. Someone will pay."

"But that doesn't have to involve you."

"Doesn't it? The only reason I'm alive is because you want the phone. I know who's expendable. If you had it, you'd be dumping my body in the river by now."

"Does the American have it?"

"No. He never knew what we were doing."

Sharmilla smiled. "If you don't know him, how do you know he never knew about the camera?"

Zara bit her lip.

"Who has it?" Sharmilla asked.

"Godbodle took it."

"When?"

"Monday night."

The three looked at each other blankly. Mistry said, "So you don't know where the American is?"

Zara shook her head.

He shrugged. "You might be years in jail before your case comes to trial. You know the best thing is to help us help you."

"Jail," Zara said, "can't be much worse than where I live now."

"I guess you'll find out," Fernandez said.

# Chapter 14

Seven people crowded around a rickety rectangular wooden table in a small room on the third (and highest) floor of the Girgaon police station. There was space at the table for six. An air conditioner rattled in its rusted-out frame in the window, spitting out wet, tepid air. Prashant Dashpante, head of the Congress Party in Maharashtra, sat at one end of the table. He was short and fat, with a ring of collar-length black hair hanging like a wreath from his otherwise bald and sweat-spotted head. He wore a tailored suit of white linen that strained to cover his belly. Before him on the table was a tumbler of brownish whiskey with no ice. There were gold rings on all ten of his fingers. He clutched the glass in his right hand and drummed the rings against the glass. Gabi Fernandez and Romesh Mistry sat to his right; to his left sat Sub-Inspector Rane and another khaki-clad police officer, Inspector Yadav, also a muscular, dark-brown Marathi with thick black hair and a moustache, burly arms and big hands. At the opposite end of the table was Uttam Ganesh, a senior official with the BMC—Bombay Municipal Corporation—the over-arching governmental conglomerate running Bombay. If Dashpante looked like a toad, then Ganesh looked like a chameleon with tea-colored skin; his hair was parted on top and dyed rust-brown with henna; his face and nose were thin, his ears tiny, his body sparse, his fingers long and slender. The caramel-colored suit he wore hung loosely on him like a shedding skin. He also had a whiskey, with ice. He stirred it absent-mindedly with his finger. Against the outer wall, beside the window, slightly to the left of and behind Mistry, sat Sharmilla—the odd person out.

They were discussing the aborted questioning. Rane wanted to claim that finding the girl who knew the American was an accomplishment, but it brought them no closer to Godbodle's killer or the missing phone, and Dashpante and Ganesh were angry about that. Yadav had ransacked the brothel and confiscated every cell phone in the house. Mistry had dispatched a man to the office of the telephone service provider to catalogue Zara's phone calls, but the telephone offices wouldn't open until ten, and it even then it might take hours to track down her account. It would be easier if they knew which phone was hers, but no one had told Yadav to find a particular phone or to keep them separate, only to collect all the phones, which he did with ruthless efficiency. They were jumbled in a yellow plastic bag on the table. Every now and then, one played a Bollywood dance tune. It was the same song, always, with the same nasally voice singing  about a poor girl loving a rich man who didn't notice that she existed.

Fernandez lit his cigarette and the room filled with smoke.

"Had I been allowed a few more minutes," Rane said, "I could have beat it out of her." He glared at Sharmilla.

The others turned to look and she replied, "You would have got something out of her, but who knows what? She's more clever than you think. Look at the trouble she's made. You can't treat her like a common bar girl."

Rane shook his head. "No one's clever when you put the boot to them."

You had her for an hour," Sharmilla said.

"There are better and faster ways to find him," Mistry added.

"She'd have cracked like a roach if wondergirl hadn't run in and mucked it up."

Sharmilla bristled. "You can't just beat her to death," she said. "And you can't rape her in a police station."

Rane laughed. "Why not? Wouldn't be the first time."

"Enough," Ganesh said. "I'm interested in solutions. We have enough problems already."

Yadav and Rane glared across the table at Mistry and Shamilla. They were old-school Bombay cops and this techno-psycho-mumbo-jumbo was a waste of time to them. If you want to know something, you beat someone until he gives you a name, and then you go down the line that way until you found who you were looking for. Beat enough people and you got what you wanted. But then again, in the back of his mind, Rane wondered. In this day and age when a picture could be snapped and shot around the world in seconds, who knows? Maybe there was something to be said for new police technologies. The changing times had upset the politics of things. He sensed that the balance of power in the department was teetering.

"Small pebbles," Yadav said, "start big landslides. Best to put a stop to this quickly."

Rane observed that Mistry had edged his chair back and aside so that he was sitting close to Sharmilla. Their romance was supposed to be a secret, but Rane did not need to intercept telephone calls to know. He read body language. He knew by the way they drifted towards one another. He had also seen the way that girl—Zara—hesitated when Rane looked into her eyes. The innocent may show fear or stupidity, but the guilty *think*. The wheels turn and you can see it. That's what gives them away. There was something else she told him—albeit inadvertently. The way she looked at the bucket. Find what people fear the most, Rane knew, and they will tell you anything. She feared water. He'd bet his next month's paycheck on it. If he had had a little longer—he scanned the room and scowled.

Mistry feared Rane, Sharmilla feared Dashpante, Yadav feared Ganesh. And Ganesh and Dashpante? Who knew what they feared? Each other? Some higher-up? Dashpante pulled rank, but Ganesh was old Bombay money. Very old Bombay money. And he was nobody's fool. Mistry, also a sub-inspector, was Rane's rival for promotion. But Mistry, to Rane, was a punk—one of those prissy college boys better suited to gracing fashion magazines than police work. So what if he had earned higher marks on the AIS exam.?What had he done since then? Made training videos? Worked on cooperative sub-committees? Yadav was in line for Godbodle's old job as inspector, but he needed the blessing of the BMC to move up the ladder, and the way to get that was to close the case quickly.

And Sharmilla—her position was purely political. Women. There was a lot of resistance to having a woman cop, but in Rane's opinion, not enough. If she made sub-inspector—the thought was too much for Rane to stomach. Wouldn't it be the shits, Rane thought, if they promoted her just because she was a woman? That was his fear. You do your job well and then they promote someone else because they're a woman or come from a scheduled caste or some other political bullshit. Rane looked from Dashpante to Ganesh. All this commotion over a little blackmail, he thought. He wondered whose pictures were in the phone. Well, he thought, that's another way to move up the ladder—if you're ballsy enough to pull it off. There certainly were a lot of ups and downs riding on one little cell phone. Dashpante was noncommittal. The politician would wait until he sensed which side would win and then act like it was his idea all along. Ganesh sided with Yadav and Rane. Ganesh has no conscience, Rane thought, or more to lose. He kicked Yadav under the table.

Yadav, eager to deflect attention from his own gaffe, said, "Why take the chance? Maybe the phone records are there, maybe they aren't. Who knows what we will find, and how long it will take to find it? Let's have another go at the girl without all this psychology shit. Let's see what she can tell us."

61

Sharmilla shook her head. "This isn't 1993, and there's a foreigner involved. If the American embassy starts asking questions, you'll want things clean."

"It is precisely because we deal with a foreigner that we have to move," Yadav said. "Who knows how long he will be here? As for clean, we can always take care of that."

True, Rane thought. Bags of dope have a convenient habit of finding their way into suitcases at just the right time. And the Americans were always pleased when the Indians bagged a dope-peddler. Rane said, "The Americans don't give a shit what we do to Indians as long as we don't fuck up their citizens. And even if we do, well, he should have known better than to get mixed up with a whore. They'll figure he got what he deserved."

Sharmilla rolled her eyes. She didn't spend six years getting her bachelor's and master's degrees in psychology to beat prisoners. She wanted to be part of a new and improved India, India Inc, they call it, but being a woman, everything she said was under a double layer of scrutiny. "There is right," she said, "and wrong. And two wrongs don't make a right."

"But," Yadav said, "two Wrights make an airplane." He grinned but no one laughed.

Fernandez lit another cigarette.

"Who knows," Dashpante said, "what heads will roll if we don't get to the root of this, and quickly."

Ganesh downed his whiskey in one quick toss and choked. When he regained his breath he said, "Somebody has to make a decision. Might as well be me." He turned to Rane and said, "Go see the girl."

Rane left cracking his knuckles. Yadav followed.

Dashpante went to meet with other Congress Party officials. With elections looming, Delhi was breathing down his neck. He had to spin some damage control.

Sharmilla and Mistry collected the sack of phones and left to work on the phone records. Alone in the hall Mistry turned to Sharmilla. "Next time," he said, "follow instructions."

She paused, then turned, and they walked, shoulders touching, down the hall. At the stairs at the end of the hall she stopped. "It's wrong," she said.

"Get over it." Mistry laid a hand on Sharmilla's shoulder. "If you're going to be a cop you have to keep your cool. Lawyer. What the hell were you thinking? Work yourself out of a job and see how much good you do."

"You promised," she said.

"You may not like Rane or his ways," Mistry said, "but he's effective.

You have to give him that."

In the office, alone, Ganesh stirred the ice in his whiskey, licked his finger, took out his cell phone, called up a saved file and stared at the image on the screen. The girl was pretty, but the picture—that was ugly. He dialed Rane's number. "When you have finished with the girl," he said, "get rid of her. Make it look like a suicide."

# Chapter 15

The processing desk at the Arthur Road Jail was midway between two iron-grated doors in a narrow building painted cat-piss yellow. The walls were high—five meters, at least—and there were barred windows spaced a few meters apart near the ceiling and running the length of the room. The rest, except for a calendar behind the desk, was blank wall. There were three guards in the room when Zara arrived, but the officer at the desk telephoned for more. He recorded Zara's name in a battered red ledger and blotted her fingerprints on a sheet which he filed in a grey metal box. He took her bracelet and ring and chain with the Mary pendant. He also took the safety pins holding Zara's gown together, and she was left in a circle of men with little more than a thin wrap clutched shut. They stood her by the wall and snapped her photo with a Polaroid. They gathered around and watched the image appear on the paper. Grinning, they took away the remains of her gown and took another picture of Zara, alone and naked, and then another, with a crowd of leering guards encircling her. They picked her up, spread her legs, and took a close-up of her pussy.

Four guards led her naked across a small, gravel lot into another piss-yellow building walled with rusting iron bars dividing the building into narrow rows of cages. The cells, except for the first one, were jammed with inmates. In it, two unfortunates slept on the concrete floor. Both were covered in blood and bruises. Zara wondered if they had been beaten by the cops or the other inmates. Did it matter?

In the back of the building was a row of narrow, stone-walled cells with heavy metal doors. The guards opened one and shoved Zara through. Inside was a blue plastic bucket for a toilet and nothing else. At least, she thought, I'm alone.

The cell was so narrow Zara could touch both walls at the same time. When the guards were gone she studied the door. It was worn smooth by the hands of countless others who must have, like her, stood behind it and wondered, Now what? The walls were of heavy stones plastered with flaking concrete and painted the same sickly yellow as the processing room. There was a rusting electrical conduit crossing the ceiling by the back wall. It fed a single-bulb light fixture and entered and exited through holes no bigger than Zara's fist. Too high to reach, and if she could have, too small to crawl through. And the light bulb was out. The only good thing was that with all the stone, the room was cooler than outside.

She sat on the floor with her back to the wall and studied the burns on her breasts and arms. They were red and black and blistered, and she scraped at the loose flesh. She wondered what it would be like to fly on an airplane. She'd traveled by bus and by train, but never by plane. She was not sure she would want to. Still, she had seen TV shows where happy families waited in large, clean lobbies, and pretty, smiling, stewardesses walked down the aisles handing passengers meals and drinks. Maybe, she thought, someday.

She woke to the slam of metal on metal. The door opened to reveal a half-dozen guards. They jerked Zara to her feet and into the hall, then punched her to the floor. They kicked her, and she curled up, covering her face. The beating stopped. Hands lifted her and shoved her face towards the wall. They yanked her hands behind her back and cinched them with a plastic tie. She heard a voice: "Remember me?" Zara turned.

Rane held out a bucket of water. She kicked at it but he jerked it back just in time. He handed the bucket to another cop, ground the knuckles of his right hand into the palm of his left, and punched her in the stomach. Zara sank to her knees at his feet.

Rane set the bucket in front of her. "Tell me about the American," he said.

Zara shook her head.

Rane took her by the back of the neck and squeezed, his hands like a vice. She thought he might crush her spine. When she didn't answer, he forced her face into the water. Ten seconds, twenty, thirty. She squirmed and kicked, shut her eyes and prayed.

Rane lifted her head from the bucket. "Tell me his name," he said.

"I don't know," Zara answered. "I told you already."

"What do you know? Give me something."

"He's an American."

"From where?"

"I don't know."

"What does he do in India?"

"I don't know."

Head in the bucket. Twenty seconds. Forty. A minute. Zara choked. Rane lifted her, sputtering, and dropped her on the floor. She lay at Rane's feet gasping and stared into his face.

"Give me a name."

"He never told me. We called him English."

Rane studied her face. "Is that it?" he asked.

"It's all I know. I swear it." She looked away.

He knelt beside her, fingers on her chin, forcing her to look him in the eye. "Where does he stay?"

"I—"

Rane put a finger to his lips. "Don't tell me you don't know. You must know something. A building? A neighborhood? Does he stay in a hotel or as a paying guest? Think."

"He stays in Bandra."

"Where?"

"I don't know."

"And what does he do?"

"He," she looked past Rane to the bit of light shining in through the open door, "works for the government."

Back in the water. Twenty seconds. Forty. She choked. She lay face down on the floor and puked water. Rane's caressed her bare ass, slipped his fingers between her legs. He rolled her over. "You are lying to me aren't you?"

Zara nodded.

"You really don't know anything about him, do you?"

She shook her head.

"You do or you don't?"

"I don't."

"That's it, then," he said. He sighed and stood, turned to his men and said, "Hang her. Don't forget to cut the ties when she's dead." He left.

A cop placed a folding metal chair in the cell. He stood on it and threaded a rope over the conduit. The other end was already knotted. One lifted Zara onto the chair and held her while another stood behind and slipped the noose over her head and cinched it tight. The chair fell away. The conduit sagged just enough that Zara was left standing on tiptoe dragging little circles on the floor.

Rane reappeared. "Are you sure you know nothing?" he asked. "This is your last chance."

Zara closed her eyes and thought about her family: her mother and father and brothers and sisters and niece. She had worried that they one day they would find out what she did for a living. They thought she was a maid at a hotel. That's what the agent said when he recruited her. An easy job at a tourist hotel. A nice job. Good money. She sent home 2000 rupees a month. Fifty dollars, English said. Half her monthly earnings. And that's what they lived on—seven adults and a child. Her calf muscles ached from straining to stand tip-toe. The noose tightened. The edges of her vision faded to red. Her family. They would never know what happened to her. The cops would dump her somewhere. Someone would find the body. The city would give her a pauper's cremation. The money would stop. Her family would worry, grieve, and eventually, forget. They'd get by without her. Funny, Zara thought, that when she was a little girl, she never expected to die hanging in a Bombay jail. Spittle ran from a corner of her mouth. She could not have talked if she'd wanted to.

Rane shrugged and left.

Zara swayed, strained, holding on, not knowing why. Because. The guards watched. Occasionally one prodded her in the gut with a *lathee*. They were too indifferent even to grope her. Once or twice she weakened, but always a surge of adrenaline renewed strength to her calves and feet. But at length her muscles cramped, she sagged, her vision grew black, and the darkness overtook her.

# Chapter 16

Ashok was sleeping when the phone rang. He grumbled and groped for it. There were four cell phones on the night stand—three of Ashok's and one belonging to Ranjani. He found the offending phone and silenced it. Ranjani was in the middle of the bed and another man—a boy, really, and a white boy, at that, a teenage model Ranjani met on a photo shoot—was on the far side. Some Brit with long hair bleached white. The boy was broad-shouldered and slim-waisted, his chest shaved. Ranjani was curled up tightly with him, her breasts pressed against the boy's back. Ashok saw a tattoo on the boy's left shoulder he'd missed in the dim light last night, or in the excitement of the moment. On the far side of the bed was a tripod with a camera, one light blinking red, meaning the camera was on, and another blinking amber, meaning the DVD was full. While Ashok watched, Ranjani, still sleeping, let her left hand drift under the covers down the boy's stomach to his groin and linger there. The boy moaned and rubbed against her.

Ashok rose quietly and lit a cigarette. He picked up a glass of whiskey from the dresser and swirled the contents, then drank it. Beside the glass was a mirror with a pile of cocaine laid out. He dabbed at the cocaine with his finger, then took a razor blade and lifted a small pile to his nose. Ranjani was awake now, licking the boy's neck, and the boy was stirring, too. Ashok felt a stab of jealousy, looked down at his own belly, not big, not fat, but showing the first hint of what he knew age would do to him. The boy hadn't a spare inch anywhere. The boy rolled over on top of Ranjani, and even though the covers shielded their lower bodies, Ashok knew the boy was inside her, imagined Ranjani's cunt sloppy and warm and wet from last night's fuck session. He saw the tattoo on the boy's shoulder clearly in the morning light, a perversion of one of Michelangelo's cherubs, not staring wistfully into space, but handcuffed to a board, with the exaggerated bare-chested figure of a muscular devil behind him. Below was written in flowing red script, behind every great man. . . is a great behind.

Ashok decided he did not like this boy, did not like the way Ranjani buttered up to him. If she'd been Ashok's toy, then this boy, Mark, seemed to be hers. He watched with a mixture of aggravation and arousal. Above the bed were hung a dozen knives of varying design: a crooked *kris*—a tiger knife—a *ghurka,* a curved knife of Omani design (perfect for slitting throats), a triangular-bladed *Rajasthani* knife that tapered to a long, thin point. If he killed Mark, Ashok thought, he would cut the tattoo from his shoulder and have it framed. Ashok climbed into bed, positioned himself behind Mark, steadied Mark's hips and prepared to enter him.

The phone rang.

He ignored it.

The phone was still ringing when Ashok came. When Ashok lay still Ranjani pushed herself from under the pile and answered. She handed the phone to Ashok. He looked at the number. There was only one call in the whole world he would take before noon. "Hello," he said.

A voice said, "I need you to take care of something for me, today, right now. I trust only you. This has to be done right."

# Chapter 17

Zara awoke on the floor in the corridor, draped in a filthy sheet. Sharmilla stood over her screaming into a phone—a stream of syllables so harsh and fast Zara could not understand a word. Mistry was in there, too, looking twitchy, turning in a circle and shouting into his phone, and there were four very nervous cops standing just outside the door. Three were constables with *lathees*, the fourth clutched a revolver to his chest. A woman cop in a smartly starched khaki uniform pushed past them with a pair of jeans and a faded red tee shirt. She threw them at Zara's feet. Sharmilla looked at Zara and said, "Get dressed. Quick!"

Zara stood as best she could. She eyed the jeans and wondered what prisoner was sitting naked in a cell right now wondering, Why did they take my clothes? The jeans were tight, the shirt wet and dirty. She smelled it and wrinkled her nose. Still, it was better than being paraded around naked again. She winced as she dressed. Her neck burned, her arms and legs throbbed, her face ached, and her stomach and ribs—she could barely bend over. A wave of blackness came, and she almost passed out. She thought she might be sick. The woman cop steadied Zara until the spell passed.

Sharmilla pointed down the hallway, motioned for Zara and the cops to follow. Zara couldn't keep up. The cops looked at Sharmilla who said, "Help her." Two of them moved towards Zara, but she shook her head.

"I'm not leaving until I get my bracelet and ring."

Sharmilla rolled her eyes. "What?"

"And my chain."

"Forget the bracelet and chain!"

Zara shook herself free of the cops and crossed her arms.

Sharmilla laid her hands on Zara's shoulder and said, "I can't promise we'll make it out the gate. We have to leave *now*. Things may change in a hurry. This place is not safe."

"You think I don't know that?"

Sharmilla stared.

"Let them hang me. What do I care?"

Sharmilla said, "They took your things when you arrived?"

Zara nodded.

Sharmilla turned to Mistry and said, "Go find her things. A ring and a bracelet and a chain." To Zara, "Come on, he'll get them."

Zara said, "No."

Sharmilla flushed red, and set her jaw. "On my honor, he will bring your things." She raised her right hand. "I swear. Now please. . . "

Zara hesitated. Sharmilla took a ring off her left hand and pressed it into Zara's hand. Zara looked at the ring. The gold was dark and heavy, the diamond flashed even in the dim light of the hallway. She handed it back. "All right," she said. "You have sworn."

At the end of the hall, an iron gate. Sharmilla hammered on the door with her open palm. A guard's face in a small steel opening. The clank of keys, a creaking hinge. Another hall, short, to a proper door. Sharmilla pounded. A clank of metal, the door opened. Daylight. A courtyard. At one end a gate, at the other, rows of squat wooden barracks. A thousand grimy, sweat-shiny faces watching hungrily. Across the courtyard past a handful of guards to a gate. A small parking lot, a black Mercedes double-parked.

Sharmilla jumped into the driver's seat, shouted, "Get in."

The car was unlike anything Zara had seen. It was so quiet she was not sure the engine was running. And the seats—soft, clean leather, like new. It was like from a movie. They skidded sideways into traffic, tires squealing. She drives, Zara thought. She smiled. She had never known a woman who drove. It was the first thing she liked about Sharmilla.

Sharmilla knifed in and out of traffic like an angry cabbie, only faster. She pushed a button and music began to play. To Zara, the music was like what she imagined angels played in heaven. Sharmilla's phone rang non-stop. She swore; she cursed cars, drivers, cops, lights, pedestrians, dogs, old women, children, the ancestors who spawned them, their offspring to follow.

Zara giggled. In the brothel, girls cursed, but she never expected to hear a woman like Sharmilla use those kinds of words.

Sharmilla looked at Zara sideways, touched her mouth self-consciously, then smiled in return.

They headed south.

"The music?" Zara asked.

"Turandot," Sharmilla replied.

Zara shrugged.

"An opera."

"Ah," Zara said. "Oprah." She remembered seeing a picture of Oprah on TV. The American star. She was black. That was all Zara knew. She sang well, Zara thought. Different from Hindi music, but nice. She wondered if English knew her.

Sharmilla switched off her phone.

Zara watched for landmarks, sank down in the seat as they passed khaki-clad cops with whistles directing traffic on street corners. She recognized a church, and then they passed close by the Crawford Market, and she saw down the road to one of the nice shopping districts. They had passed to the east of Zara's house, headed towards South Bombay. She watched the way carefully. Traffic built and they slowed.

Sharmilla leaned on the horn. A beggar-boy pressed a handful of magazines against the window and she shooed him away with an oath. There was a small hill up ahead and, when the main road turned right, Sharmilla turned left and climbed up a narrow side street, then turned right down a winding, tree-shaded street lined with bungalows. She passed through a tall, iron gate and stopped in front of a detached garage.

"Where are we?" Zara asked.

"My house."

Two servants in white suits appeared. One opened the door for Sharmilla, the other stood off to one side and stared. The front door of the bungalow opened and another servant appeared followed by an older woman in a shimmering royal blue silk sari. Sharmilla bounded out of the car and up the front steps, kissed the woman on the cheek, and they looked back at Zara, hobbling around the car and looking up the stone walk at the front steps. The women talked. The older woman nodded. They beckoned gravely at Zara who climbed slowly, the servants following.

At the top of the steps Sharmilla took Zara by the left arm and guided her into the house and up another flight of stairs, then down a short, carpeted hall to a bright bedroom with large, clean windows overlooking the backyard garden. There was a bed and Zara, without asking, sat, then collapsed onto the bed. It was soft, the sheets crisp and white and clean. They smelled of soap. And then, in this clean room, she smelled the shirt she wore and knew that these people, Sharmilla, her mother, the servants, smelled them, too. She closed her eyes. She could, as her mother used to say, "Sleep in a stranger's grave."

Sharmilla sat on the edge of bed, patted Zara on the arm. "What a day, eh?" she said.

Zara grunted.

"Sit up," Sharmilla said. "We have to talk before you rest."

A white-clad servant entered with a steaming silver teapot from which he poured two cups of *chai*. He offered them a small plate of biscuits. Zara drank, then downed two biscuits. "Would you like to wash?" Sharmilla asked. "Why don't you take a minute to wash before we talk? You'll feel better."

The room had an adjoining bathroom. It was even nicer than the one in English's flat. A sit-down toilet. The floor and walls of black marble. The sink gleaming white with gold fixtures. There was a window of louvered glass. It overlooked the garden, but it was a long jump, perhaps nine meters to the ground. Over the sink was a medicine cabinet and Zara opened it and found make-up, medicines, cotton balls, a hair net, brushes, razor blades, a cup with a picture of Minnie Mouse, and a green plastic box in which she found condoms. She stifled a laugh. It was the last thing she expected. There was a shower stall with hot water, *Chandrika* soap, and some jasmine-scented shampoo. While Zara showered, a woman-servant took away the jeans and tee shirt and left clean clothes on the counter. The bra was too small for Zara and pinched the burns on her breasts, so she discarded it, but the briefs were serviceable. There was also a plum colored *salwar-kameez* with blue trim, the shirt long and loose, the pants also long, but they fit at the waist.

The servants brought a chair to the room and set up a small table with a plate of rice and vegetable curry, cucumbers and dressing on the side. Zara sat down, but before she could eat she heard shouting. It was Mistry and Sharmilla, evidently far back in the house. The words were indistinct, but Zara was sure they were arguing about her. A minute later they appeared at the door, breathing heavily.

Misty handed Zara the bracelet, the ring, and chain with the pendant of Mary.

"Thank you," she said.

"You're welcome," he replied.

Zara sat on the bed and ate with her hands.

Sharmilla walked to the window and looked across the back yard. Mistry went out. When he left Sharmilla crossed the room and sat in the chair opposite Zara. "Are you better?"

Zara nodded.

"Are you tired?"

"Yes."

"I need to ask you a few questions. Only a few, I promise. Can we talk?"

"Sure."

"If I'm going to help you," Sharmilla said, "We have to clear up two things." She took a cell phone out of her purse and handed it to Zara. "Is this yours?"

Zara turned the phone over in her hand. A cheap Nokia, purple plastic with a silver face, big buttons. It was hers. They must have found out from one of her friends. She wondered if the cops bribed or beat them. She said, "No."

"Are you sure?"

"Yes."

"We were told it was yours."

Zara shrugged. "Who told you that?"

Sharmilla took out her phone, a slim, silver phone that opened in the middle like a pocketknife, and dialed a number. "Wrong one," she said.

Zara finished the curry, wiped her hands on a napkin, stood up and walked to the window. There were iron bars on the outside. She tried to remember the ride in the car, but she was so tired. Which way was the main road? She looked at the sunlight, but it was mid-day, hard to read direction from the shadows. Below was a balcony. It might be possible to climb down to it, and from there to the ground below. The garden was walled, the top of the wall set with jagged chunks of broken glass. On the other side of the wall the ground fell or was cut away, the hill leveled for an apartment building rising behind the bungalow. Or maybe it was a tourist hotel. Hard to tell. Zara counted six floors, each divided into repeating patterns of windows and balconies, windows and balconies. A man on the third floor balcony stood at the railing and smoked a cigarette. The door to his room was open and he had brought out a chair. Zara sat down on the edge of the bed. "What time is it?" she asked.

Sharmilla looked at her watch. "Ten till twelve."

A servant knocked softly and brought more tea. He took away the empty plate.

Sharmilla sat beside Zara and patted her arm. She looked at the bruises on Zara's face and neck and shook her head. "You're tough," she said. "Did you know that?"

Zara was not feeling tough, though what she felt she could not quite name. Confused? Shocked? Funny, she thought, how fate prepares you for fate. What was it her horoscope had said? Take your problems one at a time? She stared out the window.

After a while, Sharmilla said, "Tell me about the brothel."

"What about it?"

"How you got there. From the beginning."

Zara's hand strayed to the pendant, now under the pretty *salwar* blouse. Every day, she thought, we hang by a thread. If we knew our fate, could we bear it?

# Chapter 18

Zara took a deep breath and said, "I grew up in Hyderabad."
"I've been there," Sharmilla said. "What part?"
"Near the Lad Bazaar."
"Was your father in the jewelry business?"
"No, we were poor. He worked in a stall making cane juice. He cut cane all day with a big knife."
"And your family?"
"There were six of us, five boys and me."
"And your mother?"
"She died when I was small."
"I'm sorry."
"*Inshallah.*"
"'*Inshallah*'? I thought you were a Christian. I mean, with the pendant and everything."
"I am Muslim, but a friend gave me the pendant."
"I see."
"May I have more tea?"
Sharmilla poured Zara another cup. "And?" she asked.
"When I was seventeen my father arranged my marriage. A boy from our community. He worked for a builder."
Sharmilla's phone rang. She looked at the number, held up one finger, and left the room. Zara stood up and limped to the window where she leaned against the bars and tried to work out some of the knots in her back and her legs. The man with cigarette got up and went into his apartment. He left the door open.
Sharmilla returned.
Zara asked, "Are you married?"
"Engaged," Sharmilla said.
"Mistry?"
Sharmilla rolled her eyes. "Is it that obvious?"
Zara smiled. "It is a love-marriage?"
"I was supposed to be asking you questions."

"But is it a love-marriage? I was just wondering. I—" Zara looked down at her bare feet. "I never knew anyone who had a love-marriage."

"Yes," Sharmilla said. "My family is progressive. My father was a little hesitant, at first, but mother was all for it. So it's a love marriage. But you —your marriage was arranged."

"Yes."

Sharmilla sat on the edge of the bed. "Did you love him?"

"I wanted to. I kept expecting to. I tried to be happy, but he was not much of a husband."

"What happened to him?"

"He lost his job and took to drink. After that, he mostly chewed *pan* and gambled with his friends."

"Children?"

"No."

"You lived with his family?"

"Yes."

"And they mistreated you?"

"What do you like about Mistry?"

"What?"

"What is it that you like about Mistry? I mean—besides that he is good-looking and smart and nice."

Sharmilla looked towards the door and then at Zara. "Please," she said, "We need to focus on you right now. Romesh is nice, and he is good looking. And he's smart and modern and he's going to be very successful. And he treats me well, as does his family. But I was asking about you."

Zara shrugged. "At first they treated me like a servant, and then they demanded dowry from my father. He had nothing to give them. After that they began to beat me, to threaten me. Did his family ask a dowry of you?"

"No, no dowry. What did they—they threatened you with what?"

"They said they would burn me."

"And what did you do?"

"I ran away. You don't think Romesh would burn you, do you? He doesn't look like the kind of man who would burn his wife, though I think he has a temper."

Sharmilla stood up and went to the door, looked down the hall, then returned to the bed. "Romesh would never hurt me."

"How did you meet him?"

"Whose story are we telling here?"

76

"Sorry. I'm just curious. I never knew anyone who made a love-marriage. You see it in the movies. In the movies the poor girls always end up in love marriages with handsome rich guys, but I never knew anyone that lucky."

"So how did you run away?"

"I stole a few *rupees* from my father-in-law's pockets and got on a bus."

"Where did you go?"

"Goa. It was the first bus I could catch. I rode all night. It was early morning when I got there. I was hungry and thirsty. I walked through the town and came to the ocean. I washed. It was salty, but the best I could do. There were churches there and I asked a priest there if there was—"

"You asked a priest?"

"Yes."

"If you are Muslim, why didn't you go to the mosque?"

"The *Imams* would have been suspicious a girl traveling alone. That is forbidden. They would have sent me back, and that would have been the end. Look." Zara held up the Mary pendant. "I knew a girl once who was a Christian. She was always talking to me about the man who walked on water and fed people fishes and told stories that made the rich people mad. So I decided to pass myself off for a Christian and ask for help at a church. A priest listened to my story, but he said he already had all the widows and old women he needed to take care of the chores. I think he didn't believe me. He tried to send me away, but I got down on my knees and touched his feet, and there were tears in my eyes, and he said that at least he would see that I received a meal and a change of clothes. While I was eating, a man came in from the school and said that the pot scrubber had run off in the night with the cook."

Sharmilla looked at her watch and frowned. "So you worked as a pot-scrubber?"

"Yes."

"Where?"

"In Benaulim."

"And what was the name of the school?"

"St. Francis."

"And the priest?"

"Father Greepa."

Sharmilla chewed on her lip. "Did you study in the school?"

"No."

"Why not?"

"They spoke English and Konkani, only."

"You speak English."

"A little, but I don't read or write."

"So you worked?"

"The school was open six days. On Sundays I had only to clean a few pots for the headmaster and his family. After that, I was free to go. I used to walk on the beach. I liked to wash in the salt water. It made my skin feel new. One evening—it was in May and very hot—I had walked a long way to a quiet place, and I thought that no one was around so I went into the water. But when I came out, there was a man watching. He was English—"

"The American?"

"No, he was English."

"A different man?"

"Yes, different."

"What was his name?"

"David."

"His whole name, first and last, do you know it?"

"No. First name only."

"So what happened?"

"He offered me money to sleep with him."

"And you did?"

Zara hesitated. "I had no money, and no way to earn any."

"Didn't they pay you at the school?"

"I got a place to sleep and my meals. The headmaster bought me a *sari*."

"But there is a law in India for workers, a minimum wage."

"There are many laws in India. If everyone followed them, things would be different."

"So this Englishman, David—"

Zara shrugged. "He lived in a cottage on the beach. He took me there and paid me to cook and clean for him."

"And sleep with him?"

"Yes. We lived like that for a year. Then one day the police came. David was away and they wanted to know where he was. David never told me his comings and goings. I said, 'He has gone to see some friends.' The police waited until David came home and then arrested us."

"What for?"

"Drugs."

"Do you do drugs?"

Zara shook her head. "No drugs."

"Did David do drugs?"

"No."

"So where did the drugs come from?"

Zara shrugged. "Who knows? If David did drugs, he never did them in front of me."

"What happened to him?"

"I think maybe he was deported. I'm sure he had money and lawyers. Maybe he blamed the whole thing on me. If you have a good lawyer, anything is possible." Zara looked at Sharmilla. "Are you a good lawyer?" she asked.

Sharmilla smiled and said, "The best."

"Then," Zara said, smiling in return, "maybe you can help us get our wages."

Sharmilla laughed and poured more tea.

"How did you meet Romesh?"

"I met him in school. We were classmates."

"I never went to school. If I had, maybe I would have met someone nice."

The door opened and Mistry and Fernandez came in, and another man Zara did not recognize. This third man wore a cream-colored suit and white shoes. He was older, short, and quite fat, with a thin ring of long gray hair circling over his ears. There were rings on every one of his fingers, even the thumbs. "Is this her?" he asked.

Sharmilla stood up when the men entered the room. She said, "Yes, this is Zara." She turned to Zara and said, "This is Prashant Dashpante, Secretary of the Congress Party of Maharashtra."

Zara looked at Dashpante, and Dashpante looked at her. He said, "So what have we learned?"

"We're just talking," Sharmilla said, and then, to Zara, "Mr. Dashpante is here to help you. There was a big demonstration today, and tomorrow you and your friends are going to be front page news in the *Express of India*. You have created a scandal, and the Congress Party wants to help you."

Dashpante made a face at Zara like he had found her wriggling in his

79

soup and said, "We're going to see that you get justice. We'll find jobs for you and your friends, get money in compensation for what you've suffered. You've made a strong statement for the women's rights, and I can assure you, this comes straight from the top. I want you to think of the Congress Party as your friend. He offered her his hand and smiled. Zara smiled in return and shook it vigorously. Mistry snapped a picture.

After he leaves, Zara thought, he'll go straight to the toilet and wash his hands.

# Chapter 19

Dashpante paused at the door and asked Sharmilla to direct him to the loo. When he was gone, Mistry opened the briefcase and dumped a pile of cell phones onto the bed. "Which one is yours?" he asked.

Zara poked through the pile. She recognized some of them—they belonged to her friends. The cops, she thought, in their infinite stupidity, collected every cell phone in the house, and then they left them on all night. She picked through them. Some worked, but most had dead batteries. She turned two over. They were alike, black plastic bodies with pink decorative front plates. She tried one—nothing. She said, "I can't tell without a charger."

Sharmilla and Mistry both had chargers. They tried one phone and then the other. Neither, Zara said, was hers. Sharmilla frowned and crossed her arms. Mistry glared.

Zara read the watch on Sharmilla's wrist and was glad to see that it was almost 1:00. She pictured English, like the travelers she had seen on TV, stretched out on the plane in a comfortable, big chair, with a pretty hostess serving him a drink and some snacks. She flipped through the address book of another phone. "No," she said. "That's not it either."

"Don't you know what your phone looks like?" Sharmilla asked, her face darkening.

Zara shrugged.

Sharmilla said, "What's your phone number?" Zara told her a number and Sharmilla dialed. "Are you sure?" she asked.

"Yes."

Someone answered. Sharmilla asked who was speaking and a man on the other end of the line asked who was calling, and they got into a tiff. Evidently, the man hung up. Sharmilla asked Zara the number again. Zara had no idea what she'd said.

Sharmilla rolled her eyes. "Here we go again."

Mistry said, "We'll get it, eventually." He called one of his subordinates and asked how the records search was going.

Sharmilla sat down next to Zara and said, "If I'm going to help you, you have to be honest with me. Do you trust me?"

"Yes."

"Then you won't lie to me?"

"No."

"Which is your phone?"

Zara said, "It's not here."

"Then where?"

"I don't know. It was expensive. Maybe the police took it. They are very good at collecting things, and even better at keeping them."

Then her phone—the one Sharmilla first showed her, the phone she had palmed into her the pocket of her *salwar* suit—rang. Oops, she thought.

Sharmilla scowled.

Zara took out the phone and answered, "Hello?"

It was English. He was speaking excitedly, saying something Zara mostly didn't understand. The connection was crackly, but she made out three words: fucking, flight, and cancelled. She thought about this for about two seconds and shouted, "No come you house, big police problem!"

Sharmilla grabbed for the phone but Zara fended her off. She dove across the bed towards the window still shouting, "You go! You go! You go!" Mistry tackled Zara from behind and pinned her arms and they rolled, all three of them, thrashing, from the bed to the floor. Sharmilla tore the phone from Zara's hand and shouted, "Hello, who's speaking?"

There was a long pause.

Mistry let go of Zara and stood up. Zara lay on the floor staring at the ceiling praying silently, Make him hang up. Make him hang up. Make him hang up.

Sharmilla tossed the phone to Mistry. "He hung up."

Mistry took the phone, hit the call-back button, and waited. "Switched off. We got his number, though."

Sharmilla looked at Zara and said, "That was a pretty trick."

Zara stood up painfully. "What did you expect?" she said. In the tussle, the cut on her lip had reopened.

"Why did you lie to us?"

82

Zara laughed.

Sharmilla went to the bathroom and came back with a damp cloth and handed it to Zara. Zara dabbed the blood from her face. "Do you find it funny?" Sharmilla asked.

"Coming from you, yes."

Sharmilla looked hurt. "I thought we were going to be friends," she said.

"You're not my friend," Zara replied. "You were never my friend."

The color drained from Sharmilla's face. She shook her head. "You have no idea," she said, "how much trouble you've caused, and how much trouble you're in, and how much trouble I'm in for sticking my neck out for you."

"Don't I?"

They locked eyes, then Sharmilla and Mistry collected the cell phones and left. When they went out, they locked the door from the outside.

When they were gone Zara thought, If they catch English now it's his fate. She knew the phone company would have his name and address. Indians were meticulous at keeping records. But they were even better at losing them. It would take time for the cops to track him down. She went to the window and checked the bars. They were lagged fast into the wall. The man in the building across the garden was watching from his chair again. Down below, in the garden, three *peons* on their hands and knees crawled on the grass plucking weeds. Zara lay down on the bed and wondered what to do next. It was almost dark when she woke.

# Chapter 20

Sharmilla and Mistry came in followed by two sour-faced lady constables in starched khaki uniforms. Zara sat up, momentarily disoriented, and swung her legs over the edge of the bed. Her head was pounding and her swollen lips had bled on the pillow. Sharmilla had changed into jeans and a long, woven lady's *kurta*, dark blue and embroidered with white and gold thread. She pulled up a chair opposite Zara, straddled it man-style, and said, "Let me tell you what I know, and you can tell me where I go wrong."

"May I have some water?" Zara asked.

"Later."

"May I use the toilet?"

"Later."

The lady constables stood by the door. Mistry nodded at one and she went out.

Sharmilla said, "Your name is Zara and you are from Vijaywada, not Hyderabad. You never married and have never been to Goa. There was never an Englishman named David or a priest named Father Greepa. You never cleaned a school, and you've never been arrested for drugs. Your father is a crippled laborer and you used to work in a factory owned by a man named Devron Ali making *bede* cigarettes. You came to Bombay two years ago and went straight to work in the brothel." She flipped a crude color photocopy of a Polaroid into Zara's lap: Zara naked in a bed with two men. "What do you think of this?" Sharmilla asked.

Zara looked at the picture. Her face hardened. "Where did you get this?"

"It doesn't matter. We have a lot of cops out asking questions about you."

84

The lady constable returned and handed Zara a glass of water. She drank. "They do it to all the girls," Zara said. "It's their way of blackmailing us." She crumpled the picture and threw it on the floor. "Pretty, isn't it?"

Sharmilla picked the paper off the floor and smoothed it, then folded it and put it into her pocket. She cleared her throat, "This man, the one you call English, his name is Paul Shea, and he turned up six months ago and put the idea in your head that you should get out of prostitution. He put you up to this sewing thing, didn't he? And when it didn't work out, he put you up to the blackmail, right? And when that didn't work, he called Godbodle and threatened him. They agreed to meet, but what Paul didn't know was that Godbodle didn't go to the meeting alone." Sharmilla paused and arched her eyebrows. "Well?"

Zara said, "You are right about what didn't happen. You are wrong about what did. And I have been to Goa."

"With Paul?"

"Yes."

"When?"

"Last year. We rented a hut on the beach and went in the water every day. We ate fish at night from little hotels along the water. We took long walks every evening. That was how I knew about the church and the school."

"How did you get there?"

"By train."

"And you came back. . . "

"By bus."

"But you never worked there?"

"No."

"What does the American do for a living?"

"I don't know."

"Where does he live?"

"I don't know."

Sharmilla shook her head. "What has he told you?"

"He's divorced and has four kids."

"Where do they live?"

"I don't know."

You don't know or you don't remember?"

"Isn't that the same thing?"

"No. What you don't know, you've never heard, what you don't

85

remember, you know but can't recall. If he told you, I might be able to help your memory."

"You can do what you want, but I can't tell you what I don't know."

Sharmilla said, "That's not what I meant."

"Isn't it?"

Sharmilla sighed. "Why did you lie to me?" she asked. "Don't you know I'm here to help you?"

"Maybe the same reason you lied to me."

"But I haven't lied to you."

Zara said, "Let me tell you what *I* know. You're no more a lawyer than I am—you're a cop. You were watching me from behind the black glass at the police station. What Rane can't beat out of me, you would coax. But I'm not going to tell you anything, either."

Sharmilla made an angry face and said, "Okay, I lied, but I am still trying to help you."

"Right. I should trust you."

"If I lied, I meant it to be kind."

"Lies are lies," Zara said. "But when poor people tell them to the rich, they are wrong and you put us in jail. When rich people tell them to us, they are kind and for our own good."

"You're hopeless. Did you know that?"

"If you think I am hopeless, you don't know me. I could tell you what hopeless looks like, but I haven't given up and died."

"Yet," Mistry added.

"It doesn't matter now," Sharmilla said. "We have the phone and we have Paul's name and number. It is just a matter of time until we have him."

Zara looked at their faces closely. "You'll kill me then?"

"Of course not," Sharmilla said, "why would we do that?"

Zara shrugged. "Why wouldn't you?"

Sharmilla stood up to go, but she paused at the door and looked back.

Zara said, "Can I tell you a story?"

"A story?" Sharmilla checked her watch. "Sure, why not. All we've got from you is stories."

# Chapter 21

There used to be a girl in our house named Ratni; a stupid country girl from up north, Bihar maybe, or Uttar Pradesh. This was two years ago, back when I first came to Bombay. I had trouble sleeping then. I had nightmares. I was frightened all the time. I cried a lot. I had pains in my arm where I cut my wrists. My body hurt from all the fucking, and from everything else. I didn't have a nice room or a soft bed.

Our house—a long time ago it must have been nice, back when the British ran things, maybe. Now it is run-down. At night I lay on my back and looked at the ceiling. There was a fancy crystal light fixture. It was the only nice thing in the house. I don't know why it was even there. Somebody must have forgot it. Now the plaster is molding and flaking off, and there are mice in the walls. Cockroaches crawl across the floor at night, and they bite us when we sleep. Once in a while the bites get infected—that's how I got these scars on my leg.

I used to pass my time listening to the other girls in their sleep. Lakshmi liked to sleep on the outside because it was cooler, but she liked to have either me or Montaj close by, touching her back. Sometimes she would ask us to hold her until she fell asleep, and sometimes, when I slept beside her, I would wake up and find that she had rolled over and was holding me, like I was her big sister or something. Lakshmi's dreams were dark, she jerked and twitched and cried. When I asked her what she dreamed she said she never remembered. But you know how we lie.

Shilpa and Riya were like twins—inseparable, even in sleep, though they were the quietest, like ghosts, almost. Mumtaz talked in her sleep. Neera slept like a rock. Malika snored like a snorting ox, fat thing, and her body shook like an earthquake. Rachel was my friend until she died, but Ratni was the most interesting of all the girls. She was going crazy and nobody knew why. Some nights she was still as a corpse. Other nights she

87

thrashed and moaned and talked and laughed. Once in a while she got up and got dressed, put on her makeup and tried to go outside. We kept the gate locked, and she would rattle it until Malika or Abishek or Krishna got up and made her lie back down. The mornings after she did this she would wake up angry. She stamped her feet and insisted that we got her in the middle of the night, and made her up as a trick. Sometimes she accused us of using her sexually, and she would demand to be paid. Malika beat Ratni for this.

One night, after I had been in the house for about a year, I had the feeling Ratni was up, and I asked, 'Ratni, are you awake?' and she answered, 'I'm here.'

For some reason, this struck me as funny and I giggled, so she said, 'What's so funny?' and I said, 'Where else would you be?' Then she told me a story.

'Once upon a time there was a mighty Raj who lived in a big bungalow on a beautiful hillside, and all the people in the village loved him. He had a wife and four children—three boys and one girl, and the girl was the youngest and she was his favorite. They threw parties which all the politicians and movie stars and big-shots dared not miss. They had cars and drivers and servants and took long vacations in places like Switzerland and Disneyland. They were so happy that the gods became jealous and decided to plague the Raj, and so they did two things. The first thing was they cursed the little girl so that her eyes went this way and that, and all the letters on the page jumped about when she tried to read. And the second was that they took a big ball of dung and made it into a beautiful woman, and made the oldest son to fall in love with her. But this woman was already married to another man, an evil boy from a family of blood-drinkers, and when the evil man and his brothers found out about the affair, they became very angry. First they took the young girl's older brother and beat him with iron rods so that they broke his arms and legs and messed up his mind. Then they came to the house in the brother's car, drove right past the guards to the front door, and they took the little girl and drove away with her.

'The father was very upset. He called the authorities and he called his politician friends, and he promised to pay a ransom for her release. But the brothers of that evil man said that money could not restore their honor, so they raped the little girl all night long, and did terrible things to her, and tied her to a tree by the highway and left her there, naked, for passers-by to see.

'What could the father do? His son was broken and his daughter ruined. In his time of need, all of his friends deserted him. He and his servants put on their best clothes, and went to the house of the blood-drinkers demanding justice. There was a big fight, and later that night the servants carried the man home with all the blood gone out of him. The mother committed *suttee* on her husband's pyre.

'The girl's brothers made peace with the blood-drinkers, and kept the house, but in time, they did not wish to bother with a simple-minded girl who would never be married. One of them sent his servant out with the girl and a can of kerosene. But the rain came and the servant could not light the match. Instead, he fucked the girl and drowned her in the river.

'But Hanuman, the Monkey God, took pity on the poor naked girl floating in the water, and caused her to be tossed up on the steps where the laundry *dhobis* did their washing. A washerwoman found the girl and sucked the water out of her lungs, and kept the girl for her own. The girl scrubbed clothes on a stone in the river, and then, while they were spread to dry, the woman taught the girl to knit and crochet, and they sold the napkins and tablecloths and things they made in the market. When the girl turned fourteen and menstruated, the washerwoman took her to the city and sold her to the pimps. Now she sleeps with men all night and knits all day.'

After this I quit paying attention to what Ratni said. But at least one thing was true: Ratni knitted all the time. She was not a pretty girl, though she might have been, if she took care of herself. She was short and fat, but she had pretty skin and hair. And because she was simple, she let the men do things to her that the rest of us would not. She let them fuck her in the ass, fuck her without condoms, she did French. Whatever they said. All she wanted was to finish and get back to knitting.

One day, when Ratni was lying in the upstairs room during her MC, Lakshmi came to me and said, 'Do you ever wonder what Ratni does with all her knitting?' and I said, 'No, I never thought about it.' Lakshmi took me by the hand and led me to the big AC room in the back and stood on the bed and pushed back a ceiling tile and said, 'Look up there.'

I took the little table and set it on the bed, and when I stood on the table and looked, the ceiling was full of knitted things, napkins and cloths and baby's dresses and all kinds of stuff. I guess that having no other place to keep them, Ratni threw them up in the ceiling. None of us had thought about what she did with it all.

Lakshmi thought this was funny, but I felt sorry for Ratni. She made these things all day, and then she hid them in the ceiling at night.

A few days later, Lakshmi and Malika got into a fight about money, and Ratni was sitting in the corner knitting. In the middle of the argument Ratni chipped in that she had not been paid for all the men she slept with that night—and there were none—but she complained anyway. Lakshmi told Ratni to go fuck herself, the usual kind of thing Lakshmi said. But instead of keeping silent, Ratni threw herself on Lakshmi and knocked her to the floor. Lakshmi was screaming. Malika was beating Ratni with her stick. Abishek the cook tackled Ratni and wrestled the needles away from her, but by the time he pulled her off, she had stabbed Lakshmi. We carried Lakshmi to the hospital and she took stitches, and Malika said that Ratni would have to pay her medical bills. After that, Ratni was not allowed to knit anymore.

From that day on, Ratni began to walk around in a daze. She mumbled to herself, laughed for no reason, played with her fingers in the air, and it became harder and harder to get her to talk or watch TV or make sense. The men began to complain that she was too dumb even to fuck, and Malika took her to the doctor and he said there was some disease that was messing up her mind. He sold her some pills but they didn't help.

It was either throw Ratni out on the street, or let her knit again. Malika was going to throw her out, but I begged her not to—I don't know why—but I had to promise to try to help Ratni get better. So Malika let Ratni knit again as long as one of us was there to keep a close eye on her. That was how I learned how to knit—helping Ratni. And knitting with me seemed to help her. She would talk and sometimes laugh, and some of the life came back in her. After that, all of us girls—except Lakshmi—began talking to her more and sitting with her. For a while, it was like old times again.

Then one night, when the room was quiet, and it seemed no one was awake, I heard Lakshmi ask, 'Ratni, are you awake?' and Ratni answered, 'I'm here.' Lakshmi said, 'Can I tell you a story?' and Ratni said, 'Okay.'

Lakshmi said, 'Once upon a time there was a family of shitheads who lived in a crumpled matchbox on a dung heap on the edge of town. The oldest boy in the family was so ugly he knew he would never get a wife, so he used to drag his little sister into a hollow by the river, and ass-fuck her cross-eyed. One day the girl had enough of his foolishness and doused the boy in kerosene while he slept, and set him on fire. Then she jumped into the river and tried to drown herself, but a stupid washerwoman saved her. The poor father, who did not know what else to do, took his daughter to a mental hospital where they promised to lock her up forever. But instead they kept the girl for a little while, and then told the father that she had died of a disease. After that, they sold her to a whorehouse where she weaves tall tales.'

The next day, Ratni braided a rope of yarn and hung herself in the upstairs room.

When we divided up her things, I asked for the needles and thread. We had seen this thing on TV about an NGO that taught girls like us how to knit. I thought about all the knitting hidden in the ceiling above, and it was me who got the idea to sell them. And that was how I got into this mess.

# Chapter 22

S harmilla listened quietly while Zara talked, and when Zara was done Sharmilla nodded slowly and drew a deep breath. She opened her mouth, but before she could speak a white-suited servant appeared in the doorway with a tray of covered silver bowls. He set the tray on a small table in the corner and ceremoniously removed the covers. He placed a serving spoon in each bowl, and left the room. There was rice and *dal,* a potato curry, some *aloo gobi*, a small dish of curd, and steaming *chapattis*. There was a glass of water and a cup of tea. The smell of curry saturated the room.

"Are you hungry?" Sharmilla asked.

Zara nodded.

"I'm sorry there is no meat. Since my father died, my mother is a strict vegetarian." She gestured for Zara to help herself. "Go ahead. I'll eat later with my mother downstairs."

Zara spooned her plate full, then nodded in towards the loo.

"Of course," Sharmilla said.

In the loo, Zara quietly locked the door and stretched, arching her back and then touching her toes. She wiggled her spine as loose as she could, and cracked the knuckles on her fingers. She opened the medicine cabinet and took two condoms, dropping them into the pocket of her *salwar* suit. She looked out the window.

The back yard was deserted, and the man on the balcony in the building across the yard was gone. The door to his room, however, was still open.

She bent the little metal strips holding the glass slats in place and removed the three lowest slats from the window, climbed onto the toilet, and gingerly wriggled out, feet first, and then clung to the ledge digging her fingers into the windowsill and trying not to look down. There was just a bit of roof jutting out over the patio to her right, immediately below the bedroom window, and she jumped for it and reached it—barely—but not solidly enough to catch her balance. She toppled backwards from the roof to the ground and landed awkwardly on the grass, partly breaking the fall with her right hand. The pain was instantaneous. She might have broken her wrist, but there was no time to nurse it. She gritted her teeth and tried to shake it off, but that only made it worse. She could not move her hand or fingers. She gripped the injured wrist with her good hand and looked around.

A stone fence topped with jagged shards of broken glass surrounded the back yard. Zara could not climb it one-handed. Even if she could climb it, and get over the broken glass, the house stood on a hill and was terraced —cut away—to level the property for the apartment beyond. It might be another five or ten meters to the ground on the other side of the fence. Maybe more. She had no way of knowing—and there was no gate.

Zara hobbled to the house and tried the back door. It was unlocked and opened to a dining room. Close by, in the kitchen, the cook and several servants gossiped about a neighbor's daughter's upcoming wedding. The kitchen door opened and a servant came out. Zara ducked and shut the door behind her. Along the wall was a spigot with a hose coiled beside it. Zara crossed the yard unraveling the hose behind her and tossed the end over the fence. She returned to the back door, and picked up a small rug left for people to wipe their feet before entering the house. She threw the rug on top of the fence so that it covered the broken glass. She dragged a potted plant to the fence with her left hand, and standing on the pot, managed to scramble to the top of the wall where she lay on the carpet, half on one side, half on the other. It was a good ten meters to the ground. She shut her eyes. The hose reached only about half-way to the ground, but there was a shrub below that might break her fall, if she could reach it. She gripped the hose with her good, left hand, spun around on the wall so she could drop feet-first. From the top of the wall she looked up and saw Sharmilla, open-mouthed, staring at her from the window. Zara slid down the hose as far as she could with one hand, and when her grip failed, she jumped.

The shrub broke Zara's fall—sort of—but she tumbled to the ground where she upset a small table laden with potted plants. The table collapsed and the pots shattered. The noise was deafening. She scrambled to her feet. This building was also fenced, but at least there was a gate, and Zara ran to it. It was bolted and she rattled it in a panic before she realized that it was not padlocked. It opened to a flagstone path that led alongside the house and out to the street. There she found a cab idling in the shade and told the driver she'd give him a blow job in exchange for a ride.

"First the blow job," he said, pointing at his crotch. He grinned like he'd just won the lottery.

93

"Not here," she replied.

He reached across the seat and opened the door.

She did it in an alley a few kilometers north, insisting that the cabbie wear a condom. A good thing she took them, she thought, for he had not bathed in a long time. Afterwards, she told him to take her to the Zaveri Bazaar and was surprised—and grateful—that he did. There she sold her bracelet and ring to a seedy gold merchant who she was sure cheated her. Still, she had 3,300 rupees. Down the road she stopped in a small shop and bought a cheap, pale blue cotton *salwar kameez*, a small clasp purse, and a pair of sandals. She changed into her new clothes still nursing her wrist and folded Sharmilla's *salwar* suit and packed it inside a plastic bag. Outside the shop she bought two *samosas* and a cup of *chai* from street vendors. She bought a used cell phone and called English. His mobile was off.

She called home. Her mother answered. "Amma," Zara said, "You have to leave the house right now. Take everyone and run. Don't ask. Don't tell anyone where you go. The farther the better."

Her mother did not understand. She argued, she cried, she asked over and over again, "What is the trouble?"

"I can't tell you," Zara said, "but people will be looking to hurt you."

Her mother was almost incoherent. She wailed, "I should have never let you go to the city."

"I'm okay," Zara said. "This will pass. I promise. I just want to make sure that you are safe."

Her mother was stubborn. She had no place to go. She was not going to leave. She would pray until it passed.

"But you must," Zara said, "at least for a few days. Go to Chennai, stay with Kaka Ibrim, or stay on the beach. But you must leave the house. I will meet you there."

Her mother refused. "Come home," she said. "Your family will protect you."

"I won't," Zara replied. "I can't. There is something here I have to take care of." She found another cab and told the driver "Malabar Hill." Along the way she thought about her hard-headed mother. It was just like her. Women don't run, she thought. Twenty years with a no-good alcoholic husband will do that. What could the gangsters do that her husband hadn't? Put an end to her misery?

English stayed in a flat in a gated high-rise, a white concrete tower of perhaps thirty stories. He said it belonged to a friend who worked in Dubai. Zara did not know the name of the friend or how English knew him, or why the friend let English stay in his flat. The guard at the gate recognized Zara but told her, politely but firmly, that *Sahib* was out. She crossed the street and sat on a bench under a tree. It was no use arguing. The guard would never let her in.

It was almost dark. Zara's wrist throbbed as the swelling and the pain increased to just short of excruciating. She walked to a small store and bought a bottle of cold water and some biscuits. She asked if there was a chemist nearby and the proprietor said no. The closest one was far down the hill. But he had aspirin and she bought a few sour pills wrapped in heavy foil. After a while, the pain eased.

Traffic was heavy. Servants were running after-dinner errands, husbands and wives chauffeured home from work, or were out for their evening social activities. Above the parking garage in the building where English stayed was a playground, and children shrieked and called, taunting one another. A cricket ball flew over the railing and a boy shouted down for it. The guard at the gate ran the ball down and threw it back. A group of college students walked by, boys and girls together, a few daring to hold hands. They were young and beautiful and carried books. They were dressed in the latest fashion: tight western jeans and tee shirts. The girls cut their shirts short so that a sliver of their belly showed. One daring girl cut hers so short a bellybutton jewel glittered. The boys who could grow beards wore stubble. All of them had jelled and teased their hair. It was good, Zara thought, to be young and rich and in school with your whole life unfolding like a lotus in front of you. But there was so much about life they didn't know and might not survive if they faced it. Zara wanted to go to school, too, once. But things don't always work out like you plan. One door closes and another opens. Sometimes the path leads up, and sometimes it goes down.

# Chapter 23

Ⅰt was the hottest day in May, the hottest month of the year. Your mother and auntie lay on the bed dozing and moaning from the heat and complaining about old age. The neighborhood was dead. Even the dogs had disappeared. Everyone laid low but you. You stood by the door wide awake and eager, for in a little while your friend, Esweria, would come home from school. Though she was only three years older than you, she was the oldest kid on your block in school and still young enough to hang out with you. For this, she was like God to you, even though she was only in the third standard. So every day you made excuses or made a nuisance of yourself until you mother let you out of the house and you ran to the end of the street and waited for Esweria. Then, when she came, you followed her to her door asking endless questions about her day. The rest of the kids on your block were mostly frightened—or at best, disinterested—about starting school. They suffered Esweria only because she was the oldest and toughest, thus the leader of your group of friends. But you taught yourself to tell time just so you could meet her, and to count the calendar to watch the year pass, knowing that at the end of the month of May, you would begin school, and then you and Esweria could walk together in the morning, and home in the afternoon, your *tiffin* jangling from a string over your shoulder, a bundle of books clutched tight to your chest. And then you would see for yourself if the many things Esweria claimed—and with such authority!—were true: if the world really was round like a ball and many days train-ride across, if men dug in the ground to find the bones of dragons, and how to unlock the mystery of words. You would talk about your lessons with her. You would confide in one another. You would be friends. You would be smart. And all the other kids, and everyone in your family, would look up to you.

In the evenings, after it cooled, Esweria produced a broken slate and a nub of chalk she found in the rubbish heap behind the school, and practiced making letters while the rest of the kids licked their fingers and drew muddy imitations on flat stones you ripped from the wall that separated your block from the railroad tracks. Esweria darted among you playing teacher, correcting your letters and hitting you on the back with a switch for "misbehaving." This was how you learned to write your name: Zara. You were struck with the realization that that those four letters stood for you. Then, as you proudly watched the letters on your stone, the sun dried your name away.

You somehow had come to believe that words should be important to your family, even though none of them could read or write. You were sure that you would be better off if you did. For one thing, you are Muslim, and the Imam in his sermon said you were under obligation to learn the words of the holy Koran. How could you live a good life without the knowledge of the Word of God? Also, this was a time of great fear and uncertainty. There had been trouble with the Sikhs. Their temple had been attacked by the army, and in retaliation, Indira Gandhi's Sikh bodyguards killed her. After that, there were many people shouting in the streets, handing out tracts, and painting words on windows and walls, once writing them on the face of a drunk sleeping off his spree in the gutter. And sometimes crowds gathered in the streets and men in orange turbans shouted until the crowds ran wild, breaking glass and setting fires. On the television grim-faced men appeared—Rajiv Gandhi and his gang—and they said they were doing good things for India, but that these things were difficult, and people needed to endure these hard times until the situation got better. They made a name for these times: Emergency. It was what you called it when things went wrong.

For months there were riots and strikes, angry mobs marching this way and that, and shouting. They shouted that the government had to go. They shouted that the government had to stay. They called for more strikes, and they cried that the strikes were too much to bear. And when they came down the main road from which the small lane turned that led to your home, your father barred the door and switched off the lights, gathered you in his arms and prayed that they would pass, for even though you were Muslim and had not had any part in this misbehaving, the memory of the partition riots were still fresh in the minds of many, and your father knew that for some, any excuse to kill Muslims would do. Though you were on good terms with your neighbors, there was always the lingering fear that someone would betray you. "A word is all it takes," he said. *A word.* How could they have such power?

On quiet nights your mother, heavy with your youngest brother, leaned over the stove in the dark and boiled milk for *chai* and cooked rice and *chapattis.* Your father washed his face and put on his clean white *kurta,* laid out his *namaz* rug, and bowed towards Mecca and recited his prayers. You rocked your baby sisters on your knees and sang to them fragments of the lullabies your mother sang to you. How did you remember them? You just did. The words came to you like nothing. Later, in the dark, when you lay on the floor to sleep, your father and mother whispered the words they did not wish you to hear, the fear bleeding through the tone of their conversation, even if the meaning escaped you. And you swore that when you went to school, you would do whatever it took to be the topper in your class, and you would know everything about everything, and all of the answers, and your family would never suffer hunger or fear again.

Your father was a laborer; the son of a laborer, his father the son of a laborer. No one in your family had ever been to school. As far as you knew, they'd been laboring since time began. In the mornings he rose and took his place in line in the railway yard. If a truck or a boxcar needed loading or unloading, he passed bags of rice or limes or bales of tobacco or burlap sacks stuffed with cotton up or down the gangways. When he was young, your father was strong, and he was always one of the first men chosen for work. But later he was run down by a truck and his right leg crushed. Though the doctor set the bone, the leg was shortened and askew, and your father limped badly and was always in pain. After that it became harder for him to find work. Eventually, he turned to drink and quit trying. But during this time—this Emergency—there was no work at all, and the *chapattis* your mother made became smaller and smaller, and the tea so thin you could count the leaves swimming in the bottom of the cup. Then one day, in mid-May, the landlord came and said that if you did not pay the rent, he would send his *goombas* to throw your family into the street. After he left, your mother cried.

Even at your young age you were aware of the people living on the street, and eyed them with a mix of terror and pity. They came from the country and the outlying villages, especially when there was famine or drought, and they built little shelters of plastic or cloth, and cops harassed them during the day, and the rats and mosquitoes plagued them at night, and they knew nothing but hunger and fear and shame.

So the following Monday, the first day of the last week in May, on the very day when your friends all went to the market to buy their tablets and books and uniforms for school, your father took you by the hand and walked you across the railroad yard, loping along with his peculiar up-and-down gait, you holding his hand, hurrying along beside him. Together you pushed your way down a crooked maze of alleys crowded with rickshaws and handcarts and ox carts and men rushing here and there with their burdens, or zipping through on motorbikes, or in cars with their horns blaring, until you arrived at a crumbling brick building with a rusting tin roof; a factory, you would learn, for making *bede* cigarettes.

Inside was a large room with a threadbare rug gray with age, and a desk under a creaking ceiling fan. Behind the desk lurked a fat, greasy, middle-aged man with a lick of black hair hanging down over his eyes like the young heroes in war movies. He had skin the color of coffee; a thick black beard, tube lips, and a round face with a long, wide nose. His eyes glistened like polished stones. He wore a black shirt without a tie, open to the middle of his hairy chest; around his neck, a thick gold chain. He drummed the desk with sausage-like fingers. To his right stood two young men in jeans and tee shirts. His sons. They waited, you thought, like vultures.

Your father bowed his head and said, "*Salaam Aleichem*, Devran Mohammed Ali."

Devran nodded and replied, "*Aleichem Asalaam.*"

Your father recounted the difficulties he had endured since his injury, and how they had worsened under this "emergency". He recited the praise he had heard spoken of Devran Mohammed Ali—his business acumen, the care and love with which he presided over his family, his devotion to Allah, his charity.

Devran listened, nodded at the appropriate places, licked his lips and stroked his beard. His fingers glittered with gold rings set with colorful gems. When your father finished, Devran gestured that you should sit and he sent his servants for *chai*. While you waited, he came around his desk and stood you up, took your hands in his. His fingers were warm and damp, and you felt suddenly cold. He pressed hard on your palms, ran his fingers down yours, bent them forward and back, felt the muscles of your neck, your shoulders, massaged the small of your back through the thin fabric of your blouse. His hand slipped to your buttocks. You shut your eyes and wished he would go away. You will always remember that touch, repulsive and thrilling at the same time. A man put his hands on you. It was frightening and wrong and enlivening and confusing and somehow right, and that—the right and wrong part—was what stung the most.

When he was done, you wiped the sweat from your hands onto the front of your dress, though you tried not to let him see. The servant returned with tea in small white cups. Devran took a pen and paper from the top drawer of his desk and wrote, opened the bottom drawer and counted out a stack of limp, worn bills. After your father made his mark, Devran pushed the money across the desk, and your father put it into his pocket without counting. Your father knelt before you, took your face in his hands, kissed you, and said, "You will remain for the day with Devran Ali. I will come for you this evening." You learned, years later, that an able-bodied child sold for a thousand rupees. Twenty-five US dollars.

Devran led you to the back of the shop. It was dusky and dim. A single bulb hung by bare wires in a room six meters square. Inside, twenty-three sweating girls worked kneeling in four even rows, over concrete blocks turned flat-side up. None looked as you entered. Beside each block were three baskets and a ball of fine pink thread. One basket contained soft green *tandu* leaves, one had tobacco and herbs mixed, and the third was for finished cigarettes. In the back row was one block with no girl, and Devran led you to it and forced you to your knees. You did not want to stay. You wanted to follow your father. Devran placed one hand on the small of your back. His fingers dug again into the flesh of your buttocks. With the other hand he adjusted your feet and knees so that your butt sank to the floor.

"It is better for your legs," he said.

You stared at the back of the girl in front of you.

Then he slapped you in the back of your head so hard that lights swirled in front of your eyes. The rings on his fingers made the blow sharp. He caught you by the hair and yanked your head backwards so that you faced the ceiling, bent almost to the floor. He leaned over you, his face snarling. He said, "When a man speaks to you, you answer, Yes, *Sahib*,"

Your tongue froze. You could barely breathe.

He shook you by the hair and said, "Say it."

"Yes, *Sahib*," you croaked.

"Good." He let you go and patted you like a dog.

Devran snapped his fingers and a girl moved to your side, took a leaf from the basket and sprinkled it with tobacco. She shook the leaf to spread the powder evenly, then rolled it into a tube. She unrolled it half-way, crimped both ends, and re-rolled it. She wound a bit of thread around the narrow end so that the leaf would not unravel, bit the thread in two and tied it while holding the fat end in her mouth. She spit the cigarette into the empty basket and gestured for you to try. It took you three tries to make your first. After that, you rolled one cigarette every ten seconds, fourteen hours a day, seven days a week, for sixteen years. You rolled them when you were sick. You rolled them when you were well. You rolled them at night when you dreamed.

# Chapter 24

I t was nearly midnight when the cab dropped Paul in front of his apartment. He climbed out, read the meter, paid the cabbie, said, "Keep the change." The driver had been honest. He drove Paul home without giving him the roundabout or getting stuck needlessly in traffic. Paul turned towards the entry, where the guard had sleepily opened the gate just wide enough for a man to pass through. As he crossed the street he thought he heard someone call his name. He stopped, looked back, saw a figure swaying in the shadows across the street. Zara walked into the light.

"Eh, English," she said.

They hugged in the middle of the road, Paul aware that she favored her right arm. Paul asked, "What are you doing here?"

"You police problem."

Paul laughed at the absurdity of this, even though he remembered Zara's reaction that afternoon when he called. He arched one eyebrow in a gesture that almost always made Zara smile, but she didn't smile. She looked haggard. "Do you mean, you have a police problem?" He tapped her gently on the breastbone. Her English sometimes required descrambling.

She shook her head and tapped Paul on the breastbone, "No, *you* police problem. You go hotel. No you house go."

"Come with me," he said. He took her by her good hand and guided her through the gate. They passed the guard, walked to the lobby, rode the elevator to the twelfth floor.

Zara was exhausted; she leaned against the elevator walls. Inside his apartment he poured her a glass of water and she gulped it down. He poured her another and she gulped it, too. "I'm afraid I don't have any food left in the house," he said.

She went to the window and peered anxiously through the curtains. She said, "You phone switch off."

"I went out with friends."

"Okay, okay. Police come my house look you."

Paul was tired, too. He had been staying up extra hours to make it easier to get through the jet lag his flight home was sure to cause. There was a ten-and-a-half hour time differential between Philly and Bombay. If he left Bombay at noon he would arrive in New York sixteen hours later but it would be six-thirty in the morning. A couple of hours to clear customs, a couple more hours to connect to home, and it would be noon when he reached his house, but midnight on his body clock.

He sat down on the couch and looked at Zara. She might be telling the truth, and she might be telling something like the truth, and then again, the whole thing might be a scam designed to relieve him of a few more rupees before he went home. But it didn't feel like a scam. There was something earnest in her voice, and there was nothing fake about the way she favored the arm. Besides, he was supposed to be—he looked at his watch—about half-way between London and New York right now. What the hell? She couldn't have known the flight was going to be cancelled, could she? "Come here," he said.

She sat beside him. He took her right hand and she winced. He turned the wrist palm up and stroked it gently with the tips of his fingers. It was swollen half-again its usual size, though not the discolored blue, green, and purple he would expect if it were broken. But there were other bruises, too, and what looked like burns on her arms. She was not wearing the bracelet he gave her. That was odd, too. He expected some kind of a robbery story.

As if reading his mind she said, "I sell."

He looked at her neck for the chain and the Mary charm. They were there. Then it registered for the first time, in the light in his living room, the bruises on her neck and face. They were hard to see through the brown of her skin, but she was pulpy and tender. Her lip was swollen. It had been split "Who did this to you?" he asked.

"Police."

He stood up, crossed the room to the window, pulled back the curtains and looked out. The street was deserted, only a few cabs parked on the road, the drivers sleeping in the back seats, their legs hanging out the open doors. He opened the window. There was a bit of a pre-monsoon breeze and the cool air felt nice. He turned on his mobile and when it powered up, he punched in a number.

After a half-dozen rings a sleepy voice said, "Hello?"

"Dr. Maneshka, please."

When the doctor picked up Paul said, "I hope I'm not waking you."

"Not at all," the doctor said. "I was just reading."

This might be true. More likely, it was a kind lie. But the doctor was a doctor, and late night calls came with the profession. "Look," Paul said,

"I have a friend here who showed up at my apartment and she's hurt her wrist, and she looks like she's been beaten. She says the police did it. Can you see her?"

There was a long pause. Paul realized that his story must sound like bullshit, some late-night spousal-abuse thing. But he and the doctor were friends, and the doctor should know Paul was not like that. Still, Paul felt the blush rising on his cheeks.

"Of course," the doctor said. "Do you know where Jaslok Hospital is, on Pedder Road?"

"Yes."

"They have a very good casualty ward with an x-ray machine. I'll meet you there in half-an-hour."

Paul turned from the window and Zara was gone. He went into the bedroom but she was not there, either. The big suitcase was closed and standing by the closet, the little one open on the bed. There was nothing in it but his clothes and some books, nothing that would interest Zara. It didn't look disturbed. She came out of the loo and he said. "Come on," and they went downstairs and found a cab.

As soon as he told the driver, "Jaslok Hospital," Zara protested. "No hospital. I fine. You going." She barked something at the driver in Hindi. The driver looked from Paul to Zara and back again, and Paul repeated his instructions and dropped a hundred rupee note into the front seat. They drove to the hospital.

Doctor Maneshka was nearly ninety. He was a recent widower and at the age where the body's sag really showed. He was once tall, but was now bent and compressed, his flesh droopy. He was bald as a cricket bat and sported thick bifocals, but his mind was sharp and his manner kindly. Still, he looked tired all the time, and moved slowly. Once he was one of the most respected physicians in Bombay, though he'd faded from prominence now that he was semi-retired. Mostly he did charity work. He was a Parsi, and Paul met him through a mutual Parsi friend. They registered at the front desk and a nurse led them to a private examination room where Zara stripped, still squabbling.

Paul's eyes bulged when he saw the burns on her breasts and back.

The old doctor was gentle and thorough. He checked Zara's abdomen, back, neck, and shoulders while she sat impatiently, glaring at Paul. He cleaned the burns with cotton swabs and applied antiseptic ointment.

When he finished the doctor said, "The wrist is strained, not broken, and we don't need x-rays. She's getting the movement back already, though it is painful and it will take a few days before she regains full mobility. I'll wrap it to make it more comfortable for her. She has been beaten and she might have been raped. I can't tell that for certain without a more detailed examination. And yes," he said, "it looks like she's been tortured. The police do things like this. Paul, what have you got yourself mixed up in?"

Paul shook his head. "I don't have a clue."

"How did you meet this girl?"

Paul thought, but before he could answer the doctor said, "I know she's a sex-worker, so don't make up stories."

Paul didn't ask how Maneshka knew. He was a doctor and he must have seen thousands of them. "I met her in a brothel, but she's become something of a friend."

"Yes," Maneshka said. "They do that sometimes."

"Can you talk to her for me? She says I'm in trouble, but I have no idea what's going on. Why would the police do this to her?"

The doctor questioned Zara in Hindi, and Zara replied; a long, broken, melodious explanation. The words increased in volume and speed as they poured out. There was urgency in her tone. The doctor nodded from time to time, his eyebrows lifting.

As if drawn by gravity, Paul found himself by Zara's side, his arm around her.

When she finished the doctor sighed and rubbed his temples, then put a finger in his ear and scratched, checked it for wax, and wiped it on his pants leg. He stared at the floor, lost in thought. Finally he said, "She says the police came to her house looking for you because they think you killed somebody—a police inspector named Godbodle. They took her to the station and roughed her up trying to get information about you. She says she told them nothing, but when you called her the police got your number. She says she escaped to warn you to get away."

The doctor looked at Paul and Paul looked at Zara. Zara's eyes brimmed with tears and she looked like she might break down right there on the examination table.

"I think," Maneshka said, "that she's telling the truth, or something like it. Do you have any idea what she's talking about?"

Paul knew exactly what Zara was talking about—or at least *who* she was talking about—but it wasn't the kind of story you spread around. He had gone to see Zara some months back. The house was practically deserted. There were half the usual number of girls, and Zara was clearly agitated. He thought, I should have known something was up. She tried to make him leave and when he wouldn't, she took him in the back bedroom and told him to hurry. Something was up, but what that something was, well, that was anybody's guess. His first reaction was to suspect that she had another boyfriend she was meeting. Was he jealous? The more he asked, the less sense her answers made. In retrospect, she had to have known what was coming. A raid. They had just sat down on the bed when there was a commotion down the hall.

Zara perked up. "Sit down," she said. "Police problem. No tension."

No tension? Right. A cop pounded on the door and when Zara opened it he grabbed her and jerked her into the hallway. Paul didn't care for that. When he stood up the cop grabbed his arm and Paul shook it right off—a little judo move. The cop raised his *lathee* and Paul pointed and said, "I wouldn't do that if I were you."

The look on the cop's face was priceless, a cross between my-life-is-passing-before-eyes and who-in-the-hell-do-you-think-you-are? In the end, the cop lowered his *lathee* and gestured down the hall. There was a handful of cops in the main room, one sub-inspector in particular Paul remembered. He was putting on a show slapping Krishna the tout around. Nothing to do but take it, Paul thought.

And then this damned sub-inspector saw Paul and asked what had to be the world's dumbest question: "What are you doing here?"

Paul busted out laughing. "I'm the fucking cook," he said. "What does it look like?"

The sub-inspector didn't appreciate Paul's humor. He fronted Paul, and for a minute it looked like they might fight. Fuck him, Paul thought. I could mop the floor with this bastard. Then the head honcho came upstairs, a full-fledged inspector, a hoot of guy, Godbodle. He whistled the sub-inspector off and gestured that Paul should go.

Paul went, but he stopped in the alley and leaned against the wall across the street, waiting in the shadows. They might take the whole lot of them to jail for all Paul knew, but Zara was his girl and she wasn't going anywhere. He had enough cash in his pocket to see to that.

In a few minutes Godbodle came downstairs. He'd been drinking and was in fine form. He saw Paul and guessed why he was hanging around. He slapped Paul on the back and said, "Don't worry. This is just routine." Then, to prove what a good guy he was, he took Paul up and down the alley and showed him a dozen whorehouses Paul would never have guessed were there. Christalmighty, Paul had thought, the place is infested with them. Godbodle gave Paul his card, told him to call sometime and he'd take him on a tour of the city's steamy side. Paul laughed and thought, Hell, if I wrote it all down just like it happened, nobody would believe me.

In the end the cops came downstairs with two pretty girls. The girls didn't look too happy about the situation—lambs to the slaughter—so to speak, but Zara wasn't one of them, and Paul wasn't going to risk trouble by intervening on their behalf. He went back upstairs, and when Zara saw him she burst into tears. She thought the police had arrested him.

"No," he said, sitting down on the bench beside her. "I was going to bribe the cops if they arrested you." And that made her cry even harder.

So when Dr. Maneshka asked if Paul knew what Zara was talking about, he shook his head. "I have no idea," he said.

"Is there some reason the police might think that you killed this bloke?"

"Not so far as I know. I was supposed to be on a plane at noon, but my flight was cancelled. I called Zara to tell her and she said there was some kind of police problem. I took it to mean there was a raid at her house. Then some woman came on the line asking me who I was so I hung up. I actually went by her house, but there were cops all over the place, so I bailed. I mean, I've got a plane to catch. What could I do? I tried to get her out of this racket, but she won't quit. I don't want her to go to jail, but I guess it's what you call an occupational hazard. I called some friends and they said it was best to leave it be, she was probably just trying to pry some money out of me. And if she was in jail, they said there was nothing I could do in twenty-four hours except get my passport taken away. I figured she'd be out soon enough. So I went to dinner, saw a movie, and when I came home she was hiding outside my building."

The doctor listened politely, then slowly gathered his things. Paul reached for his wallet but the doctor waived him off. At the door the doctor asked, "What do you propose to do?"

Paul shrugged. "Delta is supposed to have me on a plane tomorrow. My travel agent is on them for me."

"What time?"

"Noon."

"Before you go," the doctor said, "you should check with the airline. If the police issue a warrant for you, they'll pass your name along to the immigration authorities and pick you up at the airport."

Paul thought about it. The whole thing seemed pretty far-fetched.

The doctor said, "I have a few friends in security there. I can make a discreet inquiry for you, if you wish. They'll tell me if you're on the list."

"Thanks," Paul said. "I think I'll be all right." After the doctor was gone, he looked at Zara and thought, What the hell have you got me into?

# Chapter 25

Outside the hospital, Zara looked up and down the street. There was little traffic. The hospital was near the top of a hill and a few cars and motorbikes topped the hill from the east end, heading down towards the Haji Ali Mosque and the main road towards Worli and Bandra and the north end of the city. It must be past one, she thought. Twenty-four hours, more or less, since Paul had kissed her goodbye. A lot can happen in a day. She plucked at the wrap on her wrist. The night had cooled off somewhat, but the monsoon humidity was building, and inside the bandage her wrist was sweating.

Paul pulled her hand away. "You'll unravel it," he said.

She shrugged.

"Are you hungry," he asked.

Zara nodded.

Paul flagged down a taxi. The driver was thin and unshaven, his eyes shifty, his face slimy with days-old sweat. He was a decidedly evil-looking man—the kind of driver who makes his living peddling vice. But there were no other cabs around, so they got in.

They drove down the long curve of Marine Drive, the Queen's Necklace Mumbaikars call it, turning away from the waterfront when they reached the tall buildings of the business district at Nariman Point. They stopped at last in front of a late-night restaurant in Colaba, the tourist district. In front were two uniformed security guards and a *maitre d'* wearing a Sikh fighter's outfit—a white suit with a fat green sash and a white turban. He opened the door for Zara.

The restaurant was nearly full, despite the late hour. Zara was surprised to see so many foreigners, though about half the customers were Indians, too. Rich Indians, she supposed, the socialites who like to be seen in the places the foreigners go, and whose pictures graced the *BomBayWatch* section of the *Express of India*. The women wore their best jewels and *saris*, the men, western-style business suits, the kids, the latest in jeans and tee shirts. A waiter in a black suit tried to seat them by the window near the front door, but Paul barked at him and the waiter found them a quiet table in the back. English, Zara thought, looked tired.

The waiter brought menus and bottled water. Zara looked at Paul, but he was reading the menu and did not look up. Zara looked at the menu and made sure that hers faced the same direction, tried to remember if the writing went right-to-left or left-to-right. She knew the prices were the most important thing and saw that they were in triple digits. Her eyes bulged. In Vijaywada her family lived on less than a hundred rupees a day. Rice. *Dal. Chapattis.* What else does one need? How could you eat a single meal that cost more than a family of eight could survive on for a day? She said, "No eat here. Too much expensive," but Paul said something she took to mean that the money didn't matter. "You choice," she said. It wasn't worth arguing about.

The waiter returned and Paul ordered lime sodas, salted, with no ice, a chicken *tandoori,* rice, *dal*, and butter *naan*. They ate in silence. Paul tore the chicken into pieces so Zara could eat with her good hand. He ate with a fork. Zara tried, but silverware was unfamiliar to her and she was clumsy. Paul said, "It doesn't matter," and when she persisted he began to eat with his fingers, too, scooping up rice and *dal* with bits of the *naan*.

They found a cab outside. "Malabar Hill," Paul said.

Zara protested. "No, English," she said. "No you house go. Police come."

He shook his head. "They'll never find me there."

The driver eyed them curiously in the rear view mirror. Zara sank down in the seat and rested her head on Paul's shoulder, found his right hand with her left and clasped it, worried the whole way.

The guard was sleeping and had to be roused. Upstairs, Paul undressed and fell onto the bed. Zara lay down beside him. "Jig-jig?" she asked. She did not feel like fucking, but felt she should oblige. He smiled and stroked her hair. She stood up to undress but he said, "No," and she lay back down. In a moment, he was asleep. She pressed her face into his chest and breathed in his scent. It was the first time in her life anyone said no to sex with her. It was an odd thing, she thought, to like about him.

That night Zara dreamed she and Paul went to a movie. The picture—one they had watched together a few months back—was about a monk who lived high in the Himalayas, but left his home and fell in love with a beautiful woman. Zara had seen high mountains in movies, and there was a low range of mountains only a few kilometers west of her home in Vijaywada. Paul had pointed and said that he had been to those mountains, and later on, in his flat, he showed her pictures on his computer: high, snow-covered peaks; buildings of yellow stone clinging precariously to the rocks; men with shaved heads and blood-red robes walking in long, winding lines up trails into the mountains.

In her dream Zara and Paul were dancing in a field of short, green grass. He held her by her hands and they spun around and around. But her body was aching, her wrist especially, and every step became like torture. And then she was on tiptoe spinning around and around in the Arthur Road Jail with the noose around her neck. Rane kept shouting, "Tell me about the American!" With great effort she stopped spinning and faced Rane. Her tongue was swollen. She could feel the veins in her throat beating against the rope. Behind Rane, in the passage outside the cell, Paul knelt, his hands tied behind his back, his head submerged in a bucket of water.

# Chapter 26

Zara woke with a start. Paul was up, washed and dressed, standing by the window with his back to her, talking on his cell phone. He wore a fresh white *kurta* over jeans. She sat up and saw his bags by the front door. The clock on the nightstand said just past seven.

It was strange to wake with the thought that today might be your last day on earth. How many people, Zara wondered, had that experience? Condemned prisoners? Martyred saints? Soldiers on the day of battle? She closed her eyes and thought about her mother, her sisters, her niece. She crawled out of bed and showered as quickly as she could, trying to keep the wrap on her wrist dry. Every move pained her, but the warm water felt good on her skin and she loosened up a bit. Paul came in and touched up her burns with a tube of ointment Maneshka had given them. She had no change of clothes, so she dressed in the same *salwar* suit she bought the day before. When she came out of the bathroom, Paul had made coffee, American style, strong and bitter, without much milk or sugar. He was still on the phone.

She drank the coffee and her head cleared. She realized she was holding the cup in her right hand. It was sore, but not as bad as before. The swelling was down. The wrap had worked loose. She re-fastened it.

Paul hung up.

"Going?" she asked.

He nodded, said something. Maybe his tickets were straightened out. Who knew? They caught a cab to Mumbai Central Station, stopping only once for Paul to visit an ATM. At the station Zara stayed in the cab while Paul bought her an AC ticket to Hyderabad, as close to Vijaywada as he could buy on short notice. He kissed her again, and pressed into her hand an envelope full of bills. Then he left for the airport. When he was gone she counted the money—almost 13,000 rupees—enough to live for half a year back home.

She thought about leaving for Hyderabad. She could call her mother again, but her mother wouldn't leave. And hiding wouldn't change anything. It might—at best—delay an unpleasant end. She knew who gave Sharmilla the photo, the one of her with the two men. They knew her home and her family. And if they knew, then the cops knew. And she had friends at the brothel. If she left, the gangsters would exact revenge against them. Somebody paid, no matter what. It didn't really matter who. The real crime wasn't the murder or the blackmail or the prostitution or the rapes or the torture. The unforgivable sin was bucking the system. That was why they would make an example of her—to put the fear of God into the rest. Unless, she thought, I kill them first. Right. Winged snakes might fly from heaven and do the job if she prayed hard enough. And then, standing on the sidewalk in front of the train station, Zara realized how their plan had gone wrong. That flaw, she thought, was now her best and only hope. But she couldn't fix things by herself.

Of all the customers Zara knew, there was only one unprincipled enough to help her, if he was out of jail: Sanjay. Sanjay was a thief, and proud of it. When he had money, he was a great customer. He would lie up in her house for days, eating, drinking, fucking. When he ran out of money he drove cab until he stole a suitcase or robbed somebody, and the cycle started all over again. The only interruptions were the rare instances when he got caught. Since he hadn't been to her house in a while, the odds were he was in jail. But it was worth a call to find out.

Zara racked her brain to remember the number. She guessed the best she could and dialed. Sanjay answered. "I need your help," she said.

"Who is this?" he asked.

"Zara."

"Oh, my little cutie! Have you missed me?"

"Yes, I have missed you."

"I have just this week got out of jail!"

"Good," Zara said. "I mean, good that you are out. Are you driving a cab?"

"Right now I am sleeping. What time is it?"

"Eight or so."

"What is it you need?"

"Can you meet me at Central Station?"

"Central Station? Why not your house?"

"I have a job for you."

"I can be there in half an hour."

She hung up, then stood on the corner and watched the morning traffic build. A police jeep arrived and four cops climbed out. Zara hurried away and found a *chaiwalla* down a side street. People came and went, the flood of morning commuters built. A boy came by hawking the *Express of*

*India.* He was chattering like a monkey, repeating the headline over and over. And the headline, absurd as it was, got the commuters' attention. The papers flew out of the boy's hands. NO PAY NO PLAY! SEX WORKERS STRIKE FOR WAGES. Zara laughed. Yes, confusion was a good thing. If she couldn't solve the problem, maybe she could make it worse.

# Chapter 27

Sharmilla watched from the window as Zara went over the wall. She ran from the room down the stairs, grabbing Mistry on the way, but by the time they started the car and reached the street below, Zara was gone. They looked until midnight, driving in ever-wider circles. The entire night shift of Bombay cops was on alert. They patrolled the train stations and threw up roadblocks on the highways leaving town. They broadcast her photo. How could the girl just disappear? Everybody knew where she went—to Paul—but nobody knew where Paul stayed. How could they have communicated? Telepathy? Rane and Yadav were furious. Dashpante was livid, Ganesh, beside himself. They ramped up the pressure on the phone company; threatened audits and arrests. The number the cops had provided led to a blank screen—someone had not yet entered the data. They would have to find the hard copy of the sales receipt. The tekkies promised an address by morning.

Sharmilla argued in her mind as they drove. She reproached herself for bringing Zara to her house, but on the other hand, she had to do something. She couldn't just let them kill the girl. That wasn't right. So it wasn't entirely her fault. But when the time came to find a scapegoat, she knew where she stood—which was exactly one place ahead of Zara in line. And Zara was as good as dead. Sharmilla found that thought disquieting.

In the night Sharmilla dreamed of the interrogation room, only she wasn't saving Zara, she was being blamed for killing Zara. But Zara wasn't dead. She gestured, she pointed, but no one listened. Sharmilla was behind the black glass with her mother and Rane and Fernandez, and they were arguing about who had killed Zara. Zara was in the room with her hands tied behind her back and her head in the bucket. There was a cop holding her under. Sharmilla beat on the glass. When the cop turned to face her, it was her uncle, Wet-eyes.

She woke at first light. Over coffee, she ran down a list of hiding places: Goa? Kashmir? Would they cross into Pakistan or Nepal or Bangladesh, flee to America from there? Sharmilla wondered what she would do were she in the same boat. Then the irony struck her: she *was* in the same boat. Somebody was going to take the fall for this. No prizes for guessing who. She dressed, ate, and went out to her car. On the way to the police station she wondered, Now what? When she arrived she found out. Rane sacked her. Booted her off the team.

The only reason Sharmilla wasn't arrested or fired outright was because Mistry, Fernandez, and the two lady cops were in the house with Sharmilla when Zara escaped, and they all agreed that Zara had only been in the loo for a few seconds—what could they have done?

"Gone in with her?" Rane asked.

But Sharmilla wasn't going down without a fight. "You were going to kill her!" she shouted as Mistry and Fernandez dragged her out of the conference room. "What the hell difference does it make if she escaped? You didn't want her anyway!"

"You're wrong," Rane shouted after her, "what we wanted was her out of the way. Now we want you out of the way."

The bitch, Sharmilla thought. All this idealistic, new-age, psycho-crap Sharmilla had been spouting since she was a student worked fine in classrooms and coffee shops, but it wasn't worth a damn in the real world. Was it really possible for a woman alone to turn the tide on ten thousand years of history? Dammit. Turn your back for a second and she's gone. And for the second time that morning the irony struck: It took a woman to fuck a woman. Zara had done to Sharmilla what no man had been able to do in four years on the job.

Mistry and Fernandez deposited Sharmilla on the sidewalk outside of the police station. "Go home," Mistry said. "Be glad you still have a job. They'll find a place for you somewhere. Probably in Dharavi. And next time—if there is a next time—keep your mouth shut and do as you're told."

As I'm told? By *them*? It was, Sharmilla thought, time to put up or shut up. She wasn't quitting now, not with Yadav and Rane on top. And then she thought, Neither will Zara. It was the first thing she'd liked about the girl. While she was brooding on the sidewalk, a boy came by hawking the morning's *Express of India*. He stuck a copy in her face. She pushed him away, but called him back. The headline caught her eye: NO PAY NO PLAY! SEX WORKERS STRIKE FOR WAGES. It couldn't be. She opened the paper and read the article. A communist agitator from Kerala. A march down Falklands Road. And at the bottom, almost as a footnote, a shop wrecked in the night on Warden Road.

*Threads!* was a small specialty boutique, one of a dozen tiny stores on the ground floor of an old-but-recently-renovated building in a row of old-but-recently-renovated buildings all of which housed similarly themed upscale stores: designer clothing, upscale bedding, specialty lighting, party jewelry, a dry fruit and *farsan* shop, a fashion optometrist's office, a yoga studio, a trendy shoe store—along Warden Road near Breach Candy Hospital. It didn't seem like the kind of place that would cause a fuss. On the right, the dry fruit store. On the left, the flower shop. On the sidewalk outside a boy sold newspapers, and an industrious *wala* had set up a little cook-stand where he was busily frying and selling *batada wadas* and *masala pav* to curious onlookers.

Sharmilla spotted the shop right away, not by the sign, for it had been ripped from its hinges and lay in pieces on the ground, but by the plywood over the window and the slogans painted in bold black strokes on the door, the walls, and the sidewalk. Bitch dogs eat their workers! Wages or War! Power to the People! Revenge is the Right of the Oppressed! On the sidewalk someone had stenciled a red hammer-and-sickle with the words: Pay or Die! Outside the shop, a woman with long red hair, embroidered jeans, and a gold *salwar* blouse watched while a barefoot servant-boy in shorts and a tee shirt swept shards of glass into a pile. Sharmilla stepped out of her car and approached carefully. "Mrs. Shetty?" she asked.

Mrs. Shetty started and looked Sharmilla over, but there was nothing unusual about Sharmilla's appearance. Green *salwar* with gold brocade, a gold *bindi* with a blue stone in the middle. Make-up: kohl-lined eyes with plum lipstick. She must have looked like a typical customer, for Mrs. Shetty's face brightened. "Yes. Please forgive the mess. Some miscreants came in the night and wrecked my store. Can you believe it? Look," and she gestured with her hand, as if the damage needed pointing out. "They chased off the watchman and ruined my stock. Now my help is too frightened to stay on. Tell me," she said, shrugging her shoulders, "what's a woman to do in such times?"

Sharmilla shook her head. "I don't know."

"That's a pretty *salwar*," Mrs. Shetty said. "Did you buy it from my sister? She has a shop a block down."

"No, I got this one at Shetal's."

Mrs. Shetty nodded. "They make good things, as well, but they are so expensive. They have a name to support, I suppose. My sister's things are just as good, often made by the same tailors, only cheaper, not that money counts for everything."

"Of course."

"And you are Mrs. Pillon?"

"No. My name is Oberoi."

"I see. But you are the woman with the wedding coming up, right? You wanted the brocade in purple?"

"No, I am an assistant sub-inspector with the Mumbai Police, Girgaon

Road Station. I'm here to talk about your—" she looked at the ruined store, "difficulties."

Mrs. Shetty's face darkened. "Bah," she said, and she spit into the gutter. "My stock is ruined, my store vandalized, my employees frightened off, and now you show up? You! A woman by yourself? What are you planning to do about this, eh? Where were the police last night when the *goombas* beat up the watchman and wrecked my shop? Tell me that! Look," and she pointed to the ruined padlock on the ground by the front gate. "They even brought a blowtorch to cut off the lock! How did they manage that and nobody say a word? My landlord is already starting proceedings to evict me. He heard about this before I did. Do you think maybe they called him? He wants me to pay for the damage those shit-birds did." She pointed at the hammer-and-sickle on the sidewalk. "They signed their name, damn their whore-mothers." She shook her fist at the sky. "I'll sue them so hard their children will feel it!" Mrs. Shetty's voice quaked. She waived her finger in Sharmilla's face. Spit was flying from her mouth as she shouted. "And what are you going to do about it? Why don't you go down to their office and arrest those communist friends of your? Or are you afraid that the Congress will lose the next election without their precious little half-wit allies?"

"Actually," Sharmilla said, brushing Mrs. Shetty's hand from under her nose, "that's not the difficulty I came to talk about."

Mrs. Shetty stepped back, smoothed her blouse and patted her hair. "What do you mean?" she asked. "What difficulty? As if I don't have enough problems, you bring more?" She paused, looked sideways at Sharmilla, then at the onlookers watching her rant. "Oh," she said. "Perhaps we should step inside. I'll call for *chai*."

Sharmilla shook her head. "That won't be necessary. I'm not fishing for a bribe."

"What, then?"

"Do you know a girl named Zara?"

Mrs. Shetty bit her lip. "Those fucking whores," she said, "I ought to have had them killed. That's what I should have done. Every one. They're not worth the price of a bullet, but look what trouble they cause! So they're behind this. I should have known. What, now? Don't tell me they bribed you, too? Or have they blackmailed you?"

Sharmilla arched her eyebrows. "Maybe we should have that *chai* after all. You can tell me about her."

The boy who was sweeping stopped and looked up hopefully.

Mrs. Shetty said, "Go!" and waived him in the direction of the *chaiwala*.

116

He dropped the broom and rushed away.

Mrs. Shetty watched him glumly. "He's not coming back," she said. "Wait and see."

The store was worse inside than out. The stock had been burned. A rank smell hung in the air as if the visitors had used the corners for a toilet. The shelves and displays had been wrecked with axes. The office door was broken down and the desk chopped and splintered, the phone crushed, the lines cut, the light fixtures, the sink, everything ruined. Two plastic chairs survived unscathed, as if someone had sat in them and watched the havoc play out.

They sat.

"I don't know what I did to deserve this," Mrs. Shetty said. "I run a good store and I have a lot of nice friends. We cater mostly to weddings, birthday parties, graduations, anniversaries, that kind of thing. It should be a happy place. My customers come from all over, not just this neighborhood. I cater to the best clientele in Bombay. Many of them are Brahmins or Jains. They want to know that the things they buy are clean and well-made. So I got a phone call. This girl said she heard that I sold knitting and lace, and I told her I had my suppliers, but she said she was good and could work cheap. I said, 'What the hell?' You know, it can't hurt to see what they can do, right? They came to see me. They looked okay. They wore clean clothes. They looked like working girls. That should have clued me in right away—they weren't like us."

"Us?"

"You know, they weren't educated. Still, I thought they might be a couple of poor women looking to make some money on the side. So they showed me some samples. I gave them a few small orders." She looked around the room and laughed. "Well, now I know what they can do."

"But they delivered the goods, right?"

"Yes, they delivered the goods. They were even—well—not badly made. They knew some clever tricks. I've seen work like that before. It's done in Calcutta and the northeast. But right away I knew something wasn't right. My father—he was in the Bombay Stock Exchange—used to say, 'If something looks too good to be true, it probably *is* too good to be true.' So they brought some samples, and their work was okay. I'm not going to lie about that. And I had some special orders—the summer weddings are on—and so I gave them some work and they left."

"And they delivered the goods on time?"

"No. They sent it early. That was the problem. Nobody delivers early."

"I don't get it."

The boy returned with two cups of tea. Mrs. Shetty, looking surprised, told the boy to finish sweeping. She continued, "I didn't have the cash on me."

"Who came?"

"Two girls."

"Zara?"

Mrs. Shetty hesitated. "Yes, maybe it was her. I don't remember names. A tall girl and another one, short and dark. They were edgy about the money. And they were low-class girls, their accents, their ways. I could tell they didn't know what they were doing. I offered to send the money by courier on the agreed day, but they said they'd come back for it. That's when I knew they were hiding something. Leave the goods without getting paid? Come back another time? Who were they kidding? So when they left, I sent my boy after them. He followed them to Lamington Road, asked around. He told me where they went, and what they were. The nerve of them! What else could I do? My customers are respectable. If anybody suspected that my things were made by women like that, I'd be ruined. I got rid of their stuff straight away. And when they showed up for their money, I set the servants on them and ran them out of my shop. Serves them right. Whores! And this is how they repay me?"

"What did you do with the lace they brought you?"

"I destroyed it."

"All of it?"

"Every stitch."

"How? Where?"

"I had my servants put it in boxes until the city truck came around, then we threw it out."

"I'll need the names of your servants," Sharmilla said, "and addresses where I can contact them."

Mrs. Shetty laughed. "I can give you names, and don't you know I wish I could contact them. But after what the *goombas* did to the watchman, I think they all took off for their villages." She shrugged. "What to do?"

"Of course. So there's no one, no manager, no special employees, no one, say, who might have spoken English?"

"No, this is a small shop. A one-woman operation. At least, it was a one-woman operation until last night."

"And now?"

"I think I'll close, take a vacation. I was thinking about taking some classes anyway."

"The girls, they asked you for their money?"

"I told you, we ran them off."

118

"But they contacted you again, right?"

"Yes." Mrs. Shetty said. She began picking at some loose fringe on her sleeve.

"Who contacted you?"

"I don't know. There were some phone calls."

"How many?"

"Eight or ten. It was annoying."

"Did you write down the number?"

"No, I didn't think anything would come of it."

"Were they were blackmailing you?"

"What do you mean, blackmail? Isn't harassment a kind of black-mail?"

"Perhaps, but there are other ways—less pleasant than harassment."

"Of course not. Why would you even ask such a thing?"

"You brought it up. You asked if they were blackmailing me."

"So what of it?"

"But why would you talk about blackmail if they weren't blackmailing you?"

"I only asked if they were blackmailing you. I didn't say they were blackmailing me. How could they blackmail me? I have nothing with them."

"Are you married?"

Mrs. Shetty's face darkened. "Are you implying that my husband would have anything to do with these girls?"

"They had to get your name somehow."

The cup chattered in Mrs. Shetty's hand. She set it down on the floor.

"I'm not implying anything," Sharmilla said. "I just asked if you were married."

"I am married. Happily married, with three sons and one daughter. My oldest son is at college in America, at Georgia Tech."

"I'm sure you're very proud."

"He is studying engineering. He wants to be a civil engineer and design bridges and transportation systems and such."

"Is there anything else I should know?"

Mrs. Shetty hesitated, then said, "A man came."

"Can you describe him?"

"He was big and bald. He was a Keralite."

"From Kerala? You're sure?"

"He spoke with an accent. He said that I should pay or suffer the consequences."

"Can you describe him better?"

"Better than what?"

"There must be ten or twenty million big, bald Keralites."

"He wore blue pants and a white shirt."

"That narrows it down a little."

"And he had a moustache."

"That's very useful. Did you by chance get a name or see a car or anything else?"

"No. He came and I told him to go fuck himself. Can you imagine that? What, are they unionizing whores now, as well?"

Sharmilla laughed. "Have you read the morning paper?" she asked.

"I haven't the time. Why?"

"They are. They're unionizing whores. There was a rally yesterday on Falklands Road."

"You're kidding me."

"No. By the way, do you know all of your suppliers?"

"Yes."

"And you can vouch that they are all, how did you put it, respectable?"

Mrs. Shetty nodded. "They are as clean as workers can be. That's what counts. They're not, well, they're not like whores are."

"One thing? Off the record."

"What's that?"

"Why didn't you just pay them? Wouldn't that have been—" she gestured at the shop with her free hand, "cheaper. I mean, you have the money, don't you?"

Mrs. Shetty's face reddened. "Of course I have the money. It's the principal off the thing," she said. "Who do they think they are?"

Sharmilla set down her cup. "They know who they are," she said. "I think what they wanted to know was: Could they be somebody else?"

# Chapter 28

It was ninety-seven degrees in the shade and there was no shade, not on the west side of Napean Sea Road, on the hot sidewalk, outside the twenty story condo where Mistry stood sweating like a one-man monsoon. A dozen or so *lathee*-wielding cops stood in a knot eyeing him with that special contempt enlisted men reserve for incompetent superiors. Mistry had just led a raid on a vacant apartment. Worse, it was under renovation and had not been occupied for months. The cops charged upstairs ready to kick down the door and beat Paul within an inch of his life, and instead found there was no door, no Paul, no nothing, only a dozen skinny barefoot laborers, illiterate drifters from the country, chalky white with plaster and paint. They scattered like cockroaches as soon as the police turned them loose.

Mistry got the address from the FonTel tekkies. He called his superiors and then organized and led the raid. Now Rane was on his way, and Yadav, and perhaps Uttam Ganesh as well. Mistry called and tried to ward them off, but they were in transit and said to sit tight, they wanted to see for themselves. Nothing to do now but wait until they arrived. And then? Then he takes it in the shorts. He rolled his eyes to heaven. The cops already had a name for it. When he told them he was going to arrest Paul they said, "Don't pull a Sharmilla on us." Sharmilla, he thought, you are not taking me down with you.

It was past midnight when Mistry finally convinced her that she was better off getting a decent night's sleep, and looking for Zara with a clear head in the morning. "She's sleeping," he said. "You need your rest, too." But the truth was, he needed his rest. They had been driving aimlessly for hours, turning ever-wider circles, scanning faces in the endless Bombay crowds.

"She has no money, no family, no friends," Sharmilla said. "Rane has someone watching the brothel. Where will she go?"

They knew the answer. She would look for Paul, but where was he? Still they drove. They passed a restaurant, Delhi Dabar, the only one in Colaba open that late. Mistry pulled over. Outside, a *maitre d'* in a traditional Sikh uniform with a fat green sash and a white turban nodded deferentially towards them. "Are you hungry?" Mistry asked.

"No," Sharmilla said, "my stomach's in knots."

Mistry looked at her, a glance blending pity and disdain. He pulled back onto the road and drove on.

"Just say it," she said. "Get it over with."

"I didn't say anything."

"Ima fuck-ing idiot. Ima fuck-ing idiot." It came out like a song.

Mistry shook his head. "You're not an idiot, you're an idealist. There's a difference."

"An idealist is an idiot with an education."

Mistry grunted.

Sharmilla glared at him. "You weren't much help," she said.

"I tried to warn you, but you're about the most headstrong woman I've ever met." He thought about this for a minute. "It's one of the things I like about you."

"Why couldn't I have just kept my mouth shut?"

Mistry had thought the same thing several times in the past twelve hours, but he kept that to himself. Instead he said, "It's not your nature."

Sharmilla crossed her arms. After a minute she sighed and said, "You know why."

"I guess not," Mistry said. But he did.

He drove her home, the sound of the engine, the chatter on the radio, the heat, the humidity, the missing girl, the dead inspector, the phone, the American, their jobs, the whole thing a yawning gap opening between them. He left her at the curb. "Get some rest," he said, "you'll feel better in the morning." He did not kiss her.

Once he was around the corner and out of sight he checked the missed calls he had been ignoring on his phone all night. An SMS from Rane: Sharmilla's being transferred to Dharavi. Don't discuss business with her.

He drove home and went to bed. He got up in the morning. He came to the station. He carried Sharmilla to the curb after Rane dropped the bomb on her. "Go home," he said. And then he went back to work on the problem at hand—to find Paul Shea. The tekkies came through with an address. He rounded up a crew and they were on their way. And then. . .

Mistry dismissed the cops and they piled into jeeps and departed, laughing. He supposed they would return to their posts. Eventually. They'd probably take a long lunch, have a few drinks, a good bullshit session. And then the rumors would make the rounds about the raid on the wrong address. He wondered what form it would take by the time it reached headquarters.

He closed his eyes and tried to anticipate what Rane and Yadav would say. How could he spin things? All was not lost. With the phone came a name, with the name came records, and with the records came a photocopy of a passport and a photo. The photocopy was blurry, a head shot of a man with a beard. Great. That ought to narrow it down to a couple of thousand. But the passport listed a home town (Philadelphia) and a place of birth (Kansas City) and they would trace the number back to Paul Shea's visa and entry card, and with luck, the surveillance cameras at the airport would have a better photo. And the US authorities would cough up a wealth of info—driver's licenses and such. The Americans were very good at keeping records. It might take a few days, but if he dropped the T word on them they'd jump. Linked to Al Qaida, he'll say. He'll mention a cell phone and a plot against some government office. They'll pony up the info. Paul Shea, Mistry thought, how did you get mixed up in all this? Foreigners. Ought to mind their own damn business. Ride an elephant. See the Taj. Get your picture taken with a snake charmer. Spend your money. Then, go home.

Yesterday they sent for a court order directing engineers at the phone company to give the cops a list of calls to and from Paul's number, but this would take time to complete. Days, maybe. Along with that list, Mistry asked for the locations of the calls—which cell towers picked them up. With a little luck, they could chart the calls and triangulate them. Given the time and coordinates, they would chart Paul's residence within a few meters. They'd find the building, anyway. People there would know which unit. Unless, of course, Paul had been warned and moved again. Given that Zara was loose, anything was possible.

And that was the situation when Mistry stood in the sun outside the building with the empty flat where Paul Shea used to stay. Or said he stayed. Or something. Then a jeep pulled up and Yadav and Rane and Ganesh piled out. "You're not going to believe this!" they shouted, all of them talking at once.

"What?" Mistry asked.

"Some miscreants robbed Godbodle's house. A man and a woman cleaned out his safe."

Before Mistry could take this in, his phone rang. He looked at the caller ID. Sharmilla. He answered. "This is not a good time," he said.

"I need a favor."

He sighed. "What?"

"I need to check out a phone number."

"Why?"

"I'm looking for Zara."

"Go home," Mistry said. "You're not on this anymore."

"I might have something."

Rane asked. "Who is that?"

Mistry covered the mouthpiece. "Nobody," he replied.

"Where are you?" Sharmilla asked.

"There's a bit of a fuss going on. I found Paul's apartment, but the place was empty. I just heard that somebody robbed Godbodle's place."

"Robbed?"

"A man and woman emptied the safe."

"The safe, huh?'

"Yeah. So what have you got?"

"A phone number."

"Leave it, Sharmilla, you're in enough trouble."

"Come on, Romesh, don't give up on me. I might have something. Give me a little help here."

Rane and Yadav and Ganesh crowded around Mistry. "*Nobody* seems to be asking a lot of questions," Rane said.

"It's my mother, just give me a minute!" Mistry turned his back and walked away. "Listen," he hissed. "You need to go home. Now. The best thing you can do is walk away. We have enough problems to deal with."

There was a long pause and she said, "After all we've been through? You can't do this to me!"

"You've done it to yourself, girl. Don't drag me down with you."

"You don't have to go anywhere with me. All I want is a chance. I can take care of myself. I just need a hand with a number."

"One number?"

"That's all."

Mistry sighed and took out a pen. "What is it?"

She read it back to him.

"Oh," he said, "I don't have to look that up. That's Godbodle's old cell. Where—" but Sharmilla was gone and the line was dead.

# Chapter 29

Paul stared out the back window as Zara faded into the crowd outside the railway depot. Always a crowd in Bombay. At the station, an endless flood of passengers and porters, railway workers and vendors, coming and going with bags and bundles and baskets and bales and goats on ropes and chickens squashed into cages and God-only-knew what all else. The cab pulled away, the building receded, and Paul watched Zara on the sidewalk, suddenly looking small.

When they're together, her energy makes her seem bigger than she actually is. It was easy for Paul to think of Zara as big—he's seen her haggle with shopkeepers until he thought they would give her merchandise just to get her out of the store. She's a real hell-cat when she wants to be. She insults their goods and the people who made them; the merchants themselves, their families, villages, pets, body parts, and moral decay in general. They hurl insults at each other, nose-to-nose. She walks away. They call her back, resignation (if not humiliation) in their faces. She gets her price. The merchants wrap her parcel and offer it deferentially. He has never seen her lose an argument.

Zara waved half-heartedly from the curb, the human curtain closing around her, and then she was gone. Paul turned around and watched the road. She'll be all right, he thought. She's tough. But still, there was something different about her, something sad and vulnerable. She had a hard life, no doubt about it. Did she love him, he wondered, or was he just her ticket out of India? And did he love her? Or was she just his—his what? His ticket back? Back from what? From the brink? The cab rounded a corner, and for the second time in thirty-six hours, he was gone.

The cabbie ground gears, overloading the engine and missing the clutch at every shift. He was stalling to make the trip take longer, but Paul was early enough that he was in no hurry. Paul sighed and thought, I hate good-byes. And then he grunted and thought that the last few days had been nothing but a long, drawn-out goodbye, and when he got off the plane in New York he was going to be so fucking happy he might kiss the customs agent at the immigration desk. He thought of the Jackson Browne song, "My Opening Farewell," and the cynic in him grumbled that Browne was right—life was one big good-bye from the day we're born till the day we die.

Paul missed his music when he was in India. At home he had his sound system, i-tunes on his computer, an i-pod for his car. And there was music at his friends' homes, and in the stores, and elevators, and seemingly blaring from the sky everywhere you went. His favorites were the old bands from the '60s and '70s, the Grateful Dead, the Rolling Stones, Steely Dan, Bob Dylan, Bruce Springsteen, Creedance Clearwater. But he's not one of those people who got stuck on one sound. He had, in his collection, some classical and folk, some country, a little opera, some jazz, some eclectic stuff like chanting Tibetan monks, even some Sikh hymns—they call it "meditation music." Something for every mood. Something for young ones, something for older ones, something for every-one, a comedy, tonight! Hell, he's even got a few musicals. What would life be without *The Sound of Music* or *The Wizard of Oz*?

But in Bombay there was only noise and more noise, and the only music was those silly, over-hyped Bollywood dance numbers: driving beats and trill, nasally female voices, all in cheap imitation of last year's latest Hollywood sensations. "Ever heard hip-hop in Hindi?" he wrote his friends back home. "I'd rather listen to cats fuck." Indians latch onto the latest film tunes and play them over and over and over, even put them on their cell phones for ring tones. As if reading Paul's mind, the cab driver switched on the radio and the music blared. The driver wobbled his head absentmindedly to the beat as he sped down the roads.

The trees flashed by and Paul wondered if he'd ever get all the names right—the Banyan, the Pipal, the God-knows-what-all else. Bombay was a city of gray and green, with crumbling old colonial buildings and marvel-ous, senselessly-beautiful art-deco buildings, rising modern concrete structures, and, sandwiched in-between, plenty of old Soviet-designed blocky-looking things. The effect was so crowded, so chaotic, that you sometimes couldn't tell what was going up and what was coming down. One day there was a weed sprouting through a crack in the concrete and the next time you looked there was a gnarled old tree with an idol nestled in a hollow and garlands of flowers hung around the thing by supplicants. In a weird way, Bombay reminded Paul of New Orleans before Katrina. Both cities are wet and old and rich with food and culture and night life and superstition. And trees. And rain.

Paul stirred. The damn cabs were so small, so cramped, so short, he could not sit straight up, but had to slouch and sprawl on the seat.

The farther they drove, the more Zara nagged at Paul's conscience. It was difficult for him to explain what he felt for her. Was it love? He knew that there was less than a zero chance for them to have a relationship. And yet, when they were together, something passed between them that he couldn't describe—or justify. If his friends in America knew, they would think he'd gone crazy since his divorce. Maybe he had. But then again, who can translate the language of the heart? The first night he saw her in the whorehouse they made eye contact and something passed between them, and even though he chose another girl, her never forgot that look on Zara's face. It was like she was calling him. When he came back, well, *it was on.*

In the end, it boiled down to one thing: trust. He was married once to what should have been the right woman and that didn't work out. You marry a lady and she turns into a whore. If you marry a whore, does she turn into a lady? Yet, crazy as it sounds, here with Zara, with what—by all rights—ought to be about as wrong a woman as you could find, he trusts her. Or maybe it's just that she is so impossible that it doesn't matter. How could you love a girl like Zara? But he knows (or thinks he knows) a side of her he wonders if anyone else has seen. She has showed him the place deep inside where the girl survived; the place where she kept her hopes and dreams alive. He wondered what would become of her.

He's heard hundreds of stories about the flesh trade. He knows about the agents and the lies they tell; the gangsters who exploit the girls with the complicity of the authorities. He's spoken to officials at NGOs about the business, the difficulties of rehabilitation. Hell, Godbodle drove him around Bombay and took him to a dozen more brothels, from the sordid street-stalls of Falklands Road and Kamathipura to the dance bars like Emerald (which are little more than thin cover for working girls), to the whorehouses of the working-class neighborhoods like Lamington Road, to the high-end call girls (including the Russian 'Natashas') working the five-star hotels. He knows the statistics: most of them are going to die of AIDS. And for the ones who don't, once they exhaust their beauty (and fucking a dozen men a night, that won't take long), there is no future save the long, painful plummet into poverty. And poverty in India is about as bad as it gets. You live on the streets, and then you die. But then again, she's told him her story. She did it so her sisters would be spared the same fate. And then—well, what's left? No husband will have her. She sends her money home to support her family. He thinks, How could you not love a girl like Zara?

In India people accept their fate. He and Zara had this argument all the time. "If meant," she said. The poor were the worst of all. He supposed it was because they had no hope of breaking the cycle. It was not just economic poverty. The problem rooted deeper than that. It was a vast, ancient, tangled web; a mobius strip of family and village and tribe and kin and caste and language and genetics and opportunities and social systems in a territory so overcrowded and fiercely fought over and turned in on itself that there simply wasn't room for everybody. Often the origins of the disputes went so far back in time as to border on (if not give rise to) mythology. Maybe that was why everything resolved into the will of the Gods. What was it Graham Greene's priest said in *The Power and the Glory*, "Faith is what remains when everything else is taken away?" In India, what else was there for the poor?

Paul remembered a building he saw, down by the Crawford Market—the Court of Small Causes. The title struck Paul as funny. In America they'd call it Small Claims Court, but here, everything was slightly twisted. Still, if there was a court for every cause, why not a God for every scenario? Maybe there's a God for Lost Lovers, Paul thought. If so, what would it look like? In Hindu cosmology, dear lord, they had one of just about everything: Kali the Destroyer (with her eight arms and necklace of severed heads), Hanuman (the Monkey God), Ganesh (the elephant-headed God), Durga riding her tiger, Saswati, Brahma, Shiva, and Vishnu, in all their incarnations, and a million different devils. In his mind's eye Paul envisioned a new God: a man's body with a fly's head. Perfect, he thought. Haven't seen one of those yet. He chuckled. If he had the money, he'd buy a little square of land and build a shrine and commission an idol. He'd bet a month's wages that within a year there'd be a *fakir* attached to it, and devotees, and an annual holiday, and people swearing that the fly-headed God cured their cancer. The cab slowed for a light and swung without stopping onto a cross street. Add to the list of similarities with New Orleans: the roads were a mess.

Paul smiled as he remembered an article in a recent paper. Some miscreant stole 14,000 trees in a single monsoon season. The cutting was illegal, the article said, but during the monsoon, there were people charged with removing fallen trees. Someone just came in with bulldozers and helped the trees along. And if they made a few bucks on the deal, who cared? You could always pay off a cop if you got caught. The whole place was so stinking corrupt it was beyond imagination. The BMC authorities let contracts to family, or on bribes; the contractors, in turn, doing shoddy work and paying off the inspectors. When disaster struck—a building collapse, for example—they covered it up, played the blame game, put a spin on things. Even when caught red-handed, the Indian justice system took years to grind to the inevitable acquittal. Unless you were poor.

And the local papers were so full of stories, the most damnably interesting thing he had ever read: THIRTEEN YEAR OLD FINDS CURE

FOR AIDS; VILLAGE WOMAN MARRIES SNAKE; MAN STEALS 6 CARS A WEEK FOR 25 YEARS FROM THE SAME LOCATION; THIEVES AMPUTATE HOLY MAN'S MAGIC LEG. And today's was a real doozy: NO PAY NO PLAY! SEX WORKERS STRIKE FOR WAGES. Good fucking grief, he thought. A boy pressed the paper against the window while they were at a light. Paul had to buy it. He would show it to his friends at home. "See," he'd say. "I told you this place was nuts."

Paul tried to talk Zara out of working in the brothel. He once had a slot reserved for her in an NGO that rehabilitated prostitutes, taught them some kind of skill. This was not long after he'd met her. But she didn't follow through—who knew why? Probably figured the money in hand was better than the uncertain future. The officials at the NGO said girls over eighteen almost never gave up the trade. Could you blame them? In India, the poor survive one day at a time. You eat today and pray that tomorrow takes care of itself.

Paul asked Zara to come to America, though God only knows what she would do there. She was probably smart enough to figure that out. She couldn't read or write, didn't speak much English, and had (besides native intelligence) no marketable skill. Paul had been to her home, a two-room hovel in a *chawl* in Vijaywada. Hell, he couldn't trust her in his house. She'd never seen an electric stove. She might burn the place down trying to make toast. Still, he had asked.

She replied that she would marry him, but only if he came to live in India. She'd marry him in a heartbeat, but that's not going to happen. It was conceivable he might come back, for work or vacation, but he's not moving here. Still, in his own weird way, he loved her. And he worried about the bruises and about her getting AIDS or being killed by one of her customers, and he hoped she would take his money and go home to her village and find some nice man there who'd marry her even though she wasn't a virgin. He'd like to know that her story had a happy ending, that she would raise a family and die a satisfied old woman. There was, of course, no way for him to know that. And the odds were against it.

The traffic was building. The driver stopped at a light. An old woman tapped on the window and gestured that she was hungry. Paul rolled down the window and gave her a hundred-rupee note. Two US dollars and change. Her eyes bugged and she touched her forehead and her heart.

Paul's Indian friends—the few who know about Zara—warned him that it was just a game to her. It was all about money. They said she probably had a dozen boyfriends on the side, but Paul doubted that. It didn't ring true for the girl he knew: the stories she told, the slashes on her wrists. When they were together, he knew she cared for him. He gave her something she might never have experienced: respect, maybe, or kindness. Love. And she gave him? A reason to live again? A spark of hope in a hopeless depression?

They passed Dharavi, Asia's most crowded slum, crossed the Mithi River; they were more than halfway to the airport, leaving old Bombay and entering what passed for suburbs. Paul stared out at the tangled wilderness of mangroves and tidal muck. Beyond that lay Bandra, the Beverly Hills of Bombay. One lousy hill and a bunch of phony movie stars. Then Santa Cruz. They were on a freeway, now, though the driver didn't act like he'd ever seen one before. Paul laughed. Probably hadn't. Don't get me started on Bombay cabs, he thought.

He opened the paper and turned to the inside pages. And there, at the top of page three, was a picture of Godbodle. SEARCH CONTINUES FOR COP KILLER. He read the article. The cops, it said, suspected a foreigner. They had posted an alert. "Fuck," Paul said. He took out his cell and dialed Dr. Maneshka. "Thanks for seeing my friend last night," Paul said. "But I need another favor from you. Remember that guy you said you knew—the one in airport security? There may be something to this after all. It's a weird coincidence, but I may have known that cop who got killed. No big deal, I've nothing to hide, but if they're looking for me, I'd rather find out now and go through the embassy than wind up at Arthur Road."

Maneshka said he'll call right away and Paul relaxed. It was probably all bullshit, anyway. He closed his eyes. Nothing to worry about. No tension.

Paul had called Godbodle twice: once to ask about the jeep ride and once to decline an invitation to a party. They could trace those calls to Paul. His number might be stored in Godbodle's cell. He shrugged and thought, Poor bastard. It was a tough life, being a Bombay cop. So much corruption, so little time. He pictured the classic Indian head wobble, not yes, not no, just an ear-to-shoulder sideways wiggle followed by the inevitable, What to do? Sometimes you get the bad guys, and sometimes they get you.

He thought about the night he met Godbodle, and then what came to mind was the face of the sub-inspector, Rane, the way he enjoyed slapping Krishna, and the look he gave Paul when Paul mouthed off at him—the look that said, What? You want some of this? What of it? Paul thought. If that rat bastard had laid a hand on me I'd have broken his fucking arm just for fun. Paul's heart raced and he clenched his fist. Sweat popped out on his forehead. There may have been a roomful of cops, but Paul thought he could give them a run for their money. He might be fifty but he wasn't dead yet.

Paul had also slapped Krishna around, once. It was not long after Paul met Zara, and there was some kind of dispute between them—Zara and Krishna—and they were shouting at one another in Hindi. It seemed to Paul that Zara had been promised to another customer, but there was no way of knowing for sure. Anyway, Paul and Zara were on their way into the little back bedroom when Krishna grabbed her by the arm. It hadn't taken Paul a second—he snatched Krishna's hand from Zara's arm and spun him around, then locked his wrist and dropped him to his knees. Krishna didn't like that one bit—especially the part about forced to kneel in front of the girls. It was just little judo move, but if you don't know the trick it looks like magic. Later on Krishna had made a fuss about things, paraded around in the main room waving his arms, the Indian equivalent of chest-thumping. A second time Paul spun him around, locked Krishna's right arm behind his back, then took him in a stranglehold and choked the fight out of him. And still a third time, Krishna and a friend had accosted Paul in the alley outside, and without hesitating, Paul took them both by the collar, one in each hand, and pinned them against the wall. After that, they left him alone.

In time, as Paul visited the house and brought gifts of mangos and cakes and such, he became friends with all of them—part of the scenery. But Paul knew, too, that they might someday take their revenge against Zara, so from time-to-time he tipped Krishna, or one of the other pimps, 100 rupees for beer money, just to keep them on an even keel.

His phone rang. It was Maneshka. His friend said no Paul Shea on the watch list, so he was clear to fly. A good thing, Paul thought. They were almost to the terminal.

# Chapter 30

A few blocks north of the railway station Zara stopped in front of a *sari* shop and looked at her reflection in the glass. She studied the bruises on her face and her swollen lower lip. She imagined what others would think when they saw her. A beaten wife ought to stay home until the wounds heal, not shame her family by being seen in public. That's what people thought when they saw her. Still, close by the railway station, the shop owner must see dozens of beaten women every week. They arrive by train every day carrying little more than fear and bruises. Perhaps a few rupees pilfered from the grocery money. Those with progressive relatives might find shelter. The rest? A lucky few might find jobs sweeping, laboring, or in an office or call center—if they're lucky enough to have an education. Without skills, if they are young enough and pretty enough, they might land a place in the dance bars. Others might drift into the brothels. The pimps will find them walking the street at night, hungry and frightened. The rest—the old, the ugly, the infirm—would beg on the pavement until they went back to their husbands or died.

Zara returned to the railroad station and eyed the rows of parked cabbies. It took her a minute to spot Sanjay. He was looking particularly disreputable—he must have fallen on very hard times. Sanjay was pinch-faced and flinty-looking. He had long, greasy hair and had not shaved in several days. Probably not since he got out of jail. He wore old army trousers and a grimy, grayish-yellow tee shirt. God only knew where he found them. He was reclining, barefoot, on the hood of his cab, his back resting against the windshield, his eyes closed.

"Hey," Zara said. Sanjay sat up and looked Zara over. Up close, he was worse-looking than she imagined.

"What have you in mind?" he asked.

"A robbery."

He looked skeptical.

"A small thing," she said. "Someone took something of mine that I want back. It is not worth much, but I'll pay you to help me."

"So is this a robbery or a burglary?'

"A burglary I guess."

"That is a much more difficult proposition. So tell me."

"What do you mean?"

"The place. Is it a bungalow, a flat, or in a *chawl*?"

"A flat."

"Those are the worst. Ground floor or upstairs?"

Zara hesitated. "Upstairs, I think."

"You think?"

"I have not been. I have only heard about it."

"Also bad. And it is occupied?"

"I suppose, yes."

"Double bad." Sanjay shook his head. "So we have to dupe our way inside a place you have never been and guess about this thing you are looking for." He rubbed his eyes and stretched. "You don't want a thief, you want a magician. Why don't you hire a monkey or a mongoose?"

Zara stared at the crowds flowing into and out of the railway station.

"And people don't go to all that trouble to steal things that are not worth much," Sanjay added, looking at Zara sideways. "Too much risk."

"Something can have value besides money."

"But in the end, everything comes down to money. What is it worth to you?"

"A thousand rupees."

He scratched his chin and squinted into the morning sun. "Ah, come on," Sanjay said. "I can make that before lunch driving cab."

"What then?"

"Twenty thousand," he said.

"Don't be greedy," Zara said, "I thought I was your friend."

"That was my friend rate," Sanjay said. "What, do I look like a fishmonger? You think you can talk me down?"

They argued. They insulted each other and called favors, reminded each other of all the reasons they should be grateful. They cursed, waved arms, shook warning fingers. Zara walked away and Sanjay started his cab. He stopped the cab and chased her down on the sidewalk. In the end, Sanjay agreed to five thousand and Zara gave him five hundred in advance. "Let's go," she said.

"Not looking like this," he said. "Who would open a door to me?"

They drove to a shop where Sanjay took more money and bought new clothes and shoes. When he emerged he had washed, shaved, and changed. He still looked like a thief from Delhi, but nothing much could be done about that. He was a thief from Delhi. But at least he was presentable.

"Where to?" Sanjay asked.

"Pali Naka."

Sanjay stopped in a commercial district at the base of a long hill. Zara was stumped. She did not figure on the neighborhood being this big or busy. She craned her neck and stared up at the streets winding their way to the top. There must be a thousand bungalows and God-only-knows how many thousands of flats.

Sanjay got out and lit a cigarette. One at a time he put his feet on the bumper and spit on the tip of his shoes, then rubbed in the shine with the cuff of his pants.

Zara checked her watch.

"What's his name?" Sanjay asked.

"Who's name?"

"The name of the man you are looking for."

Zara frowned. "How did you know it was a man?"

"It is not my first day on the job," Sanjay said, "or yours. I find houses all the time." He leaned closer. "Give me a name and in five minutes I find the house."

"Godbodle," Zara said. "And buy some chewing gum. You breath stinks like a goat."

Sanjay nodded. "Godbodle, eh?" He hesitated.

Zara stared back. "Did you know him?"

"We've crossed paths," Sanjay said. He walked away. Five minutes later he was back. "Get in," he said. He made a show of spitting out a fat wad of gum. And he handed Zara a small bottle of antiperspirant which she threw out the window. "You smell like a pig," he said.

"So stand downwind," she replied.

They drove. "How—" Zara asked.

"I told a delivery boy I had a stupid passenger. Happens all the time. I gave him the name and ten rupees, he gave me the address. And the Godbodle you want is dead. But you knew that?"

"Yes," she said. "I did."

"That's even worse. The house will be full of mourners."

The Godbodles' building was only six blocks away, low on the hill and facing east. The building was four stories tall, perhaps seventy years old, weathered gray, flat-roofed, with a small, walled yard surrounding it. Nothing special. Even shabbier, perhaps, than Zara had imagined. There must be half-a-million like it in Bombay. The Godbodles, Sanjay said, lived on the third floor. They drove by slowly and parked a half-block away. "Now what?" Sanjay asked.

Zara shrugged. "We have to talk our way in. Or break in." She looked at the concrete walls rising unbroken, except for stacked balconies, from the ground to the roof. "Do you think we could climb?"

"If we had wings we could fly," Sanjay said. He was also looking at the balconies. "Where is this . . . thing . . . you want to retrieve?"

Zara realized that Sanjay thought she was Godbodle's mistress—that she must want something back to protect herself, or more likely, something to incriminate Godbodle in the courts or with his wife. She looked at Sanjay and knew that he was thinking she wanted to blackmail Godbodle. Funny, she thought, how close to the truth he was.

"I just need you to make a distraction while I look," she said.

He nodded. "Things," he said, "are either in the bedroom or the office, if he has an office. And if he has an office, they are probably in the safe, if he has a safe. Do you think he has an office?"

Zara shrugged. "Do you know how to open a safe?" she asked.

"If I knew how to open safes, would I be driving a cab?"

Zara wondered if there was room in a flat for an office. What had Godbodle said about his house? Too good for the bitch—always complaining—new kitchen—a room for the kids. She decided it must have an office. He would have wanted a room to get away from the wife. She studied the windows on the third floor. "I don't see how we can get in," she said. "If we climb the balconies, someone will see."

Sanjay looked at the windows, then at the building. The entry was in the middle of the ground floor with a desk where a watchman sat beside a telephone. "I can get us in," he said. "Do you know anything about telephones?"

Zara shook her head.

"They run on wires," Sanjay continued.

"Okay."

"If you pull out the wires, the phones won't run."

"You want me to pull out the wires?"

"You distract the watchman. I'll pull out the wires. If he asks anything, tell him you are with the phone company."

"Which phone company?"

"Tell him FloTel. They run everything, anyway. Go talk to the watchman. Ask him if the telephone is working. Get me two minutes. Then come back to the cab. But don't say anything else or he'll know you're a fake."

"Do you know anything about phones?" Zara asked.

"If I knew anything about phones," Sanjay said, "would I be driving cab?" He got out and went to the corner of the building, then motioned Zara to go in.

The watchman was reading a newspaper. He looked up as Zara

approached.

"Is your telephone working?" she asked.

He looked at her blankly, then picked up the phone and listened. He nodded.

"May I borrow it?"

The watchman looked annoyed, but he passed the phone to Zara. For lack of anything better to do, she dialed the number of the missing cell phone. The lovely, lilting voice said, "The number you have reached . . ."

Zara saw Sanjay turn the corner of the hallway behind the watchman. He stopped at the wirebox—the terminal for all the telephone connections —pressed one finger to his lips, then opened the box and pulled every wire loose. The line went dead. Zara asked, "Do you have the time?"

He looked at his watch. "Ten twenty-five," he said.

Sanjay slipped around the corner.

Zara handed the watchman the phone. "How long has the service been out?" she asked.

The watchman listened, hung up, picked up again, listened, jabbed at the buttons on the phone and said, "It was working only a moment ago." He eyed Zara suspiciously. "What have you done?"

"I did nothing. I was right here in front of you. It is—" she remembered Sanjay's warning, "—a blackout. It will last only a short while. I'll be right back."

She went out and found Sanjay leaning over the open trunk of the cab. He handed Zara a green canvas bag with two screwdrivers, a crescent wrench, and a pair of pliers. "Here you go," he said.

"You're coming with me?" she asked.

"Not on your life. I said I would get you in, now you're in. After that you're on your own." He held out his hand for his money.

"I'm not going to pay you!" Zara said. "I hired you for the day."

"You hired me for a burglary. What else can I do? You want me to fix their phones? I told you, I know nothing about phones. If you don't pay me, I'll tell the watchman you're a thief."

Zara stared at him in disbelief. "You lying, double-crossing bastard."

"What? You wanted an honest thief? Okay, I'm an honest thief. I got my 5,000 rupees and a change of clothes. That's a pretty good day's work, if you ask me. Maybe tonight I'll come up and you can make your money back." He winked.

Zara's eyes began to tear.

Sanjay looked away, then back. "Stop it," he said. His tone softened. "Look, it's not so bad. You got some tools. Go into the house and nobody will pay you any attention. If they send a servant to watch you, give him something to do."

"Like what?"

"I don't know!" Sanjay snapped. "Tell him to hold something. Just as soon as you make him work he'll find an excuse to leave. Servants are easy."

"Ten thousand," Zara said.

"What?"

"Fifteen."

Sanjay shook his head, no.

"It's all I've got."

He looked up at the building and then back at Zara.

"And anything you can steal from the house."

Sanjay narrowed his eyes.

"Jewelry, computers, anything. Whatever you can lift. I only need a few minutes without anyone watching me."

"Pay me now," he said, holding out his hand.

Zara shook her head. "When we are finished."

Sanjay frowned, then threw back a blanket in the trunk and took out more tools, a pry bar, some wire cutters, more screwdrivers, a hammer, a file. He took out a hacksaw and looked at it, then shrugged his shoulders and dropped it in the bag, too. He shut the trunk and took a deep breath. "Okay," he said. "Rigorous imprisonment here I come. Let's go."

They nodded officiously at the watchman, who was still listening hopefully to the dead telephone, and rode the elevator to the third floor. They found the flat and knocked on the door. A servant answered. "We are here to fix the telephone," Sanjay said.

The servant said, "One minute," and shut the door. Five minutes later it opened and a woman in a white *sari* said, "What has happened?" She wore her *sari* draped over her head.

"The lines," Zara said, "the lines have frozen a fuse. We need to change them."

The woman looked perplexed.

Sanjay pushed Zara aside and said, "Are you Mrs. Godbodle?"

"I am."

"She means that the fuse in one of your phones has blown, not frozen." He glared at Zara, then smiled apologetically. "A trainee," he said. He shrugged his shoulders.

"Ah. They are training women to repair phone lines now?"

"What to do?" Sanjay said. He wobbled his head from side to side.

"Keep an eye on her."

"Yes, madam." Sanjay nodded.

137

Mrs. Godbodle opened the door and let them in. She called for a servant to watch them. "The fuse box is down the hall," she said.

"And how many telephones?"

"There are four. One in the bedroom, one in the kitchen, one in the living room, and one in the office."

"With madam's permission, we shall begin in the bedroom?"

She pointed down the hall, then shuffled off to the living room.

Through the open door Zara could see a crowd of women, all in white *saris*, sitting together on the floor. From another room—the kitchen, perhaps—she heard the murmur of men's voices.

The bedroom was narrow and cramped, with dark furniture and a bed with twin mattresses laid side-by-side in single frame. The phone was on a stand by the bed and Sanjay took the receiver and listened, then unplugged the phone from the wall and turned it over. "Give me a screwdriver," he said.

Zara looked at him blankly.

Sanjay hissed at her. "It's in the bag."

She set the bag on the bed and rummaged inside. She found a screwdriver and handed it to Sanjay.

He looked at Zara and then looked at the servant. He said, to the servant, "Come here and hold this."

The servant, an elderly man, in a white suit, barefoot, shuffled to where Sanjay held out the phone and took it reluctantly. "Like this," Sanjay said, gripping the phone firmly. "If I wanted a girl to hold it I would have asked her."

Sanjay unscrewed the bottom plate of the phone and slipped off the cover. He examined the circuitry and the wires, poking and prodding it with the screwdriver. He made a clicking sound to get Zara's attention and gestured towards the door. "Go to the truck and get me a number seven fuse."

"A what?"

"A fuse. A number seven fuse."

For a moment Zara wondered what the hell Sanjay was doing, but then he winked. "Oh," she said. "A fuse." She went out into the hall. She tried one door—a child's bedroom, where a couple of boys looked up from a stack of comic books, and then another—the office. It was empty.

One wall was dedicated to bookshelves. The other opened up to windows overlooking the courtyard below. There was a desk in one corner covered by a large leather blotter. At the other end was a couch with a table and two chairs arranged in a semi-circle. On the desk was a silver pen set, a tea set, and a telephone. On the table, by the couch, was a sleek black cell phone connected to a charger. Zara closed the door and crossed the room to the couch. She looked at the cell phone. She picked it up and turned it over in her hand. It was thin and quite light. It also had a camera. She touched it gently, almost as if she was stroking a pet, then set it back on the table.

She went to the desk. The top drawer contained a stapler and some pens, a box of paper clips, a rubber stamp, envelopes, an eraser, a small block of black marble, a letter opener, a souvenir card from Disneyland, and a multi-colored hard rubber ball. Nothing important or useful. The middle drawer contained stacks of papers—some in files, some loose. In the bottom drawer were more papers, but pushing the files to the side, Zara felt something solid. She dug in the back of the drawer and found a revolver, short, fat, and heavy. The gun was black and slightly oily. She held it to her cheek. The metal was cold and smelled faintly like paprika. The grips were of light brown wood crisscrossed with grooves in a diamond pattern to give it a rough texture. She looked inside the cylinder and saw bullets. She slipped it into her purse. She looked the room over. Not much there, and no place to hide anything valuable. She checked behind the pictures on the wall and the books on the shelves. There was no safe.

The doorbell rang and she froze. There was talk in the hallway, but it was only more family arriving. They complained about the phone lines being down. What new calamity? When the voices died down Zara slipped to the door and checked the hallway, then closed the door and crossed the room again to the couch. She unplugged the cell phone and turned it off, slipped it into her bra.

Back in the bedroom she found Sanjay sitting in a chair taking the telephone apart. He was whistling, but he was also sweating.

Zara forgot what she was supposed to be looking for. She stared at Sanjay blankly, hoping he would understand. "Well," he said. "Have you got it?" He seemed also to have forgotten.

She shook her head and he began to heap abuse on her. Then he stopped and lowered his voice. "Here," he said, handing her the telephone. "Hold this, and don't let the wires cross."

Zara nodded, then looked into the open guts of the telephone. She saw nothing but crossed wires.

Sanjay said to the servant, "Come," but then at the door he stopped and said, "No, you better keep an eye on the girl. Don't let her cross any wires." The servant hesitated, then did as he was told.

Zara waited. Funny how when someone tells you to hold still, the hardest thing in the world to do is to hold still. She suddenly needed to urinate. Her nose itched. A mosquito appeared and circled her face. She sat in the chair, her legs crossed, and tried not to do anything that might look like she was about to cross wires. Five minutes passed, then ten. She had the sudden feeling that Sanjay had ditched her—he would loot the house and leave her sitting in the bedroom with a ruined telephone. That would be just like him. She was about to set the phone down when he returned. He was jumpy. He had another open phone in his hand, which he thrust at the servant. "Hold this," he said. "You!" he shouted so loudly at Zara. "I told you not to cross any wires. You almost electrocuted me!"

So convincing he was that for a moment Zara looked to see if there were burns on Sanjay's hands.

He gestured towards the door. "Come with me. You!" he said, pointing the servant, "Don't dare shake those phones. We'll be right back."

They went down the hall and out the front door. Zara stopped at the elevator, but Sanjay grabbed her hand and said, "Come on!"

Down the stairs, pausing at the ground floor only long enough to take a deep breath and stroll casually past the guard to the gate. Once out of his sight, Sanjay sped up again, almost running to the cab, dragging Zara along behind her. Sanjay dove behind the wheel, Zara climbed in beside him. They drove. Sanjay slipped the canvas bag from his shoulder and dropped it in Zara's lap. She opened it. Inside were the stamped and stapled stacks of money that banks issued for large transactions. There must have been a half-million rupees. And below the bills: gold bars, coins, and chain.

"But where—"

"In the office, just like I told you."

"But I didn't see—"

"Of course not. It wasn't meant to be seen."

"But—"

"It was in the floor, under the rug, under the couch."

"But how did you—"

Sanjay grinned. "If I wasn't a thief, do you think I would be driving cab?"

Zara stared at him.

"Did you get what you wanted?" he asked.

She nodded.

"Keep your money. You brought me luck. Shall we go to your place? You want to play? I can buy us some beer. All the beer in the world."

Zara shook her head. "We have a police problem right now. Why don't you wait a few days, then come. Call me first."

"We could get a room in a guest house. We could hole up for a few days and celebrate. If you wanted, I could drive us somewhere. To Goa, or up to one of the hill stations. Have you been to Matheran?"

"No," she said. "I have some things I have to take care of. It's about the police problem."

"What can you do?" Sanjay patted her on the thigh. "Best thing is to hide out until it blows over. Believe me, I know. I've had tons of scrapes with the cops."

"I bet you have," Zara said. "And believe me, I'd like to hide. But this won't blow over. Especially now."

Sanjay searched Zara's face. He looked hurt, but as she watched, the look melted to one of resignation. He shrugged. Probably one woman was as good as another to him. He'd make do. "Where to, then?" he asked.

Zara looked out the window. They were speeding south, towards Worli. A few miles down the road was Haji Ali Mosque. There was a famous juice bar there. Lots of people around. That would work. "This is as good as anyplace," she said.

Sanjay pulled over and Zara got out.

Sanjay drove away deliriously happy, blowing kisses and sounding his horn.

Poor simple Sanjay, Zara thought. He wanted nothing more out of life than a *chillum* of hash, a bottle of beer, and woman to sleep with. As soon as he was out of sight Zara flagged down another cab. "Haji Ali." she said. Five minutes later she climbed out of the cab on the roadway in front of the Heerapana Shopping Center, opposite the long causeway that led to the tiny island and its famous mosque. She walked down the steps of the pedestrian underpass and crossed under the roadway, emerging in front of the little juice bar by the entrance to the causeway.

Zara took out the stolen cell phone and dialed a number. "I want to speak to Sharmilla Oberoi," she said. A voice replied that Sharmilla was out. "Do you have her cell number it is urgent." They did. She dialed again and Sharmilla answered, "Hello."

"We need to meet," Zara said. "But first, you have to promise that you will come alone."

"Who is this?" Sharmilla replied.

"*Array*. You must be looking everywhere for me. I call and you don't know my voice?"

"Zara," Sharmilla said. She sounded disappointed, or disgusted. "Where are you?"

"First you have to promise to come alone. If I'm going to turn myself in, I don't want to get killed for my trouble."

"Why should I trust you?"

"I'm turning myself in, why shouldn't you trust me?"

"For one thing, you escaped. For another, you've caused me nothing but trouble since I met you."

"Sorry," Zara said.

"Sorry? Sorry? Is that all you can say for yourself?"

"I had some things I had to take care of."

"Like warning Paul?"

"Yes. Like warning . . . Paul. But there was something else, too."

"What now?"

"If I can prove I have the phone, will you come alone?"

"But we have your phone," Sharmilla said. "It rang in my house, remember?"

"You have a phone. If you'd looked at it closely, you would have noticed something important about it."

There was a long pause. Sharmilla seemed to be mulling over the phones they showed Zara yesterday in her house. "Shit!" she said. "There was no camera!"

Zara smiled. "You're learning."

"*Rama! Rama! Rama!* How many phones do you have?"

"I had two. You got my old one."

"And Godbodle got the other?"

"Yes."

"But you got it back?"

"I can get it."

There was another pause. "If you have the phone, I'll come alone."

"Promise?"

"I promise."

"Give me five minutes. When you see it, call me back." Zara hung up, then dialed another number and waited. When the line connected, she selected an option: download. When the download was complete she flipped through a gallery, chose a photo of herself and Godbodle, redialed Sharmilla's number, and hit send. She checked her watch. English did not say what time he was leaving, but she assumed it would be on the same noon flight that was cancelled the day before. It was half past eleven. She sat down and ordered a sandwich.

# Chapter 31

Sharmilla left Mrs. Shetty and found a constable on foot patrol at the end of the block. She showed him her ID. He eyed her with equal parts of suspicion and contempt. "I want you to keep watch on the shopping center down the road," she said, "Particularly *Threads!*. You know which store I mean, the one that was vandalized last night."

The cop, a dark, broad-shouldered Marathi with large paunch, scowled at Sharmilla and twirled his *lathee*. "You think the vandals will come again?" he asked. "What's left for them to wreck, eh?" He laughed.

Sharmilla frowned. "I'm not worried about vandals. I want to know about the employees. Find out their names and how I might reach them. Someone will know."

The cop looked unconvinced. Sharmilla was sure that he paid so little attention that if she asked him to repeat her instructions, he wouldn't remember them. "I want to know the real story behind the vandalism," she said.

The cop nodded, and a light seemed to come on in his eyes.

Sharmilla realized that he thought she had been bribed to take some action, or was fishing for a bribe. That meant if he asked around, there might be bribes in it for him, too. He nodded. Motivation. "Just do it," she said. "Talk to the employees of the other stores, especially the *sari* shop two doors down." She took the cop's name and mobile number so she could follow up, and hopefully, to encourage him to be diligent.

The cop said, "Okay," and wandered away to a *chaiwala*, where he joined a crowd gossiping about the vandalism. They were pointing towards the ruined store, where Mrs. Shetty stood outside haranguing her servant boy, who was again slowly sweeping the shards from the sidewalk. The cop nodded in Sharmilla's direction and the group turned in unison to look.

She walked to her car. It had been a long night, and already it was shaping up to be a longer day. She took a bottle of water from the back seat and drank. She was tired, dehydrated, having a low-blood-sugar moment. Her career as a police officer—as a woman, never a sure thing—was in serious trouble. She stood to be demoted, and likely transferred to Dharavi or some other hellish slum where her life would be pure hell. She envisioned an endless merry-go-round of spousal abuse and drunken petty crime. She wondered what gossip about her was making the rounds back at the police station. She could feel the stain spreading like a virus-rash on her career. She got a headache just thinking about it.

She walked down the road to a different *chaiwala* and bought a *chai*. By his stall was a table stacked with newspapers. A headline caught Sharmilla's eye. NO PAY NO PLAY! SEX WORKERS STRIKE FOR WAGES. Great, she thought. What next? And then she wondered, How did Zara do it? She must be blackmailing half the God-damned city. Well, she thought, it takes balls. That's what the Americans say. Balls. Well, Zara was going to find out that she wasn't the only woman in Bombay with balls.

Sharmilla walked back to her car and leaned against the hood, wondered where, in a country of a billion people, Zara would go. She doubted Zara would stay long at the American's house—wherever that was. They would find him today—no doubt about that. But would they run? And if so, where? She thought, Where would we least expect her?

Her phone rang. She checked the caller ID. She was expecting Mistry, or Rane, or Ganesh, one of them, furious with her for talking to Mrs. Shetty. The number was not one she recognized. She answered. A voice said, "We need to meet. But first, you have to promise that you will come alone."

Sharmilla double-checked the caller ID. At least she could tell the number was local. "Who is this?" she asked.

"*Array*, you must be looking everywhere for me. I call and you don't know my voice?"

Sharmilla almost dropped the phone. "Zara," she said, "where are you?"

"First you have to promise to come alone. If I'm going to turn myself in, I don't want to get killed for my troubles."

"Why should I trust you?"

"I'm turning myself in, why shouldn't you trust me?"

"For one thing, you escaped. For another, you've caused me nothing but trouble since I met you."

"Sorry," Zara said.

"Sorry?" She slapped the hood of her car and kicked the tire for emphasis. "Sorry? Is that all you can say for yourself?"

"I had some things I had to take care of."

"Like warning Paul?"

There was a pause on the line. "Yes. Like warning Paul. But there was something else, too."

"What now?"

"If I can prove I have the phone, will you come alone?"

"But we have your phone," Sharmilla said. "It rang in my house, remember?"

"You have a phone. If you'd looked at it closely, you would have noticed something important about it."

Sharmilla tried to remember the phone. Cheap. Pink. A second hand phone like some schoolgirl might carry. "Shit!" she exclaimed. "There was no camera!"

"You're learning."

Sharmilla slapped her forehead. "*Rama! Rama! Rama!*" she said. "How many phones do you have?"

"I had two. You got my old one."

"And Godbodle got the other?"

"Yes."

"But you got it back?"

"I can get it."

Sharmilla thought about this. It was a tough call, but the important thing was to get the girl. Get her and then get the phone. Priorities. "If you have the phone," she said, "I'll come alone."

"Promise?"

"I promise."

"Give me five minutes. When you see it, call me back."

"See what?" Sharmilla asked, but Zara had hung up. "Shit!" Sharmilla looked at the number. She had no clue who it was. She wrote it down and called in to the station. "I want the duty officer," she said. She prayed he didn't know how much trouble she is in. He answered, she asked him to track down the number. "Can't do it," he said.

"But it's an emergency!"

"Sorry. Orders."

Sorry orders was right. Sharmilla walked in circles, watched the cop and the *chai*-drinkers watching her. An ex-cop on the way down. Waiting on the paperwork to come through. Who else was there? She called Mistry.

"This is not a good time," he said.

"I need a favor."

He sighed. "What?"

"I need to check out a phone number."

"Why?"

She hesitated. "I'm looking for Zara."

"Go home. You're not on this anymore."

"I might have something." Another pause. A mumble. He was talking to someone. "Where are you?" Sharmilla asked.

"There's a bit of a fuss going on. I found Paul's apartment, but the place was empty. I just heard that somebody robbed Godbodle's place."

"Robbed?"

"A man and woman emptied the safe."

Sharmilla looked around. Down the street, Mrs. Shetty watched a laborer putting a new padlock on the front door. She looked at Sharmilla, then hurried away in the opposite direction.

"The safe, huh?"

"Yeah. So what have you got?"

"A phone number."

"Leave it, Sharmilla. You're in enough trouble."

"Come on, Romesh, don't give up on me. I might have something. Give me a little help here."

He paused. He was talking to someone. Rane? Yadav? "Listen," he said, his voice low. "You need to go home. *Now.* The best thing you can do is to walk away. We got enough problems to deal with."

Mistry was probably right. The easiest thing—the path of least resistance—would be to give up and go home, hope that in a few years the storm blew over. And then she thought, No way I'm backing down now. "After all we've been through?" she said. "You can't do this to me!"

"You've done it to yourself, girl. Don't drag me down with you."

"You don't have to go anywhere with me. All I want is a chance. I can take care of myself. I just need a hand with a number."

"One number?"

"That's all."

He sighed. "What is it?"

She read it back to him.

"Oh," he said, "I don't have to look that up. That's Godbodle's old cell. Where—" Sharmilla hung up.

Before she could call Zara back, her phone beeped. An SMS. A picture. Sharmilla opened it and laughed. Zara and Godbodle in bed. "That's my girl," she said.

# Chapter 32

Zara had barely bitten into her veg sandwich when the phone rang.

"Where are you?" Sharmilla asked.

"You have to promise to come alone."

"Just tell me where."

"You promise?"

"I do."

"Haji Ali Juice Center."

"I'll be there in five minutes."

Zara didn't like the sound of that five minutes. Maybe Sharmilla was down the road and maybe she wasn't. Maybe she was coming alone and maybe she called the riot squad. She should have asked where Sharmilla was before she said anything, but she hadn't. That couldn't be helped now. She wrapped her sandwich in a napkin and left money for the waiter. She crossed Warden Road back through the underpass to Heerapena Mall and crossed the intersecting road to watch from the northeast corner.

She'd barely caught her breath before a black Mercedes double parked in front of the juice bar and Sharmilla jumped out and ran inside.

Zara watched, then called Sharmilla on the cell phone.

"Where are you?" Sharmilla asked. She came out to the sidewalk and looked up and down the road.

"I'm on the other side. Come through the tunnel."

"Oh, no. I'm not walking through any tunnels."

"What? You think I'm going to kill you?"

"I'm not taking any chances. I came alone, just like you said."

"Okay," Zara said. "Wait there, I'm coming."

Sharmilla was inside drinking a *falooda* when Zara arrived. She looked Zara up and down. "Did you hurt yourself jumping?" she asked.

"Yes," Zara said, touching her wrist. "But it is better. Today I can move it at little."

Sharmilla started to say good but bit her tongue. There might be something to this psychology stuff after all. She had Zara almost as good as handcuffed and in the car. "Do you need to go to a hospital?"

"I have been."

"He took you?"

"Yes."

"We should have thought to check." She looked disgusted.

Zara shrugged. Cops and thinking are two words she would not usually associate with one another. She wondered if she should tell Sharmilla that and decided to keep her opinions to herself.

Sharmilla said, "That was nice of him."

"Yes."

"Which hospital?"

"I don't know."

"Was it near here?"

"It was late. We took a cab."

"Don't you know the roads?"

"I don't get out much."

"He must like you."

"He does."

Sharmilla finished her *falooda* and left a fifty *rupee* note on the table. They walked out to the car. "I have to arrest you for absconding and for aiding and abetting a fugitive."

Zara shrugged. "I'm already arrested for murder. How many times can they hang me?"

"Should we add burglary to the charge?"

"Sure, why not?"

"And that's how you got the phone?"

"Right."

"How did you get in?"

"I came to fix the telephone."

Sharmilla rolled her eyes. "Right," she said. She pointed at the car. "Get in." Zara got in and Sharmilla got in.

"You don't believe me?" Zara asked.

"I'll never believe another word you say."

"It's not like you haven't lied to me, too."

Sharmilla looked away. That was true, sort of. She looked back, eyes angry, and said, "I saved your life and you hung me out to dry."

"I'm supposed to feel sorry for you?" Zara replied. "I've been to your house. Why don't you come stay in mine for awhile?"

"I stuck my neck out for you."

"And I had mine in a noose."

"You know what I mean."

"You tried to con me, remember? All that lawyer shit?"

"That's not true!"

"The hell it isn't," Zara said. "You fucking rich people are all alike."

Sharmilla lunged; grabbed Zara around the neck shoved her backwards against the door. She had the advantage of surprise, but Zara was stronger than Sharmilla expected. Zara drove her good left hand under Sharmilla's chin and forced her head back. For a moment they were locked, jaws clenched, muscles straining. Then Zara went limp and Sharmilla let go and they sat up and straightened their clothes.

Zara rubbed her wrist and winced. "Look," she said, "I'm not trying to make trouble for you. I just mean, if you had to change places for a few days, you might not think your life was so bad. Let the cops beat on you for a while and see how you like it. You rescued me and I appreciate that. Why do you think I called you? You helped me. Now I'll help you." She looked at Sharmilla. "All we wanted was our wages. We went to the police first. Where were you then? What was left, but to try on our own?"

Sharmilla started the car.

"Look," Zara said, "I turned myself in to you. I had to warn English, but I didn't want to cause you any trouble. But there was no other way. And I tell you something: you need my help you as much as I need yours."

"I don't think I can take any more of your help."

Zara nodded her head. "I bet you do." She looked at Sharmilla.

"What?" Sharmilla asked.

"You're in trouble, aren't you?"

"Not—" She paused, then nodded. "A little bit. Okay, I might lose my job. But I wouldn't exactly say I was in trouble."

"And things aren't going too well with the boyfriend either, are they?"

Sharmilla looked away.

"You see," Zara said, "It's just like I told you. They figure who's expendable, and then—even Romesh. If he has to choose between you and his job—"

"Let's leave Romesh out of this." Sharmilla said. She glared at Zara. "Anyway. Now that I've got you and the phone, I'll probably get a raise and a promotion. We'll see what Romesh thinks about *that*."

"I see how it works. You keep your job and your boyfriend, and I get fucked."

Sharmilla switched off the car. She sighed. A traffic cop banged on the window and startled her.

"Move along!" he said.

She flashed her ID and said, "Fuck off." The cop, eyes wide, backed away. Sharmilla looked at Zara. "Nobody's going to hurt you," she said.

"I'll see to that."

"Right. How many times do you think you can save my life? What, are you going to do? Go to prison with me? Anyway, I said I could get the phone, I didn't say I had it."

Sharmilla stared at Zara. "You sent me a picture."

"I also got rid of the phone. I sent it away for safekeeping."

"Shit!" Sharmilla said. "You didn't!"

"Of course I did. You think I'd trust you?"

Sharmilla slammed her fist on the steering wheel. "You idiot! With the phone I could probably get you off!"

"You just said you were going to arrest me."

"I also said I could get you off."

"With the phone you could probably get me killed. Don't you understand? There's only one way I'm getting out of this."

"What's that?"

"We need to blame somebody else for killing Godbodle. And to do that, they're probably going to have to be dead. And that means—"

Sharmilla chewed on her lip.

"If you put me in jail we're right back where we started. No phone, no killer, no nothing."

"At least I'd be off the hook for your escape."

"But what would happen if we caught the real killer? What would they think of you then?"

Sharmilla looked at Zara. She drummed her fingers on the steering wheel. "And how do you propose to do that?"

"The same way I got you to come."

"With the phone?"

"Forget the phone. He'll come for me."

Sharmilla said, "You never answered my question."

"What was that?"

"How can I trust you?"

Good question, Zara thought. She opened her mouth, but Sharmilla's phone rang.

Sharmilla listened, said, "When? Thanks, Romesh. Yes, I did want to know." She hung up and looked at Zara. "They got your friend at the airport," she said.

# Chapter 33

Paul paid the cabbie, checked in for his flight, ran his bags through x-ray, and paid extra to have them wrapped in plastic. The baggage handlers, who must make a commission on the wrapping sales, said it discouraged thieves. Paul thought that the wrapping more likely identified bags with the good stuff in them. A little plastic sure as hell won't stop an Indian thief. But he paid anyway. Maybe the authorities looked after the wrapped bags a little better. Sort of like *hafta*. Pay me and I'll take care of things. Don't pay me and—

He cleared the passenger search, reached customs, filed his exit papers. A customs agent with perhaps ten teeth scrutinized Paul's passport. The teeth protruded oddly from the agent's mouth and for some reason reminded Paul of Stonehenge. *Gumhenge*. The ancient mysteries of life before floss. He smiled, thought, I ought to see Stonehenge someday, and knew when he did, he would remember the customs agent in Bombay. The agent excused himself, returned with another, his supervisor, apparently. This one wore a smart khaki uniform and had a mouthful of good teeth. They read the passport and conferred. Paul shifted from foot to foot. "Is there a problem?" he asked.

"No problem," the agents said in unison. They stamped his exit papers and handed Paul his passport.

It was ten-forty when he reached the departure lounge. Almost an hour to kill before boarding. He should have brought a book. You'd think they'd have a bookstore, a coffee shop, something. They didn't. A cavernous chamber with about a thousand hard plastic benches. He sat down and read the warning board advising passengers to throw away nail clippers, scissors, knives, guns, hand grenades, letter openers, bottles of acid, and laser pens before they got on the plane. He checked his pockets. Empty. No bottles of acid today. No guns, knives, or hand grenades, either. Must have left 'em at home. A half-dozen cops appeared at the far end of the lobby. Paul turned, out of habit, and looked over his shoulder. There was another half-dozen cops at the other end of the lounge. With a sinking feeling, he watched as they walked towards him.

# Chapter 34

Alight rain fell and Sachin cursed his luck. On the day of his big break—his first big assignment—he would arrive for his interview looking like a drowned rat. Who would take him seriously as a reporter if he couldn't even keep dry? It was bad enough that he looked so young. He didn't have a car so he was riding a motorbike with his cousin, Manesh, pressed into duty for moral support, and to masquerade as a photographer. And since he didn't have a camera, he'd had to borrow his father's. Manesh didn't know how to use the camera, but when the time came, if it came, Sachin would take the pictures. So Manesh clung to Sachin's back on the back of the bike and carried the camera, stuffed into a leather sample case slung over his shoulder. In the case with the camera body were lenses and spare batteries, wiping cloths, filters for sun and for shade, and at the bottom of the bag, wrapped in a plain red rag, Sachin carried (at his father's insistence), a tire iron. Just in case some miscreant made trouble.

"What if someone tried to steal the camera?" his father asked.

"Wouldn't they'd take the whole bag?" Sachin replied. The thought of whacking somebody over the head didn't jibe with his easy-going disposition, but it was no use arguing. Not if he wanted to borrow the camera.

Traffic was heavy. It was nearly noon and the morning commute should have been over. At a stoplight Sachin steered the bike between long lines of cars, pushing his way to the front of the queue. He stopped alongside a small, battered, lime-green Tata Indigo with six college girls crammed inside, two in the front, four in the back. Sachin made eye contact with the driver and she rolled her eyes and turned the radio up. A Bollywood dance tune was playing, something mindless but with a good beat, the theme song from a recent movie. It was on practically every station right now. Sachin knew (because he had friends working on the BomBayWatch section) that the producers of the movie paid two *lakh rupees* for the EOI to run a story about one of the actresses being a love-starved girl from a poor family in Punjab. Other than being from

Punjab, the story was a complete fabrication, with the B-watch gang overwriting the schlock that the publicity agent made up about the actress, who was actually the girlfriend of a notorious local gangster and was once busted in a high-class prostitution sting at a five-star hotel. Sachin knew that everybody was in on the game: the gangsters who financed the movie, the producer who slept with the actress in exchange for her getting the part, the paper, the radio stations, even the DJs who were bribed to plug one song over another. And now he—Sachin—was about to hit the big time, riding to his first big story on the back of a motorcycle and getting soaking wet in the process. How cool would that be, when he met the Communist Party official and left a puddle on the floor of his hotel room?

But then the music stopped and the DJ cut to a breaking news story —that the police were searching for a foreigner who had murdered a police inspector. According to the reporter, the man had strangled the inspector in a dispute over a girl. Roadblocks were going up around town and the railway stations and airports were being watched. Citizens with information were encouraged to call the police. Sachin thought, No wonder traffic is all fucked up.

He looked at the girls again, college girls, in trendy jeans and tee shirts, except for one poor, ugly thing whose mother must have insisted that she wear a traditional *salwar kameez*. The DJ came on the air again, practically screaming, "When the rains aren't backing up the sewers into the streets, then it's up to the cops to mess up traffic. And now," he said, "for another hit. Hit *pe* hit *pe* hit *pe* hit. . . "

The driver of the car cast a coy second-glance at Sachin. A chorus of horns blared and Sachin realized that he had been caught staring. The girl giggled before peeling out into a left-turn, the music of the bass speakers thumping so loudly that the whole car shook. Sachin gunned the bike through the intersection.

Finding Anantharaman had taken a nifty bit of detective work. The agitator wasn't answering his phone and the local party hadn't put him up. As far as they knew, he was still in Kerala. His wife said only that Anantharaman was, "Away on business." The police didn't know much either, but they were also looking, this Sachin knew. His contacts said there were a lot of people angry about the stir. Sachin got his break from Anantharaman's cell phone. Sachin had a friend from college who worked as a software engineer at FlowTel—one of the biggest cell phone carriers in India. He worked his friend for a print-out of Anantharaman's phone's activity. For the last twenty-four hours, the phone had been serviced through a single cell tower on Cumballa Hill. It hadn't moved, though it was currently switched off. "A quarter-mile from the tower," the friend said. No more. If Anantharaman hadn't switched off the phone and moved to avoid being found.

Sachin spent a day going from person to person flashing a picture, Anantharaman in a rough red worker's shirt flanked by a phalanx of toughs, two of whom carried tridents with hammer-and-sickle emblems. It was the kind of picture that made it easy to see why you would be asking for this man, and the man was pretty unmistakable. Somebody had to have seen him. He tried the guest houses with no success. He tried the hotels, finding one where the manager remembered Anantharaman eating a meal a few days ago. He tried the small stores selling cigarettes and candy. He found two more people who had seen him but nobody knew where the agitator stayed. He tried *chaiwalas* and *panwallas* up and down the block. He was so close, he could smell it.

At the end of the day, Sachin tried the beer bars. The first place he tried he struck gold—a guest house upstairs, not advertised, "If you know what I mean," the manager said. Sachin looked the bar over: dark, throbbing with dance tunes, the smell of stale beer, a handful of idle workers bent over their drink, a few overly made-up women in cheap saris taking up tables on the far side of the room. The manager, dark, greasy, wearing jeans and a red-and-pink striped shirt open at the throat to reveal a thick gold chain, pointed towards a set of stairs in the back. "Third floor, last room on the right." Sachin and Monesh hurried up the unlighted staircase. He knocked, heard no reply, tried the handle and found it locked. He left a card wedged in the frame right above the doorknob. That was last night.

Now he was back and the card was gone. He knocked and knocked and knocked, but there was no answer. He looked at Manesh and tried to hide his disappointment. Monesh fiddled with the camera case. He looked scared. Sachin tried the handle and—to his surprise and consternation— found the room unlocked. "He's gone," Sachin said. But they opened the door, anyway. They were greeted by a swarm of flies.

Anantharaman lay on his back in a pool of blood thickened to pudding. The window was open, the rain, now falling slantwise with the monsoon wind, blew into the room. The ceiling fan creaked overhead. A portable radio lay on the floor by an overturned table. The signal lost, the speaker hissed white noise. Anantharaman wore nothing but a red lungee, and it was open to reveal the whole naked body. The penis had been chopped off.

Manesh dropped the case and ran, stumbled and fell in the hallway, scrambled to his feet and fled screaming down the stairway as Sachin shouted after him to be brave. Hands shaking, Sachin assembled the camera and shot six quick pictures. He looked once around the room, taking in the heap of clothes, the suitcase emptied onto the floor, the dresser drawers hanging open, and finally, the body, eyes glazed, the black holes in the chest, the brass cartridges scattered across the floor. And then he, too, fled, hiding in the shadows beyond the stairway until the manager and a few patrons charged up the stairs and raced down the hall to the open door of Anantharaman's room. And then Sachin bounded down the stairs, to the bar on the ground floor and the street outside, where he arrived just in time to see Manesh disappearing around the corner on Sachin's bike.

# Chapter 35

When people asked Sharmilla what she knew about guns, she would launch into a story about a question on the AIS police exam: You are attacked by seven men. You have six shots in your revolver. What do you do? Sharmilla knew the macho students would write: Shoot six, or Shoot two with one bullet, or some variation thereof. At first glance, that might seem like the right answer. Kill six and you're one-on-one, and at you still have a blunt object to fight with. And who knows? If you kill one or two, the rest might run away. How would they know how many bullets you had? But Sharmilla wrote, Nothing. And for her justification she added, There are too many unknowns for me say. Do the men have weapons? Do they come from the same direction? How far away are they? Am I alone? If not, who am I with, other cops or civilians? Unless they were very close and walking slowly, or all in a row, I would have little chance of hitting them all. Better to hide the gun and wait than to kill one or two and anger the rest. Force should be the last resort. And force, even to save myself, might not be the best course. If necessary to save another, then perhaps.

After the test, talking over the questions with Romesh and their friends, he cringed at her answer. "You can't be a non-violent cop," he said.

"That's not what Gandhi said," Sharmilla replied.

The correct answer was, Shoot the closest one first, and then the one you think might be the leader, but Sharmilla stuck by her answer. There were too many loose ends to the question. Things were seldom cut-and-dry. Besides, it was the kind of question you ask, but in real life, never expect to face. Most police worked their entire career and never had a gun pulled on them. And when it happened, the old-timers said, it was always when you least expected it.

Like now. Where did she get a gun?

All Zara knew about guns was what she had seen on TV. It looked easy enough. You pulled back the hammer and squeezed the trigger. The gun felt heavy in her hand; the metal cool and slightly greasy. The hammer slid back and locked with a satisfying click. "You want to know why you should trust me?" she asked.

Sharmilla froze. "You have a gun," she said. It was a statement of fact. She wasn't angry. She almost laughed. It was almost like, sure, what next? You pull a rabbit out of your hat? She shook her head and said, "You have six bullets. You are attacked by seven men. What do you do?"

"What the hell are you talking about?" Zara asked. She looked around. She didn't see any men attacking. "Are you crazy?"

"There's only me," Sharmilla said. "And I don't have a gun."

Zara said, "Of course you have a gun. You're a cop."

"No," she said. "I don't."

"What kind of cop are you?"

"The non-violent kind. The kind of cop who doesn't carry a gun."

"Just a minute ago you tried to choke me."

"I lost my temper. Sorry."

"Sorry," Zara said. "Sorry."

"So what are you going to do?"

The question stumped Zara. She had had a plan, but that plan didn't include contingencies for English landing in jail. She hadn't intended to pull the gun. Not yet, anyway. The truth was that she didn't like violence, either. She didn't like scary movies, and whenever they came to a bloody part she shut her eyes. She didn't want to use the gun. She owed a debt to Sharmilla for saving her life, but she owed a debt to English, too. "I don't know," she said. A minute ago she thought she had Sharmilla convinced to help her. But then Sharmilla asked her, 'How can I trust you?' Zara held her fist to her forehead and tried to concentrate. Life was so much easier before all this happened. "I want you to do something for me," she said.

"What?" Sharmilla asked.

"You have to God promise to do it."

"What is it?"

"Promise."

"I can't promise you unless you tell me."

"Come on," Zara said. "I have the gun. You have to promise."

Sharmilla looked around. There was a crowd at the juice bar, and people moving in a human river up and down the sidewalk, and down the causeway to the mosque. It had clouded over and the wind had picked up. It looked the monsoon was about to begin. The traffic cop who smacked on the window was standing in the road some distance away talking with four other cops. "How can I promise what I don't know?" she said. "I'd like to help you. Tell me what you want and I'll see if I can do it."

Zara stamped her foot. "*Array!*" she said. "That's not how it works. I have the gun and you have to promise. Don't you know anything about this stuff?"

"I've never had a gun pointed at me before? How do I know what to do? I always wondered what I would do if I had to shoot somebody. They teach us that."

"You mean they didn't teach you what to do when somebody points a gun at you?"

"No."

"Great," Zara said. "Stupid cops. Doesn't what's-his-name take you to the movies?"

"Romesh? Sure. What do you want me to do? Dance and sing?"

"I want you to make a phone call."

"That's it? A phone call?"

"That's it."

"Why didn't you just say so?"

"Well I am saying so, but you have to promise."

"Okay, I promise. Who do you want me to call?"

"God promise," Zara said. "Touch your forehead."

Sharmilla touched her forehead. "Okay," she said. "May I?" She pointed at her purse.

Zara nodded.

Sharmilla took out her phone. "Who?" she asked.

"I don't know."

"You don't know? Great." She folded her arms across her chest. "Stupid criminals. Don't they teach you what to do when you point a gun at somebody?"

"You have to call somebody about English. I don't know who, but you do. Or you should."

"Okay," Sharmilla said. "I'll call the High Commissioner. What do you want me to say? They won't let him out."

"Of course they will."

"Not in exchange for me they won't." She looked at Zara. "Right now, I'm less popular than you are."

"At least you can stop Rane from killing him."

"Rane won't kill him. He's a foreigner."

"Yes, he will."

"What makes you say that?"

"I just know. The same reason you knew he was going to kill me. Somebody has to die so they can blame them for killing Godbodle."

Sharmilla thought. There was some truth in what Zara said. That was why she went looking for Zara at Arthur Road Jail—just to make sure they didn't kill her. She had stood behind the glass a day ago in the Girgaon

Station and watched Rane beat Zara and burn her with the electric cord. It wasn't pretty. They were supposed to give him fifteen minutes to beat the story out of her. But when he tore open Zara's gown and ripped off her briefs, something inside Sharmilla snapped and she found herself running for the door. It was one thing to beat a prisoner. Happens every day. But rape was another matter. Fifteen minutes, he had said. And then it was like he just wanted to waste time. "I could call the American consulate," she said. "They might do something."

# Chapter 36

Paul opened his eyes and brought the room into focus. He was naked, hanging upside down by a rope cinched tight around his ankles, his elbows yanked and tied behind his back. This is not, he thought, what he had in mind when he planned his trip to Bombay. He fought to breathe. His face was taut and wet. His ears buzzed. There was pain all-over, cuts on his face and what felt like crusty dried blood, the lumps and swellings that rise after a beating. But strangely enough, what he felt most was an adrenalized detachment from his body. A blurry face peered into his. He struggled to bring it into focus. It was upside down. The face was mouthing words Paul couldn't hear over the roaring in his ears. He concentrated until the face congealed: that prick sub-inspector from the whorehouse raid. Paul grunted. It figured.

Rane shouted something and a blur of figures moved around the periphery of Paul's vision. He pulled on a pair of black leather gloves and slugged Paul in the gut, and then again, a bang on the solar-plexus. It was a good, smooth uppercut. Rane stepped into the punch, driving off his back leg. The blow swung Paul up and back and he gagged, fought the urge to puke. He squeezed his eyes shut and prayed for his breath to return.

When Paul opened his eyes he was swaying gently. He wondered if he'd been out ten seconds or ten minutes. Rane was still there, but he'd taken off the gloves, so Paul guessed it was closer to ten minutes.

Rane bent down and looked Paul in the eye. "I want to know two things," he said. "Where is the girl? and Where is the phone?"

"Two things?" Paul asked. The words came out in a dry, rattling croak.

"Two things."

"Okay." Paul drew a breath and said, "Fuck you, and fuck your mother."

# Chapter 37

Everybody at the embassy called him "Charlie" and they all loved him, if not for his work ethic (which was atrocious) then for his eccentricities (which were even worse). He was short, thin, and balding, with a narrow chin and an overlarge parrot's beak of a nose. He was a dapper dresser, too, with a closet full of hand-tailored silk suits—all in officious shades of blue and gray. His daily uniform was invariable—suit, white shirt, black shoes—only in his ties did he permit any bright colors. He was particularly fond of yellow. He had a high-strung, nervous disposition punctuated by mile-a-minute bursts of insane humor, the only way, he said, to cope with all the bullshit. And he had been coping with the bullshit at the U.S. Consulate in Bombay for four years, ten months, twenty-two days, seven hours and ten minutes.

During that time he has taken exactly 112 days of vacation time, 56 days of sick leave, 28 days of emergency leave, and 94 days of official government holiday (both US and Indian holidays are celebrated). This made up exactly 30.2% of what most people would call "workdays." He'd spent every moment of the time-off he'd earned—and then some. And he'd gone through three green-white-and-orange Miami Dolphin coffee mugs and three clear glass Starbucks French press coffee makers (two each of the aforementioned broken by the incompetent *peon* who cleans his office every evening), fourteen pounds of American made granulated sugar (the Indian sugar was not granulated and wouldn't dissolve properly), and twelve boxes of Cuban cigars (he was not, as an American citizen, and especially as a government employee, supposed to purchase or possess Cuban cigars, and he didn't so much like tobacco as he liked the idea of thumbing his nose at the law. And it had the added benefit of pissing off Nina, his wife, who thought cigars low-class (along with practically every-thing else) and pretended to be allergic to the smoke. He'd had jaundice once, the flu every year, and the cramping shits almost constantly since he arrived in Bombay.

He had hated every minute of it. He hated Bombay. He hated the name Bombay, and the fact that some fanatic Maharashtrans were radical about calling it Mumbai. He hated the heat; the stench; the traffic; the water; the rain; the sun; the crowds; the bugs (especially the mosquitoes); the rats, the mongrel stray dogs, the emaciated feral cats, the pollution, the beggars, the *fakirs* spreading their pseudo-spirituality that masked a cancerous, insatiable, greed, and the crooked, arrogant, solicitous, and duplicitous Indians he had to work with every day. Especially his wife. Why, he wondered, did I have to marry an Indian? The only two things he loathed worse than Indians were his fellow government workers and the panic-stricken Americans whose idiotic blunders became his nightmare to fix. The Americans, he said, divided themselves into three categories. First were the punky teenagers who got drugged and raped at rave parties out in the boondocks, but also sometimes got busted for drugs at the airport on their way home. The second were the numbskull businessmen who got fucked on slimy deals by crooked Indians. The deals might be corporate or they might be personal, but the mechanics (and the solution) was always the same. They should have a morning after pill for people who didn't practice safe transactions. Buyer beware. And then there was the third group. Fortunately, Charlie explained, when he told this story, he had never met any of the third group, whatever they were.

The good news was, for Charlie, that in ten days (minus the seven hours and ten minutes worked today) he left for vacation—and a new posting—to Botswana. For most Foreign Service workers, a posting to Botswana would be a step down, but Charlie couldn't wait. Next to India, Botswana sounded like a stroll in the park, a cultural Mecca and Club Med rolled into one. He could tell you all about it: The Sands of the Kalahari (84% of the country is desert) where he imagined he would finally dry out his toes and get rid of the itching, creeping crud that had plagued him since he arrived in India (actually, the Kalahari was not so much sand dunes as covered with tough shrubs and grasses—except for the salt pans and marshes where water collected—although there was some sand, mostly on the southwest side of the low range of hills). And he could tell you about Gaborone, the capital, on the Notwane River, a fast-growing, modern city on the rail line from Pretoria with a paltry 200,000 people (Bombay had 30,000,000 of whom more than 2,000,000 were pavement dwellers), a university of 15,000 students (including a medical college), and a brewery making Chibuku Beer (which was brewed from sorghum and corn and sold in paper cartons which had to be shaken before opening because the product separated—and as an added incentive he had been advised that the beer was best when consumed two days after manufacture, but after six days was likely to make you sick if you drank it). He couldn't wait.

So it was early afternoon and Charlie was enjoying a cup of coffee from his newly-cracked Dolphins Mug and sitting at his desk wondering how sick you could really get from Chibuku Beer when the call came, referred to him by a senior staffer who took it from a line supervisor who took it from a phone operator. He was not thrilled. Some jackass, they said, had got himself thrown in jail.

"Type one or type two?" Charlie asked, absent-mindedly flipping the end of the favorite yellow tie.

The staffer shrugged, nobody had got that far with the questions yet. But this must be the snow job of all snow jobs—for the jackass's buddies were posing as cops trying to get him out. At least, that was what the operator said.

Charlie let the phone sit for what he considered an appropriately awe-inspiring length of time, the little red light blinking that someone was still on hold, until at last he punched the button for the speaker and said, with an aggrieved air, "Nostrandt here."

There was a pause on the line and woman's voice said, "I'm with the Mumbai police. I have reason to believe a U.S. citizen has been picked up at the airport by the police and he may be in very serious trouble."

Charlie rolled his eyes. "Most people, ma'am, would consider being picked up by the police serious trouble. I'm sure we'll get word through the usual channels if he needs our assistance." He reached for the disconnect button but the woman said, "You don't understand—they'll kill him."

Charlie paused, his finger hovering over the button, the little red light flashing. There were two voices competing in his head. One said, Let the fucker fry, I'm tired of these dipshits getting in trouble and asking me to fix it. What do I look like, Mister Wizard? But the other was the voice of the young college graduate who sought out the Foreign Service so he could see the world and make a difference. Right. I've seen the inside of doctor's offices from Albania to Zambia, and let me tell you, they got some real shit-hole doctor's offices in Zambia. No *Highlights for Children* there. The issue hung in the balance and then Charlie said, "And why would you think that, Miss—" he bit his tongue.

She paused. She seemed to be squabbling with someone about the call. "Oberoi," she said. "Assistant Sub-inspector at the Girgaon Road Station."

"Well, Miss Oberoi," Charlie said, "Why don't you talk to your bosses and have someone from the High Commissioner's Office give me a jingle and I'll look into it." He punched at the button just as she shouted, "They're the ones doing it—my bosses! That's the problem. I'm trying to warn you for his sake, and yours." The finger stopped just short of disconnecting. Charlie shut his eyes. He could feel the ridges in the plastic. Just a little more pressure and he could go back to daydreaming about beer-swilling in Botswana. Wonder what the ladies are like there? Probably black and exotic.

"For the love of God!" she shouted, "Just call somebody in the city or state government! Let them know that you know they have him in custody. Make an inquiry. He is one of yours, for God's sake!"

"We don't," Charlie said, "make inquiry without formal request from the person in custody or from his or her family. Are you family?" he asked.

"What's wrong with you!" she shouted. "He's an American! Don't you care? His name is Paul Shea. You might even know him."

Charlie leaned back in his ergonomically-designed black leather chair and put his bare feet up on his desk. He studied his toes. He had painted the nails with an oily red paste which he had been assured by a local quack doctor would kill the crud growing under them. The chair swiveled and reclined. It glided silently across the carpeted floor on rubberized rollers. It was a gift from an Indian contractor who sought Charlie's help getting his cook a visa to the states. The chair arrived and the problem holding up the visa mysteriously disappeared. The desk was teak (the wood probably cut by one of the timber bandits plaguing the national forest), the top inlaid with a solid slab of cool green marble (probably cut by child laborers toiling for starvation wages in the mines in Rajasthan). The desk was also a gift—a token of appreciation from a plastics exporter whose environmental record might have precluded his landing a government contract if the record had become known. Ah, India, Charlie thought.

And then he meandered back in time, cataloguing in his memory the parties and embassy events—the monthly poetry readings and the jazz concerts, the cultural clusterfucks that Nina loved and he abhorred (if it wasn't for the free wine and whiskey they'd be intolerable). Shea. He sighed. Shea. Yeah, I might have met a Shea. The names and faces blurred. But there was a Shea at something or another—a book release party maybe—and Charlie half-way remembered a funny, animated conversation with a tall, bearded man about riding around in a jeep with a police inspector looking at whorehouses. Or something like that. It was corrupt. That's what Charlie liked about it. Yeah, he thought, Shea. And then, So what? He dug in his ear for wax with his little finger.

"Listen to me," the woman said. "I'm telling you—the guy has links to Al Qaida. They picked him up at the airport with RDX in his bags on a plane to New York. ISI will kill him and keep it secret just to cover it up. I'm telling you for your own good—you need to find this guy and make sure your people get to talk to him."

Charlie's feet shot off the desk so fast he almost fell out of his chair. "Who is this again?" he asked, but the line went dead. For a moment he sat and wondered if what he heard was a joke. But there were guidelines about dealing with calls like this, and the guidelines were serious as a heart attack.

The senior staffer who took the call from the supervisor who took it from the phone operator stood in his door. "What do you want for lunch?" she asked.

Charlie said, "Back up the tapes on that last call and get me the number right-fucking-now." He took out his cell and speed-dialed the ambassador in New Delhi.

In three minutes the CIA computer geeks had a name and a number —a Bombay cop name Oberoi—and the location of the call within a dozen meters—close by the causeway to the Haji Ali Mosque. In five he had the ambassador on the line. "Houston," he said, "we have a problem."

# Chapter 38

Sharmilla looked at the sky and chewed on her lip.

Zara, still fiddling with the pistol, asked, "What's RDX?"

"You don't want to know."

Zara studied Sharmilla's face. She thought, She's pretty when she's not worried or unhappy. "That didn't sound good," she said.

"It was the best I could come up with. If the Americans call, it ought to keep him alive."

"Ought to?"

"What else can I do?" Sharmilla shrugged. "You said call someone, so I called someone. I can't make them do anything. All I can do is try." She looked at Zara. "Now what?"

Zara said, "How can I convince you to trust me?"

"You could stop pointing that gun at me."

Zara looked at the pistol, and then at Sharmilla. Then she slowly extended her open hand and Sharmilla took the gun gingerly and held it in her lap. "Now do you trust me?" Zara asked.

"Not really. I suppose I should have searched you, and handcuffed you. What else have you got in that bag?"

"A bunch of money and gold and stuff."

Sharmilla rolled her eyes. Here we go again.

"No, really, it came from Godbodle's. I didn't want to get charged with theft so I wanted to make sure they got it back."

"Right."

"If it helps you can shoot me."

"You want me to shoot you?"

"Yes."

"Why?"

"You can say you captured me. You can give Mrs. Godbodle back her things. Maybe they'll give you a medal."

"But I don't want to shoot you."

"You don't have to kill me. Just shoot me a little bit. In the arm or something. Then you can take me to the hospital."

"Shooting you won't solve anything."

"Why not? Didn't you say I ruined your career and cost you your boyfriend?"

"That's beside the point. I didn't become a cop to shoot people for no reason."

"Okay," Zara said. "If you won't shoot me, then help me. That's all I've been asking. We both lost our jobs. We both lost our boyfriends, and we're both in big trouble with the cops. But if we help each other, maybe we can fix things. At least, I have an idea. Unless you have a better one."

Sharmilla buried her face in her hands. "Oh, God," she said. "This was not how I envisioned police work."

"Well?"

"So what's your big plan?"

"I want you to take me to meet Prashante Dashpante."

"Who?"

"Dashpante. The big-shot with the Congress Party."

"That toad? What do you want with *him*?"

"Remember Mister the-Congress-Party-wants-to-help. Well, I need his help."

"All he wants is to use you for political gain."

"So what? I can use him, too."

Sharmilla lowered her voice. "You don't have pictures of him, do you?"

"Not that I know of."

"Then why would he help you?"

"He won't. Not intentionally. But if I piss him off, he might without meaning to."

"I don't get it."

"Tell me, when you were a kid, did you ever steal mangos?"

"We had money. If we wanted mangos we sent a servant to the market."

"Well my family didn't have money. If I wanted mangos, I had to steal them. When I was little I had a friend, Esweria. She taught me how. But climbing the tree was too hard. The best thing was to shake the tree. Or since we were too small, to wait until the wind came along. And once in a while, when the wind wouldn't cooperate, we'd tie a rope around the tree, and then hook it to the bumper of a car, and when the car drove off, it shook the tree for us. Sometimes it shook the bumper off, but that's beside the point."

"Why are we talking about mangos?"

"Somebody has been messing with me for a while now, and I'm still not sure who. I want to shake the tree and see who falls out."

Sharmilla shook her head. "I don't know. Going to see Dashpante would be like walking into the lion's den."

"I've already been in the lion's den," Zara said. "What else can they do to me? Besides, nobody's going to be looking for me there."

That was true, Sharmilla thought. "But if I take you there—"

"Yes, he'll be pissed off. Really pissed off. And the louder he yells, the more people are going to hear about it. And if they get pissed off, maybe they'll make a mistake."

Sharmilla closed her eyes and sighed. "Here we go again," she said. "My life was so easy before I met you."

"What?" Zara asked.

Sharmilla looked at the pistol in her lap. "You asked me one time why I became a policewoman."

"I did?"

"I became a cop because I wanted to help people."

"Well, here's your chance."

Sharmilla handed Zara the pistol. "I guess I can kiss that career good-bye."

Zara looked at the pistol, then at Sharmilla. "So you do trust me?"

"I've got my own. If we're going to work together, I have to trust you."

"Wait a minute," Zara said. "You just told me you didn't have a gun."

"Well what was I supposed to say? I'm a cop. Of course I have gun."

"You lied to me! Again!"

"You were pointing a gun at me."

"Did you lie about not having any training about what to do if people are pointing a gun at you too?"

"Yes."

"What did they tell you to do?"

"They said to humor them."

"You fucking bitch!"

"Well, what do you expect? Besides, you had the safety on. It wouldn't have fired anyway."

Zara looked at the pistol. "What do you mean, the 'safety'?"

"The little red button. Push it in and the gun won't fire. If you don't know how to use it, don't try," Sharmilla said. She started the car again.

"You better show me this safety thing," Zara said.

"You're not going to shoot Dashpante, are you?" Sharmilla shut the car off and folded her arms. "Because if you are, I definitely won't take you."

"I'm not going to shoot anybody," Zara said.

Sharmilla restarted the car. "Promise?" she asked.

"Promise. I just mean . . . you know . . . just in case I have to use it. Later." She held the gun up and pushed the red button backwards and forward. She cocked it and looked down the barrel.

"For God's sake!" Sharmilla said, snatching the gun from Zara's hand. "Give me that before you hurt yourself." She carefully lowered the hammer. "Here," she said, switching a little button above the grip back and forth. This is the safety. In and the gun can't be fired. Pull it out and it—" The gun went off and the passenger side window exploded. The car was instantly filled with acrid blue smoke. People in line at the juice bar screamed and scattered. Down the street, the traffic cops dove for cover.

"Shit!" Sharmilla shouted, throwing the gun into the back seat. She jammed on the accelerator and, tires squealing, fish-tailed out into traffic. Ten minutes later Zara still couldn't look at Sharmilla without laughing.

Sharmilla glared at her. "Shut up," she said. "I totally fucked up my car."

# Chapter 39

Paul lay face down on a block of ice, his arms pinioned, his body chilled stiff. Someone was standing on his back and grinding their heels into his shoulder blades. Son-of-a-bitch, Paul thought. These fuckers are going to kill me. After a while the person stepped off and a pair of hands flipped Paul over and he fell from the ice to the floor. A single light hung above him, so bright it burned his eyes. Around it, staring down at him, Paul made out the silhouettes of five faces. Or maybe the silhouette of one face five times. It was hard to tell. He felt like he was floating. He had only to close his eyes to be far away, wherever he wanted. He wanted to be someplace warm—a summer vacation to Florida when he was a boy came to mind. Destin Beach, back in the early '60's, when there were ten hotels and miles of undeveloped white sand.

Someone lifted him into a sitting position. They cut his hands free and forced a clipboard into them. He could not hold the clipboard, and it fell to the floor. They slapped him. They jerked him to his feet and dragged him to a chair, set Paul in the chair, shoved the chair up to a desk, and dropped the clipboard on the desk in front of him. On the board was a typewritten paper. Paul couldn't focus well enough even to tell what language it was written in, much less read it.

Rane sat down on the desk opposite Paul. He was smoking a cigarette and carrying a glass of whiskey. He took a sip and shook the glass so that the ice cubes spun. "Sooner or later," he said, "You will want this to be over." He polished off the drink and set the glass down. "If you sign soon enough you might live, if not—" He shrugged. "Signing will at least put an end to your misery."

Somehow Paul knew there were only two things that would bring an end to his pain. Because they weren't likely to turn him loose, he tried not to think about the other thing. If they were going to kill him, he didn't want to reward them. Nor did he want to make it quick and easy. The longer he was in custody, the more likely that Frank or Sunil or someone would start asking questions. They might be calling about him already. And the only way Paul knew for sure to stay alive was not to give Rane anything. Eventually someone would get him out. And when they do, Paul thought, I'm going to hunt this fucker down and kill him.

"Sign the papers," Rane said.

Paul laughed.

Rane looked at him like he was crazy.

Maybe he was crazy. Pain does funny things to people. But so does the will to survive. It latches onto the oddest memories. The only thing Paul could think of was the old Cheech and Chong routine: "Sign ze pay-purz, old mannnn. Vy von't you sign ze pay-purz?" He repeated the punch line in a falsetto voice: "Becauz you haf brrrrroken my fingerz."

Rane looked around the room as if to say, What the hell is he talking about? Before he could snatch the clipboard away, Paul slashed the pen across it and ripped the paper.

# Chapter 40

The rain poured through the passenger side's shattered window, and Zara climbed into the back seat to keep dry. Traffic was backed up. The word on the radio was that the police had a suspect in custody for the killing Inspector Godbodle. Other than that, the cops were tight-lipped. But then there was new story—that a CPI agitator from Kerala —the same one who caused a stir leading sex workers on a *bundh*—had been found mutilated in a seedy guest house off Grant Road.

Sharmilla looked at Zara in the rear-view mirror.

Zara stared out the window at the rain. "He should have left town," she said.

"So they killed him for organizing the protest?"

"Maybe. Or to get the phone. Or to get to me. Maybe they thought he knew where I was."

They reached Juhu, where Dashpante lived. He owned the top floor of a new condo along the beach. The building was gated and guarded. "How do we get in?" Zara asked.

Sharmilla smiled. "We're here to fix the phone."

Zara rolled her eyes. "Right."

"I'm a cop," Sharmilla said. "They'll let us in." They asked at the front desk but the guards refused them. They called Dashpante. After a short, sharp conversation, the guard said, "*Sahib* is not at home." He folded his arms and looked at them with an air of insolent finality.

Sharmilla thought about this, then dialed a number and forwarded the SMS Zara had sent her. A minute later the phone at the desk rang. The guard answered, said, "Yes, *Sahib*," and gestured towards the elevator. "Twenty-two," he said.

They took the elevator. Before Sharmilla could knock, a servant in a white suit opened the door and led them to a cavernous room with a ceiling a full five meters high. A chandelier with a hundred glittering prisms splashed whirling specks of color on the walls around the room above a dining table of hand-carved teak. A dark blue Kashmiri hand-knotted silk rug in a red, gold, and ivory traditional mogul design lay on the white marble floor in the center of the room. The interior wall was devoted to dark, oversized paintings depicting women in doorways or alleyways, all of the paintings done in somber browns and purples, muted shades of rust and dark green. The outer walls were glass, framed by dark red curtains pulled back and tied with thick gold braids. Zara went to the window and looked down. Behind the building was the beach, curving out of sight into the gray of the falling rain. Far below was the turquoise oval of a pool. To the north and south the high rises of Bombay stood in rows like tombstones.

Dashpante appeared wearing western slacks under a big red robe. He looked from Sharmilla to Zara and back. "Hello, again," he said, nodding at Zara. "To what do I owe the honor of your visit?"

Zara looked around the room.

When it is clear that she would not answer, Dashpante said, "Do you have any idea how much trouble you've caused? We've got half the police force out scouring the streets for you."

Zara shrugged and said, "Sorry."

"Sorry?" Dashpante echoed. He held up a cell phone. In the display was a photo. "I take it you have the rest of these?"

"I can get them," Zara said.

"You can get them?"

"That's what I said."

"Only yesterday you said that you didn't know where the phone was."

She shrugged. "That was yesterday. Now I know where it is."

"What do you want?" Dashpante asked.

A white suited servant appeared with tea and biscuits. Dashpante gestured to a small couch near the window and Sharmilla and Zara sat down. He took a chair from the table and sat opposite them.

"We want our wages from Mrs. Shetty."

Dashpante grunted. "That's it?" he asked.

"No, there's more."

"I thought so. Like what?"

"I want English on a plane out of the country with all the charges against him dropped. I want you promise me—" she looked at Sharmilla, "promise *us* immunity."

Dashpante said, "I don't think you are in any position to dictate terms. Have you forgotten who I am? Tell me where the phone is and I'll have it in ten minutes. Then I'll get you your American. I'll even see the charges against you dropped, and I'll see that Miss Oberoi is restored to good graces. But first, I get the phone."

"I don't have it."

"So where is it?"

"I said I can get it."

"Why shouldn't I just hand you to the cops and let them deal with you?"

"Because I left the phone with someone I trust and I told him that if he didn't hear from me by morning to give the phone to your worst enemy."

Dashpante's eyes narrowed. "The BJP? The Shiv Sena? The dons?"

"The press."

Dashpante grunted. "Who did you give the phone to? The American?"

"How could I do that when you have him in custody?"

Dashpante stood up and went to the window. He called for his servant and said, "A whiskey." When the servant had gone he looked at Zara and Sharmilla, sitting side-by-side. He said, "I suppose, since you're working with the cops, that just about anything is possible. You burglarized Godbodle's house?"

Zara nodded.

"And you started that stir—the one yesterday on Falklands Road? The one for which our communist friend was killed."

"Yes."

"What do you know about him?"

"He came to help me."

"And now you want me to help you? After what happened to him, I'm not sure I want my name mixed up in this."

"You're already mixed up in it. You promised, remember?"

"That was yesterday, this is today."

The servant appeared with the whiskey.

"I see," Zara said. "I guess we should go then."

"Not so fast," Dashpante said. He gestured that they should remain seated. "Suppose I did help you? What then?"

"You meet my terms, you get the phone."

"How can I trust you?"

Zara asked Sharmilla, "Do you have your phone?"

Sharmilla dug in her purse and produced it.

Zara got up and stood beside Dashpante. She said, "Smile" and then holding the phone at arm's length, snapped their picture. She handed the phone to Sharmilla, who dialed a number.

"Just a minute," Dashpante said. He grabbed for the phone but the SMS had been sent. He looked at the number. "Who is this?" he asked.

"Rane," Zara said.

"What's this all about?"

"Mangos."

Dashpante ran his fingers through the remains of his hair. "Mangos?" he said, looking at Zara. "Are you mad?" He drank his whiskey and threw the glass across the room. He looked at Sharmilla. "What the hell is she talking about?"

"Haven't you ever stolen mangos?" Sharmilla asked. She turned to Zara and said, "We'd better go."

"Of course not. If I want mangos I send a servant to the market."

Zara stood up, but Dashpante blocked the way. "I could have you both dead and buried in less time than it takes my servants to draw my bath," he said. "You think you can come here—to my house—and order me around? I ought to have you both shot."

Sharmilla's hand went to her purse but Zara elbowed her. "That won't get you the phone," Zara said. "I need time and a few small favors. It's not much to ask of a big-shot politician like you. You want the phone and I'll get it. In the mean time, you get English out of the country. After that, you have to trust me."

"Trust? You?" Dashpante looked incredulous. "A filthy fucking whore from some rat midden in the south?" Dashpante looked hard at them before turning to the servants who had appeared at the door and waving them away. Lowering his voice to a whisper, he asked Sharmilla, "Do you trust her?"

"More than I trust you." Sharmilla's phone began to ring. She opened it, then snapped it shut. She tugged at Zara's sleeve and said, "We have to go. *Now.*" She tried to walk past Dashpante, but he sidestepped and cut them off.

Sharmilla slipped her hand into her purse. Zara pulled her pistol from the pocket of her *salwar kameez.* "See us as far as the gate," Sharmilla said.

"You wouldn't dare," Dashpante replied.

"Oh, wouldn't I?" Zara asked. "We could have you dead and buried faster than—whatever."

At the elevator Dashpante said, "You'll never get away with this."

"Nobody gets away with anything," Sharmilla replied. "The best you can hope for is that somebody else pays. Whose sins do you want to pay for today?"

They rode the elevator down quietly and walked past the guards to the front gate. As they sped away in Sharmilla's Mercedes, Zara asked, "Who called?"

"Rane."

"What did he say?"

"You don't want to know."

Zara looked at Sharmilla. "I'll find out eventually. Might as well tell me now."

Sharmilla took out her phone and showed Zara the picture of Paul slumped in a chair. A khaki-clad arm pressed a pistol against his head. The message read: LIKE PICTURES? Sharmilla said, "We have to ditch the car."

# Chapter 41

Paul woke in a room with bare white walls and a single bright light set in a fixture in the ceiling. He was still naked, lying on his back, now strapped to a gurney, and he hurt like hell all over. He couldn't have thought about moving even if he hadn't been tied down. His skin felt like it was on fire, and his mouth and throat were so swollen and dry it was painful for him to breathe. Beside him stood two grim-faced women cops in starched khaki uniforms. Women. All business, from the look of them, but not bad-looking. He tried to make sense of this when one of them drew a syringe of clear liquid. Here goes nothing, Paul thought. He wanted to fight, but there was no gas left in his tank. One woman held his arm while the other found a vein. The warmth that washed over him was a relief. He wondered if this was how Godbodle felt when the end came. And then, as his lips began to tingle, and the edge of his vision faded to black, he remembered another old joke, one about a skydiver whose parachute wouldn't open. He was plummeing to earth when he saw, on the ground below him, a bright flash followed by a loud bang. Then he saw another man hurtling up towards him. As they passed, the parachutist shouted, "Know anything about parachutes?" and the other man shouted back, "Know anything about Coleman stoves?" As the darkness closed in around him, Paul saw a bright flash and heard a loud bang.

# Chapter 42

Rane saw the sleek, black Mercedes parked conspicuously in the drive at the Girgaon Police Station but gave it no thought until he reached his office and found his secretary pale and sweaty, typing feverishly. If she was working, there must be trouble. He leaned over her and saw that she was re-typing a report that she'd turned in last week about peddlers encroaching on Grant Road. One glance from the secretary told him everything.

The commissioner was in Rane's office seated behind Rane's desk. To the commissioner's right were Fernandez, Yadav, and Uttam Ganesh. Since they had taken all of the chairs, Rane stood.

The commissioner said, "You lost control."

Rane shook his head and replied, "These things take time. What do you expect? I'm conducting an investigation."

"So I'm told," Ganesh replied. "I went to a symphony once and it had a conductor. But the show was over in two hours."

"We're crossing suspects off the list."

"Crossing off? Or knocking off?" Ganesh asked.

"I don't know what you mean."

The commissioner stood. "Another body, that agitator—what's-his-name?"

Rane stared at the commissioner blankly.

"Anantharaman," Fernandez said.

"Yes," the commissioner said, "that's the one."

Rane scratched his chin. "How and where?" he asked.

Yadav said, "Shot in a guest house off Grant Road."

"When?"

"This morning."

"Suspects?"

The commissioner said, "We were hoping you could answer that."

Rane shrugged. "I hadn't heard," he said. "I've been busy. And not with . . . Ana what's-his-name." He sat down on the edge of his desk and reached across it to take a cigarette from a silver box, then lit it with an overlarge, ornate silver lighter. He looked at the men staring at him from their seats. "Don't look at me." he said. "You know where I've been."

"And what have you to show for your efforts?"

"Not much," Rane said gloomily. "Every time I get—" His phone rang. He looked at it and blanched.

"What?" the commissioner asked.

"Nothing," Rane said. He typed a quick reply and flipped the phone shut. "Every time I get started, somebody gets in the way." He looked at the four officials and said, "You know who I mean. I had to give the American up."

"You knew that was coming," Ganesh said.

"I did not know!" Rane said. "Every time I start questioning someone, some jackass gums up the works."

"You don't suppose—"

"Who else?" Rane said. "Who else is there?" He turned the lighter over and over in his hand while he smoked.

The three officials looked at each other. "Doesn't matter now," Fernandez said. "The embassy is making a stink about his condition. We can blame it on prisoners, but that won't hold, not after they've talked to him."

"And when will that be?"

"We can hold out for a while. Another twenty-four hours, maybe. Nostrandt calls every half hour. Delhi calls every hour on the hour. I expect we'll hear from Washington when it gets daylight over there."

Rane shrugged. "So what? Find some hash and plant it on him."

Ganesh said, "Someone dropped the T-word on him."

Rane smiled. "That's even better. Plant some RDX and timers. Say we stopped something big. They'll thank us. You can ask for money."

"This isn't a joke," the commissioner said.

"So who's laughing?"

The commissioner drummed his fingers on the desk. "It's bad enough about the phone. This could become an international incident."

Rane rolled his eyes.

Ganesh said, "If that phone falls into the wrong hands—"

"It won't," Rane said curtly. "They have it—one of them has it."

"Them?"

"She's hooked up with you-know-who. We should have jailed her."

"Really?" the commissioner asked.

"You know or you wouldn't be here," Rane replied.

The commissioner smiled. "And how would you know that?"

"The same way you know," Rane said. "Because Dashpante called you." Rane walked to the window and looked down at Girgaon Road. The wind was whipping the rain into sheets. Kids were dancing in the road, arms open to the sky. The water was running in knee-deep rivers along the curbs. "It was your idea to bring her in to begin with. I told you—women aren't cut out for this kind of work. They're too emotional. As far as I am concerned, they are only good for one thing. That and typing. I don't know what she's up to. The whore might have her convinced that—who knows —that someone else has the phone."

"Who else might have it?"

Rane shrugged. "Who else is there? No one, that's who."

"She broke into Godbodle's house. Do you think she found it?"

"Yes," Rane said.

"But we—"

"But we *what*? She knew where it was. We didn't. What were we supposed to do? Rip the place apart? We did the best we could."

"It would have been easier," Ganesh said, "If they had just paid the damn girl to begin with."

"Cheaper anyway," Fernandez added.

"It doesn't work that way," Rane said.

"The problem," the commissioner said, "is that Godbodle had it. Who else knew? The girl knew, and the American might have known. And he knew Godbodle. Who else could have known?"

Rane slammed his fist down on the desk. "I tell you the girl has the goddamned phone, or knows where it is. Give me the American and I'll make her cough it up."

The commissioner shook his head. "He's too hot for that right now. It's gone political."

"Fuck politics," Rane said.

Yadav said, "We need more men—and perhaps some extraordinary powers."

The commissioner looked at Fernandez and Ganesh. "Can I justify this?"

"There is a way," Rane said. "And it will silence the Americans, too."

"Silence? Which ones?"

"All of them."

# Chapter 43

The rain began to fall in slanting curtains driven by gusts of wind. Traffic crawled. A car in the opposite lane had fallen into an open manhole and broken an axle. A line of police jeeps, with blue lights flashing, was caught in the jam headed in the direction of Dashpante's condo. At the sight of them Sharmilla jerked the wheel and turned off the main road onto a side street that burrowed into a slum. Traffic there was even worse, with pushcarts and three wheelers and cabs and bicyclists and pedestrians all jammed into a single, narrow lane. The water rose, pooling into lakes in the roadway. "Shit," Sharmilla said. It was already up to the hubcaps on the Benz. There was no use driving on, and no way to turn back.

"Don't worry, I know this place," Zara said.

Sharmilla looked at her. "You've been here?"

"No, but it's just like home. Look." She pointed. "Muslims."

It was true. The signs above the shops were written in flowing green Arabic script.

"Come on," she said. "Let's get out."

Sharmilla looked at the rising water—mud brown and carrying the flotsam of a six-month drought: paper and bottles, oil, scum, and sewage. The neighborhood kids danced and skipped about in the rain. A fair number of adults, too.

They climbed out of the car, Sharmilla cringing as she stepped into the water and the muck underneath it.

"It won't kill you," Zara said.

But then again, Sharmilla thought, it might. Tetanus. Cholera. Dengue. Rabies. Malaria. Leprosy. Leptospirosis. The list of diseases found in Bombay's slums read like a who's-who of lethal microbes. And the smell. Dear God, she thought.

Zara had taken off her shoes and was twirling around in a ring of kids. "I haven't done this in years!" she shouted.

Sharmilla looked at the water and wished she'd rolled up the legs of her *salwar* suit. "This cost me like, 5,000 rupees."

"So what?" Zara said. "Mine cost 250 and got just as wet."

"My point exactly."

"Come on," Zara said. "I'll buy you a new one. It's the least I can do to repay you."

"But what about my car?"

"I might buy you a *salwar*, but I'm not buying you a car."

"But I can't leave it here."

"Why not? You said you wanted to ditch it. This place is as good as any."

"But I wanted to ditch it where I could get it back."

"You might get it back."

"Not likely," Sharmilla said, looking around. Already the women were attracting a crowd of onlookers. "If the flood waters don't get it, the thieves will."

"Nothing to do about that," Zara said.

They found a *chaiwala* with a blue tarp hung over his stall, huddled drinking tea and watching the water rise.

"We can't stay here all day," Sharmilla said.

"You're right," Zara replied.

"The cops are looking for us."

Zara shrugged. "Let them look. Come on."

They crossed the street and found a couple of small stores. Zara chose a place hardly bigger than one of the closets in Sharmilla's house. Inside were shelves displaying *caftans* and *burqas*. Sharmilla huddled under the eave while Zara went in. Zara came back to the door with a black caftan and held it to Sharmilla's shoulders. "You gave me a suit," she said. "Now I'll give you one." She pointed to a curtain at the back of the store. "Go in there and change."

# Chapter 44

They walked carefully back to main road and found a three wheeler, paying him an outrageous fare to take them to the nearest train station. Sharmilla tugged at the burqa, lifting the veil to look around. "You can't keep doing that," Zara said.

"I can't see," she said. "How do you wear these things?"

"You get used to it."

They bought tickets south to Grant Road Station. On the platform Sharmilla slapped her forehead.

"What?" Zara asked.

"Our cell phones," Sharmilla said. She dug hers out of her purse and turned it off. "They'll track us."

"They can track you with that?" Zara asked.

"Yes. Is yours off?"

Zara dug her phone out, and the one she had taken from Godbodle's. She started to switch them off but Sharmilla said, "I have a better idea." She turned her phone back on and said, "Give me your phone."

Zara gave her the phone.

"Now give me your bag."

"No."

"Come on, give me the bag."

"No, I need it."

"It's just a bag."

Zara shook her head. She clutched it to her chest.

"But I need a bag."

"So go find one. I need this."

Sharmilla looked around. The wind had whipped paper and bags and junk into a pile on the opposite side of the station. "Come on," she said. They crossed the pedestrian bridge to the northbound platform and rummaged through the pile until they found a plastic bag. "Perfect," Sharmilla said. She put the phones in the bag, and when the next train arrived she got into the women's car. As the train pulled away, headed north, she jumped out. "Let them track us," she said.

They caught a southbound. The women's car was less crowded than the regular coaches and they found a seat on the left side of the train where the rain wasn't blowing in. Sharmilla fussed with her burqa.

"Leave it alone," Zara said. "Act natural."

"What's natural about this thing? I can barely breathe. I'm sweating half to death. Every step I take I'm worried I'm going to trip and fall."

"Just walk slowly. Take little steps, but strong."

"I know how to walk."

"Come on, it's not so bad. There must be fifty million women wearing these things."

"Well, I've never been one of them. If my mother could see me right now—" Sharmilla played with the embroidery on her sleeve.

Zara swatted at Sharmilla's hands. "Leave it alone, you'll unravel it."

Sharmilla's caftan was black with white embroidery. Zara's was black on black. "How do I look?" Sharmilla asked.

"Fine."

"You should have bought better ones, mine's falling apart."

"You whine a lot."

"I wonder what I'll do for work when this is all over."

"Run for president?"

"Oh, shut up."

"Find a husband and raise a family—that's what I'd do."

"Romesh and I used to argue about that. He wanted an old-fashioned woman, but I thought I should do something to make a statement."

"A statement? Why? Would anybody listen?"

Sharmilla frowned. "You know what I mean."

"Maybe it isn't our fate."

Sharmilla stared out the window. "They'll find my car soon."

"So what?" Zara said.

"And they'll find the phones."

"Maybe."

"They will. And when they do, they'll guess we're going south."

"So what?"

"So where are we going?"

Zara shrugged.

"We're going to your house, aren't we?"

Zara nodded. "It's as good a place as any. We shook the tree. Let's see who falls out."

# Chapter 45

Whenen Paul opened his eyes he was expecting to see Rane, but the image confused him—a dark face in a bright room, softly out-of-focus. "Rooney punts for England," Paul said, though he was not sure why. He squinted. His tongue was thick and tasted bitter—garlicky. But the image that came into focus was the gentle, smiling, almost-black, perfectly round face of a middle-aged woman wearing an old-fashioned nurse's cap. She was, Paul realized, checking his blood pressure. She pressed her lips together and looked perplexed at his rambling. She did not, Paul thought, speak English. She released the pressure valve on the wrap and for the first time Paul felt the throb of pain in his limbs.

When she finished, the nurse wrote down the measurements on a chart hanging on a nail at the foot of Paul's bed. At the door she paused and said, in a lovely British/BBC accent, "You have the foulest tongue I have ever heard," and walked out.

Paul wondered what he'd said in his sleep.

He was not tied but his chest was bandaged, and as he struggled to sit up the muscles seized and he realized that he had a broken rib. At least one. And the bones in his shoulder blades didn't feel too good, either. He looked to his left and saw a soldier with a sten gun slung over his shoulder sitting in a chair and reading the afternoon newspaper. The soldier was also quite dark, with a thin little caterpillar-moustache. He wore a khaki uniform with a maroon beret with some gold braid looped over his right shoulder, so Paul guessed the soldier was some kind of special muckety-muck and not a cop. That was good news. Maybe.

The soldier looked at Paul and Paul, not knowing what else to do, waved. The movement was cut short by the pain stabbing in his ribs, and he winced.

The soldier grunted and went back to reading his paper. The nurse returned with a syringe full of clear liquid. No, Paul thought. Not in the ass.

As if reading his mind, the nurse smiled. Revenge, Paul thought, must be sweet.

# Chapter 46

The article lay on Kumar Singh's desk, but Kumar had not looked at it since Sachin responded to his summons. In fact, Kumar had only looked at Sachin once, when the young man first walked through the door. Kumar said, "Sit down," and turned to the window, where he stood, hands behind his back, gazing at the rain, ignoring Sachin for a five full minutes.

For once, Sachin was not nervous. He had written a good story. He had been the first on the scene, discovered the body, described in detail the thickening quality of the blood on the floor, the pudding-like texture, the garnet color, the musical quality of the buzzing flies, the way they fed on the dead man's lips, the eyes that no longer reflected light, the bits of torn skin escaping the swollen edges of the bullet holes, the way the light played off the brass cartridges on the floor, the scent of old gunsmoke in the air, and the reek of death that clung to Sachin's clothes long after he had fled the scene. It was not just another article, it was poetry on the page.

He looked around and wondered if someday this office might be his. Over there, where the bookshelf stood, Sachin would have a glass-faced mahogany cabinet for his art collection: vases perhaps, a brass motif of Shiva dancing, or Ma Kali, a Ganesh carved of black marble and inlaid with colored stones, perhaps a ceremonial sword or knife. It would be a display that reflected good tastes, the abode of an artist, not the lifeless collection of conventional wisdom Kumar hoarded.

At length Kumar said, "So how does it feel to see a dead body?"

Sachin swallowed. "I would rather have seen Anantharaman alive," he said, "though the body makes a better story."

"Dead men make poor subjects for interviews."

"They are known for remaining silent, aren't they?"

"Do you know," Kumar said, "why Sikhs always go about armed?"

Sachin thought. He had heard the lesson in school. "Because they must at all times be prepared to defend their faith?"

"And their honor," Kumar said, his face grave.

"And honor, of course."

Kumar left the window and sat down, reclined in his chair. "And there is another reason," he said, "that being, to remind us of the nearness of death. One step in the wrong direction and all that we have can be undone. All it takes is one stroke." He drew a long, curved dagger from his top drawer. The blade was a dull gray steel mottled with dark lines; the guard a bright silver and ornately carved; the handle, white ivory, inlaid with a Mogul design in gold. He laid the knife on the desk, the blade pointed towards Sachin. "Dead men," he said, "can be made to tell a great deal, if you know how to ask. Dead men *want* their stories told. That way, their death is not in vain. When you have been in this business as long as I have, you learn how to listen—even to the dead. Here are the things you did not observe in your article: was the body face up or face down? Towards the door or away from the door. Were the hands clenched or unclenched? Had he shaved? Was the skin blackened under the nails? Was the bed made? Were all the cigarettes in the ashtray of the same brand, and were they burned to the filter, stubbed out, or both? What was on the table—glasses, plates, or both? Was there a pen or pencil in the room? A phone? A charger or case for a phone? Were there light bands of skin on the fingers or wrists? Did the dead man wear shoes, and if not, where were they? Was there a towel out? Was the sink wet? Was the dust under the bed disturbed? Can you answer these questions?

Sachin closed his eyes and tried to re-live the moment he walked into the room. He had had so little time. "There was a struggle," he said, "the table was on its side and one leg was broken."

"Where was the leg?"

"I don't recall seeing it only that it was missing."

"And the sink?"

"I didn't look."

"Under the bed?"

"What is so important about under the bed?"

"Where do you keep your suitcase when you stay in a hotel?"

"I didn't look, but the suitcase was on the floor and open."

"And the nails?"

Sachin remembered the hands, the way Anantharaman lay spread like Jesus on the floor. "The hands were clenched," he said, "but I did not examine the nails."

"He fought back."

"I would think so."

"Were there glasses out? Plates?"

"No."

"Then he did not know his attacker."

Sachin smiled. "You are very clever, sir."

Kumar shook his head. "It is not so much being clever as being experienced." He paused, nodded sagely, eyed Sachin curiously. "I was taught when I was young. And the phone," he asked, "Was there a phone?"

"Everyone carries a phone," Sachin said. "There must have been one."

"In the room?"

He thought about the room again—recalled the bedsheets in disarray, the open suitcase and the pile of clothes, the creak of the ceiling fan, the way the wet curtains flew in the wind, the sound of the rain, the open red *lungee*, the black, swollen stump where Anantharaman's penis should have been. He shook his head. "No phone, no charger." And then his phone rang. He silenced it.

Kumar clasped his hands and rested his chin thoughtfully on them. "Now that you've proved yourself adept at finding people, there's someone else I want you to find."

Sachin nodded.

"She is a clever one, that girl." He looked at Sachin. "Is she pretty?"

Sachin nodded.

"First she organizes whores for the communists. Now what?"

Sachin shrugged.

"My people tell me you were a bright boy in college," Kumar said. "The trick is to ask the right questions. Remember that. We'll run the story of the killing. It's not too bad. A bit flowery in the descriptions, but my copyeditors will take care of that. Find her. If she calls again, listen. Not just to what she says. Traffic, trains, bells, muzzenins, whatever you can make out. All the clues add up, eventually. This might be the story of the century. I want that girl. Bring her to me. Do that, and your place at the *Express of India* is assured."

# Chapter 47

The southbound train packed in passengers at every station until Zara and Sharmilla were jammed on a bench in the women's carriage in the middle of a group of gossipy college girls headed home from a day of classes. The gossip was the usual mindless stuff—what boy was hot, which girls were sluts, who was failing classes, and who had cheated on their last exams. But then the topic shifted to the latest in a lurid crime wave sweeping Bombay. One of the girls leaned forward and whispered, "My uncle has a shop on Grant Road. He was there when they carried the body out. Somebody cut off—you know—his thing."

Zara caught Sharmilla's eye. She leaned close and whispered, "Did you ever kill anyone?"

"No," Sharmilla said.

"Did you ever want to?"

Sharmilla stared out the window as the train slowed for another station. "Yes," she said. "I did, once."

"Why didn't you?"

"I was only six."

"Six?" Zara nodded, as if wanting to kill someone was a normal part of childhood. Almost as an afterthought she asked, "What happened?"

A glaze seemed to come over Sharmilla's eyes. "Doesn't matter. I hope I never have to. Don't know if I could."

Zara took a deep breath. "I'm going to kill Rane."

"I think your friend is okay."

"He didn't look okay."

"Well, maybe not *okay* okay, but Rane's not going to kill him. He's bluffing."

"Maybe."

"I didn't take six years of psychology for nothing."

Zara made a face.

"What?

"You've been wrong about just about everything."

"Like what?" Sharmilla asked. Right away she wished she hadn't.

189

Zara counted on her fingers. "English, Godbodle, me "

"Okay, I underestimated you."

"You underestimate Rane, too."

"Him? Why?"

"He'll kill English if he gets the chance. And then he'll come for me. And after that who knows?"

Sharmilla shook her head.

"You know how to read?"

"Of course."

"You learn in books how to read between the lines?"

"Yes."

"I learned to read between the sheets. It's not what people say, or what other people say about them. It's not even what they don't say. There's just something about some people that you learn to watch out for. You see it once and you never forget it. It doesn't matter what clothes they wear, what car they drive, or how much they make. Some men are just bad."

The train had come to a complete stop and the women in the carriage became increasingly restless. Many of them were *burqa*-clad and sweating under the heavy layer of cloth. Sharmilla pulled at her veil and Zara swatted at her hand again. "I should have scraped off that *bindi*. Be careful or it shows."

Sharmilla said, "He'll kill me, too?"

"He's wanted you out of the way for a long time. Any excuse will do. How do you like it?" she asked, "Living on borrowed time."

Sharmilla opened her purse and checked the pistol inside. You are attacked by one man. You have nine bullets. What do you do?

"How long do you think before they find the car?" Zara asked.

"They've probably got it by now."

"And how long before they find the phones?"

"If we're lucky, somebody will steal them and it will take the cops all night."

"And if we're not lucky?"

Sharmilla shrugged.

The conversation among the college girls became suddenly quite animated—they were pointed and shouting to other students outside the car. Zara held a finger to her lips and concentrated on the shouting. The train had stopped just short of the station. There was a large crowd milling around outside, and the girls and some of the women outside were calling to one another. "They're searching the women on the train ahead of us," Zara said. "They're making them lift their veils."

# Chapter 48

Rane had a secret—a side to him that nobody knew. When he was angry or tired or depressed or lost or lonely or confused he changed out of his uniform and put on jeans and a nondescript shirt and rode the train. He got on at Grant Road Station, rode to Central Station, then backtracked south past the stinking *koliwalas* of the fish market and the scattering of beer bars and guest houses downhill from them. He passed the *panwala* at the corner by the Old Paper Marts, and the third-rate Chinese restaurants owned by feuding brothers who hadn't spoken to each other in thirty years. There he crossed the road and turned west, towards the sea, and stopped at a tiny shop no wider than its open rollaway door. There a man Rane's age repaired shoes and umbrellas and belt buckles and purses and the snaps and zippers on jackets and coats. The man's name was Pitambari. No first name and no last. Just, Pitambari. He was the neighborhood *Chamar*, the leatherworker. He was also a chess master. From morning till afternoon he worked with his hammer and anvil, pliers, pinchers, awl, needles, scissors, and glue. At two on the dot he put down what he was doing and set up his chessboard on an old fruit crate. The board took up nearly the whole of his closet-sized shop. Opponents would already be waiting in queue. One would sit down opposite Pitambari and a crowd would gather as though it were a sporting event. And it was, of a sort. There was even a peanut vendor and a *chaiwala*. If there were no major sporting events in the offing, the neighborhood bookie came around taking bets on how many moves Pitambari's opponent would last.

Pitambari had never played in a tournament, never read a book on chess. In fact, he could neither read nor write. Rane had never beaten him. No one in the neighborhood had ever beaten him. No one had even heard of Pitambari being beaten. Legend has it Pitambari had *never* been beaten. If he had, it was not in his shop, not on the scratched and faded and uneven wooden board he called his own. Pitambari chose which color he would play, and he played every game that day in whichever color he selected. If he played white, he used the same opening for every opponent.

If he played black, he varied his defense, though he inclined towards one, given the opportunity to use it.

Pitambari did not play with the grave silence of the traditional chess master, but rather, held forth like a court jester, part sage, part fool, an endless fountain of profundity and trivia uttered with a toothy grin. He dispensed advice on chess, marriage, diet, religion, war, the stock market, education, the raising of children, the care of elders, farming, astronomy, astrology, art, medicine, history, and nuclear physics. He was short and bald, dressed every day in tan trousers and a white, short-sleeved shirt worn open to the third button. He repaired shoes but went shoeless himself, wearing only a pair of old rubber flip-flops when it rained. The walls of his shop were lined with unclaimed shoes left by customers, but Pitambari would neither wear nor sell them.

Rane arrived and took his place in queue.

The crowd was discussing a recent incident in the neighborhood where a wandering *saddhu* had been obstructing traffic by urinating in the middle of the road. Pitambari leaped from the chessboard to the sidewalk and struck the classic oratory pose: left arm folded across his chest, right arm raised, index finger pointing heavenward. "In India," he said, "every man is a king, and every place a toilet!" He scanned the chessboard amid a chorus of laughter, saw that his opponent had moved. He countered and returned to the crowd.

Six moves later his opponent conceded. The queue shifted. A heavy rain began to fall. Pitambari stood on the sidewalk, puzzled. "The rain has come early," he said. "You know what they say about the umbrella business? We're the only shopkeepers open late when it pours."

He mated the next player in a fourteen move blitz and the queue shifted again. Rane lit a cigarette, watched the traffic pile up. So he gave up the American. The bastard wasn't talking anyway. Every now and then and you find one like him. Who knew what made them tick? Addicted to pain. He'd die before he said anything.

The ambassador called from Delhi. Rane wondered how the hell he found out. The girl? She was nothing but a whore from the country. She didn't have the brains to call the embassy. It could have been Shea's relatives or friends, but even if they knew he missed the plane, how would they have known he was in jail? Wasn't he traveling alone? So who, then? Mistry's girl—Sharmilla? It must have been her, the bitch. She'd been a thorn in Rane's side from day one. All this new-age psychology shit. They should have drowned the whore in jail when they had the chance. And Sharmilla was not so smart either. Sure she had them tracking her phone for the half hour or so it took them to catch the snotty little college kid with the thing in his backpack. Scared the hell out of him. But she slipped up with car. Practically left it in front of the shop. Hiding under the veil. I got a veil you can hide under. When I catch you, he thought, I'll fuck you in the ass just for spite. See how you like that. And I *will* catch her. They've thrown up blockades on practically every corner. He snapped his fingers and five hundred policemen manned barricades, pictures went out over cell phones and the internet. He'd strip-search every damned Muslim woman in Bombay if that's what it took. Let them scream. In the mean time, he'd done all he could. Nothing to do now but wait. You set the trap and see what falls into it.

But that's only half his problem. Now the state police have that fucking American, and the attache will raise holy hell when he sees the bruises. These foreigners—especially Americans—they bruise so easily.

The crowd applauded. Pitambari won again. It was Rane's turn. Pitambari was playing black. The last time they played, Pitambari was also playing black, and Rani thought he had twisted Pitambari's arm into a draw, but the master wriggled loose and queened a pawn in the end game. It only took one false move, Rane thought. He'd been reading up on Fischer vs. Spasky and the world championship played forty years ago. Fischer revived an opening line long-thought dead: the Queen's Gambit. Rane played pawn to queen four. Pitambari countered and Rani offered the gambit, pawn to queen bishop four.

"Woman trouble?" Pitambari asked.

"I'm fishing," Rane replied.

They played on. After a few moves, Pitambari said, "Ahhh, fishing. I know all about fishing. There are three kinds of fishing, did you know that?"

"Three kinds?" Rane asked, disinterestedly. He studied his next move.

"Most fish are caught in a net. That's one. But some people fish with bait and hook. Less effective, but more sport. It requires much skill to catch with the hook. There is the matter of using live bait or a lure, and the knowledge of where to cast."

Rane moved. He had his bishop on the diagonal he wanted, and this seemed to trouble Pitambari, who fell into a deep silence.

Bait and hook, Rane thought. Live bait or lure. The girls will get through the net, he thought. He'd underestimated them again. And he lost the only bait he knew they would come up for. He cursed under his breath. If he only knew where they were going.

Pitambari countered with the knight. Odd, Rane thought. Spasky did the same thing. Had Pitambari's memory failed him? Or had he thought this through to some new line of play? Rane shifted his queen one square.

Every piece on the board takes up space: the space it occupies, the space it attacks, and the space it defends. Rane was driving a wedge into the heart of Pitambari's defense. Pitambari was being squeezed to either side; his forces, so-to-speak, being divided. Chess was all about control, about making your opponent volley in reply to your serve. If I can keep the pressure on, Rane thought. And then he asked, "What's the third kind?"

Pitambari looked puzzled. "Third kind of what?"

"Fishing."

"Oh, yes. That. The third kind," he said, "dynamite." Pitambari moved his king's knight to the king's second.

"Dynamite?" Rane asked. And then the curtains parted in Rane's mind and he saw something oddly abstract. He needed to crack Pitambari's defense, but he could only attack with his queen. But at the same time, he saw—as if by magic—that he could eliminate a troublesome bishop and cement a potential escape route on Pitambari's queen's side. It was a classic sacrifice with all the risks, but if Pitambari took the bait, all the following moves were forced. Eight moves to mate. Rane counted them. He played it out again in his mind. He broke out into a sweat and wiped his face. He ran through the moves a third time, and a fourth. He had to be sure. Pitambari had shifted his attention to the crowd. He was discussing the process of making powdered coffee, and the dangers associated with drinking it. Arsenic. Wasn't that what killed Socrates?

Rane took the bishop. Pitambari returned to the board, a puzzled look creeping across his face.

Rane thought, Godbodle didn't have the phone, and neither did Anantharaman. There's that kid from the *Express of India* snooping around—he might have got it. And then there's the damned *Shiv Sena* —wouldn't *they* love to have it? But who do they know? The dons? He could have sworn the American had it, but it wasn't in his things, and if he had known, why hadn't he broken? He should have broken. He couldn't care about the whore that much. No man could take a beating like that and not talk. Rane smiled at the memory of the beating. Fucking American. It was not so much the beating he enjoyed as the feeling after, when the flood of relief comes over the prisoner. They blubber, they cry, they apologize for making you hit them. They wrap their arms around you like a long-lost lover and, sobbing, and tell you whatever you want to know. All you have to do is ask. Do you do drugs? Yes. Have you stolen from your employer? Yes. Will you lick my boots? Yes. Did you fuck your sister in the ass? Yes. They'll tell you anything and thank you for listening, for making them talk. The girl must be bluffing, he thought. She wanted them to think she got the phone from Godbodle's, but there was no way. They searched the house twice. She had to be bluffing.

"You're bluffing," Pitambari said. He took the queen.

Rane could barely breathe. He was certain that somewhere he miscalculated. He took a pawn, check. Pitambari moved his king.

Check, again.

It was all about anticipation, about forcing moves.

And again.

If he only knew where they were going.

Check.

And then he knew. It was so obvious—he should have known all along. Where would you *not* look for them?

Pitambari froze, his hand hovering over the king, the awareness of his miscalculation dawning on his face. A sea of onlookers closed in around the doorway, the crowd holding its collective breath. They were witnessing the impossible.

Rane would like to have waited, to have seen the look on Pitambari's face when he tipped his king. But instead he rose and stepped out into the rain, the crowd parting soundlessly, almost reverently. He flagged a cab and snapped directions to the driver. As they pulled away he looked back, saw a single face looking out from the crowd with an expression something like awe. He took out his phone and dialed. "We need to meet," he said, "tonight."

# Chapter 49

Outside the train, wet, short-tempered cops swinging *lathees* smacked a crowd of Muslim women into a line against a wobbling chain link fence. On the other side of the fence—which threatened to collapse at any moment—a mob of Muslim men gathered sticks and stones and hurled obscenities at the cops. The rain came down in sheets, soaking all of them. One by one the cops went down the line lifting veils. Zara and Sharmilla shed their caftans and *burqas* in the carriage, and jumped from the opposite door, landing in calf-deep water and falling, sprawling across the next set of tracks. They stumbled across the rails just ahead of a screaming northbound express, but their dash caught the eye of a cop at the far end of the train who shouted for them to stop.

They climbed over the fence on the far side of the tracks and crossed the road running parallel to the trains, then cut down the slope to the western expressway, which was clogged with stalled traffic. Ahead and behind them more cops appeared, zigzagging through the cars. Sharmilla was knocked down by a cyclist driving between the lanes. The cyclist, in turn, struck a car and fell. Sharmilla got up limping. Zara took her by the arm and pulled her along. Behind them, shouting. A fight broke out between drivers.

They skidded in loose muck down an embankment on the far side of the freeway, scrambling to their feet and running south towards the Mithi River. They dodged two cops and ran against traffic in the westbound lanes of Link Road. More cops appeared ahead, piling out of a jeep and blocking their path. Sharmilla cut to her right, Zara following, and they crawled through a culvert under the side road, then climbed another fence and ran down a dirt road across the grounds of an abandoned mill. Behind them, a jeep stopped at the locked gate and a handful of cops shouted.

Sharmilla stopped. Zara bent over gasping for breath, hands resting on her knees.

"We can't go this way," Sharmilla said, panting. "This road," she pointed, "leads to Bandra-Kurla, the biggest police station."

"What then?" Zara asked.

Behind them, the cops scaled the fence.

"This way!" Sharmilla shouted, pointing south. They turned off the road and ran through an abandoned warehouse, where a half-dozen ragpickers and tribals were roasting rats on wires around a flickering campfire. Out the back gate, police running at them from both sides of the building, down another muddy road that sapped the strength from their legs with every sucking step. At the end of the road, a rotten, sagging wooden pier—soft, slimy green boards jutting out over the river. They skipped over the holes and weak spots to the very end and stopped there, looking back. Ahead, only the wide, swirling expanse of oily brown water churning its rain-swollen way, overflowing its banks and flooding a mangrove swamp on the far side as it poured towards Mahim Bay. Behind them, the cops advanced in a line down the pier.

You are attacked by seven men. You have six bullets. What do you do? Without hesitation, Sharmilla jumped. She turned, treading water, and looked back at Zara standing on the pier. "Come on!" she shouted.

Zara looked down at the woman in the water, her face long, her lips trembling. "I can't swim," she said.

Sharmilla shook her head and fought the water. She didn't seem to hear.

"Come on!" she shouted. "We don't have all day."

Zara shook her head. "You go." She pulled the pistol from her bag and turned to face the cops.

Behind her she heard Sharmilla call, "Trust me. I'll carry you."

What is trust? Zara looked down the pier at the police—short, broad men with *lathees*. They stopped, a dozen meters away, when they saw the gun. Zara raised the pistol and fired. And then she jumped.

# Chapter 50

There are two things Zara never understood. The first was why, when Devron Mohamed Ali put his hands on her, it felt dirty and shameful and thrilling all at the same time. The second was why, in her drowning dream, she was never afraid. The feeling was, if anything, peaceful—like an end to her troubles. In both of these things she could see that what the body said and what the mind heard were often two different things. There was what the body willed, and what the heart willed, and when they opposed one another, something had to give. Fate, she thought, must be just like that.

In the water, face down, suspended beneath the surface, Zara was not afraid. Quite the opposite—the feeling was exquisite, rapturous, like something you'd waited your whole life to experience. Or perhaps, more like something you'd fought your whole life against, knowing that it was inevitable. Was this how Jesus felt in his moment of dying on the cross? The body would cease to function in a minute or two. The tides would sweep it out to sea where it would be absorbed back into the elements from which it came, its features forgotten, its history, erased. In the end it did not matter how or where. Dying, Zara decided, was the most beautiful thing in the world. It was the end of all care. The last chore finished. The final door closed. And a hand grasped the back of her blouse.

Above her was the gray, wind-swept sky from which a billion glistening drops of rain hurtled to earth. Ahead of her, she knew, Sharmilla swam with a strong stroke, angling with the current towards the mangroves on the far side. Add to the list of things Zara liked about Sharmilla: she can swim. To the near side, the policemen stood on the edge of the pier, black silhouettes against the slate sky. Zara still grasped the pistol. She raised her hand and fired and they scattered like mice. After that, she closed her eyes and let herself be carried. She could not tell if the crossing lasted two minutes or twenty. She floated like a kitten, hanging relaxed in the mouth of its mother. Stroke. Stroke. Stroke. Faces passed before her. Her family. Devron Mohammed Ali. The agent who sold her to the brothel. The men who raped her. Mrs. Shetty. Godbodle. Rane.

English. She had dreams as a girl, but those dreams resolved themselves into a single request. Help me. You can only go so far on your own. And even if you overcame every obstacle in your path, in the end you find yourself alone. We are connected, not so much by success, but by our failures. Our human weaknesses cause us to depend on one another. That is how life was meant to be, the fate that we can't change. But we can accept it. And the accepting, Zara thought, changes everything. She had survived poverty, ignorance, degradation, and fear, but until Sharmilla pulled her across the river, she had missed life's most important gift. No one has greater love than this, Jesus said. Maybe that was why he said to wash in the water. Maybe that was why he walked across the sea, because as creatures of the dry earth, we were not meant to swim. When Zara felt the muddy bank beneath her, and Sharmilla let go of her blouse and dropped beside her, exhausted, Zara took Sharmilla in her arms and sobbed. She did not weep for sadness and she did not weep for joy. It took a whole lifetime to save up those tears. She wept with relief. For the first time in her life, she had been saved.

Crossing the mangrove swamp and headed towards the slum dwellings of Dharavi, Zara decided that if she survived until morning she would do three things. She would learn to read. She would learn to swim. And she was going to do something with her life to help others. What that was, she didn't know. But she knew the door would open.

# Chapter 51

In the mangrove swamp, Zara and Sharmilla stripped and rang the filthy river water out of their clothes as best they could. They lay on the clothes and let the rain wash them clean while they recovered. After a while, the rising river forced them to their feet. They dressed and struck out across the swamp, feet sucking mud, until they came upon an aging water pipeline that led south into Dharavi, the world's largest slum. They climbed onto the pipe and walked like children—arms held out like wings for balance. In Dharavi they found a *chaiwala* and lunch *dabha* and drank tea and ate *samosas*. Sharmilla had abandoned her purse in the river. Zara had held hers, but when she opened it, mucky water poured out. She paid for the food from a wad of soggy bills. The vendor wrung them out and placed them in his little steel cash box, a disgusted look on his face.

Sharmilla had lost everything: money, gun, even her shoes. She had cut her feet crossing the swamp, and she rinsed the blood in the rain and worried about infections. Zara bought her a pair of rubber flip flops, but there was no chemist in sight, no place to purchase bandages or antibiotics. A little boy passing by offered them a filthy red rag. Sharmilla wrapped it around her foot and tied it the best she could. They sat on plastic buckets outside the lunch *dabha* and watched the rain. "We must look like hell," Sharmilla said. She ran her fingers through the tangles in her hair and looked at her hand. It came away brown and greasy.

Zara giggled.

"Shut up!"

"Don't you wish you had a *burqa* now?"

Sharmilla shook her head. "I need a bath," she said.

"And some dry clothes."

"And a good hot meal."

"And a place to sleep."

"And a good night's sleep. God I'm tired."

Zara said, "I need to get to Gloria Church in Bycula."

"Are we hiding or praying for miracles?" Sharmilla asked.

"A little of both. Someone there will help us."

The TV inside the lunch *dabha* cut to a breaking news story. As if the rain and recent spate of murders wasn't enough, now the Mumbai police were searching the trains for a pair of suicide bombers. The story had all the usual bells and whistles. A raid on a guest house, a foreigner in custody, some timing devices, guns, and money. The Muslim community was up in arms. A crowd gathered around the door. They began to complain—the police, the rain, Hindus, the slumlords.

Sharmilla shook her head and sighed. "Do you know how many cops are looking for us?"

Zara shrugged. "They make trouble, we make trouble."

"Aren't we in enough trouble?"

"You're thinking like a cop again. Confusion is our friend. The trick is to confuse them more than they confuse us."

"What's left?" Sharmilla asked. "Half the city is up in arms."

"The other half?"

Sharmilla thought about this. "The Shiv Sena?"

"That works. What could we do to piss them off?"

Sharmilla said, "Their headquarters is not far."

"So what are we waiting for?" Zara said.

"What do you want to do? Set it on fire?"

"Okay. But could we do that in this rain? We'd have to get inside."

They looked up at the sky. The rain showed no sign of letting up.

"It could do this for days," Zara said.

Sharmilla shook her head. "That place will be guarded like the Prime Minister's house. And if the Saniks caught us, they'd make a session with Rane look like a foot massage."

"All we need is something to get them in the streets."

"Those guys are always pissed off about something," Sharmilla said. "They're on TV every other day."

"We might not have another day."

"We don't have to write the article. All we have to do is piss them off."

Zara took her finger and made marks like writing in the mud in front of her.

Sharmilla said, "I think I'm catching a cold."

Zara wiped out the marks and drew a picture in the mud with her finger.

"Whenever I start to come down with a cold, my mother makes me ginger tea."

"There you go whining again. What, you want me to buy you some tea? Or do you want me to fetch your mother?"

"No, I was just thinking about her, that's all."

"What would your mother do if she was sitting here right now?"

"She'd go shopping for clothes." Sharmilla snapped her finger. "That's it!"

"What? You want to go shopping?"

"There you go, thinking like a criminal again. Think like a cop for a minute. When you're looking for a couple of terrorists on the run, you don't expect them to look like movie stars. When cops on the street look at rich people, we sneer at them. They work for us. They have no right to look."

Zara opened her purse and took out a roll of soggy 1000 rupee notes. "Do you think a store owner would take these?"

"What the hell?" Sharmilla asked. "Where did you get that?"

"I told you. Godbodle's house. But I didn't want to spend it—I wanted to give it back."

Sharmilla stood up. "You're fucking kidding me!" She pushed Zara's hand back into the purse. "Don't go waving it around. Don't you know where you are?"

"Of course I know where I am. You're just thinking like a rich person again."

Sharmilla grabbed Zara by the arm and pulled her away from the bench. "Come on," she said. "I got an idea. First we get some clothes. Then we get your confusion."

# Chapter 52

Mistry, Yadav, and Fernandez sat in the same upstairs room in the Girgaon Station where, less than 48 hours ago, Sharmilla, Mistry, and Fernandez had tried to win Zara's confidence. The tissue with Zara's blood was still wadded on the table. Mistry stared out the window at the crowds streaming down Lamington Road, trying to make their way home from work. Fernandez smoked non-stop. In front of him was an overflowing ashtray. If he dies, Mistry thought, his body will be like a smoked fish—it will never decay.

Only Yadav seemed to take everything in stride. He had a pad of grayish, green-lined paper on the table on which he had drawn a crude map of Bombay. There he marked sightings and purported sightings: x's for confirmed and o's for the rest. The x's began at Dashpante's and ended on the banks of the Mithi River. There were o's scattered from Colaba to Virar and all points in between. Across the river from where the sightings ended was a large mangrove swamp—a nature reserve—and beyond that lay Dharavi, with two million people living in four square kilometers. Talk about the needle in the haystack. And none of the slum dwellers were friends of the police. "Two million eyes," Yadav said, "and the only place on the map without a sighting. My money says she's there." He tapped the map for emphasis.

Fernandez crushed out one cigarette and lit another. "Four million."

"Four million what?"

"Eyes. People have two eyes."

"Three million nine hundred and ninety-nine thousand, nine hundred and ninety-nine," Yadav said. When the others looked at him he added, "I put a guy's eye out in a fight there last year."

"You transferred Sharmilla there," Mistry said." Precisely because it was hostile."

"They probably drowned," Fernandez said. "The river is flooding."

"We're not that lucky."

"They could have been eaten by crocodiles."

"They're not that lucky," Mistry said.

"Who," Fernandez asked. "The girls or the crocodiles?"

"There are no crocodiles," Mistry said. "Not in Mumbai."

Yadav grunted. "Some things even a croc won't swallow."

"It was only wishful thinking," Fernandez said.

Yadav looked at the map. "Two kilometers to Shivaji Park, at least," he said. "Could they have made it in an hour?"

Mistry nodded. "You can walk five kilometers in an hour, easy."

Fernandez said, "I can't."

"Well, most people can. And they certainly could."

"It's a coincidence," Yadav said.

"No," Fernandez said. "Some Muslims got pissed off about the searches. I told you it was a bad idea."

"Where's Rane?" Mistry asked.

Yadav didn't know. Fernandez didn't know. "Wherever he is, he didn't do it," Fernandez said.

Nobody had seen him since he stormed out of the station almost—Mistry looked at his watch—four hours ago. He didn't answer his phone. He wasn't at his house.

At about 4:30 someone hung a garland of shoes around the neck of the bust of Bal Thackaray's mother, smeared mud on her face, and all hell broke loose in at the Shiv Sena headquarters. The Saniks organized a *bundh* and took to the streets smashing windows and setting fires. The press was calling it 6-1-1. Terrorists, rain, and riots. What next? Earthquakes, floods, and fires? Mistry turned from the window and found Yadav and Fernandez watching him. "What?" he said.

"She's your girlfriend," Fernandez said. "Where are they going?"

"To hell in a handbasket," Mistry said. "I thought I knew her once. Now, well, who knows?"

# Chapter 53

Ashok knew exactly where they were going. He was never in doubt. It was so obvious when you thought about it. He had spent enough time in the extortion racket to know that, sooner or later, they all come home. And bad weather was the best time to find people. Everyone looks for shelter when the shit hits the fan.

He watched the riots from the window of one of his apartments, one which, coincidentally, overlooked Shivaji Park and the statue of Bal Thackeray's mother. He didn't see the vandals. According to the television, nobody did. Or if they did, they weren't saying.

He was taking an afternoon nap with Ranjani when she sat bolt upright in bed and said, "What's that?"

'That' was a long, sustained roar from the street below.

Ashok unwound from the covers and sauntered to the window, opened it wide, and despite the fact that he was naked, leaned out into the wind and rain. A mob had formed at the entrance of the park, near a small covered monument—the bust of Meenatai Thackeray. He listened to their shrieking until he understood, then he laughed until a coughing fit overtook him. He closed the window and lit a cigarette.

"What is it?" Ranjani asked, the covers clutched to her breasts.

"Some miscreants have defaced the statue," he replied. "The Saniks are going mad."

And then the phone rang. He listened. "Okay," he said. "When?" He hung up.

"Who was that?" Ranjani asked.

"Nothing," Ashok said. He inhaled deeply and then crushed out the cigarette. "A little job for later on. We weren't going out tonight anyway. Not in this traffic."

# Chapter 54

Paul opened his eyes and smelled food—something earthy and spicy. He was lying on his back staring at a white ceiling. He rolled to his left—wincing in pain—and looked at the floor, where he saw a plate with some leftover rice and *dal* and *chapattis*. The plate lay at the feet of the same soldier he saw before. The soldier had folded the newspaper and was now reading what looked to be—from the lurid drawing of a man and woman on the cover—a trashy novel.

At the sight of the food Paul realized he was starving. He also realized that the room was permeated by a dull roar, almost like the sound of the sea. He thought for a moment that his hearing was damaged, and considered that he might be still groggy from the drugs. But the noise persisted, so he asked, "What's that sound?"

The soldier looked up from his book but said nothing.

The door opened and another soldier poked his head in, said something in Hindi that Paul couldn't understand, then shut the door. The soldier lay the book down and went to the window.

Paul listened. Somebody sounded pissed off. A bunch of somebodies, by the sound of it. He lay back flat and wondered what the fuss was about.

Paul wondered if he'd been legally arrested, if there was any paperwork on his detention, and if so, whether the embassy had been notified. He remembered what Zara said—that he was in trouble. He thought, Well, this is what trouble looks like. He considered his options. He could think of two. The first was that he could do nothing until the cavalry arrived—which might not happen, given what had transpired so far. The other was that he could try to escape. He felt like shit, but the skinny guy at the window looked like a good sneeze might break him in half. Was there a third option? Flying saucers? The storming of the Bastille? During revolutions, the upstarts always attacked prisons—let their buddies out. But Paul didn't have any buddies in the revolution, if this was a revolution. On the other hand, Paul thought, whatever the heck it was, it sounded like perfect cover.

There was at least one soldier outside the door. Would there be more? If so, there was a pretty good chance they might be preoccupied. He decided on option number two. He pushed back the sheets and swung his legs over the side of the bed, sat up in spite of the stabbing pain in his ribs. The soldier turned and jabbered at Paul, gesturing that he should remain in bed, but Paul played dumb, stood unsteadily, leaned against the wall for support, and, finding his legs, crossed the room.

The soldier frowned and repeated his instructions, raising his voice.

Paul held his right hand up, said, "Okay, Okay," but still went to the window and looked out. The room was a double, but Paul was the only patient. It was perhaps twelve by twelve, clean, and painted a bright white, with bright white tiles on the floor.

They were high up in the building. How high Paul couldn't tell. Tenth floor, maybe. Hard to guess. The window faced west. Paul knew this because, perhaps a half-mile away, he saw the flat, gray line of the Arabian Sea, barely visible in the driving rain that enveloped the city. Paul couldn't even see the beach. He oriented north and south, and took in the scene in the street below. In spite of the downpour, it was choked with a mob streaming from the north to the south. They were shouting and chanting —Paul had no idea what—but he knew that the mob was Hindu by all the orange they wore. He saw one man with a trident and lots of others with swords. While he watched, a group of youths uprooted a traffic sign and used it as a battering ram to break down the rollaway door of shop selling and servicing mobile phones. A portion of the crowd veered off and a fight broke out as they looted the place. On the ground in front of the hospital, a line of steel-helmeted Bombay cops armed with shields and *lathees* watched and did nothing.

The soldier looked out the window, pointed, and said something lighthearted-sounding about the situation. He looked at Paul and then back down at the scene below. Paul looked at the back of the soldier's head, thought, Sorry, pal, and (braced for the pain) threw the best left hook he ever threw in his life. The punch caught the soldier flush on the temple. His mouth open, a look of amazement frozen on his face, he fell rigid as a tree. Halfway down he struck the iron headboard of the other bed on his right temple and he went boneless. His eyes rolled back in his head and he slapped the floor like a wet rag and lay still.

Paul relieved the soldier of his sten gun. He opened a medicine cabinet and found a roll of tape and taped the soldier's hands behind his back. He plugged the soldier's mouth with gauze and taped it, too. Paul looked at the soldier. He would take his clothes, but they were far too small. Instead he pulled back the covers and stuffed the still-limp body under the sheets and pulled the covers up to its nose.

Paul opened the door a crack and made a nonsense sound he hoped would sound something like Hindi, and waited for the second soldier to come in. When he did, Paul stuck the gun to the back of the soldiers head and said, "One move, motherfucker. See what happens."

The soldier had either seen enough movies or spoke enough English to grasp the situation. His hands flew up and he dropped to his knees and began his own stream of jabber. Paul relieved him of his rifle—a Vietnam-era version of the Kalashnikov—and then kicked the soldier to the floor, face down. This one, Paul decided, would have to do. "Strip," he said.

The soldier stripped to his skivvies and Paul taped his hands behind his back and his mouth shut, then dressed in the soldier's uniform. It was too short and too tight. He knew the disguise wouldn't fool anybody for long, but it would serve at first glance. He checked the soldiers' wallets. The two had, between them, almost 1000 rupees. He shoved the clip from the Kalashnikov into his back pocket and left the empty gun behind. He checked the clip and safety on the sten gun, and chambered a shell. He tied the near-naked soldier to the bedpost with a sheet, then looked into the eyes of the young man pleading silently with Paul not to hurt him. Sorry kid, he thought. He took the Kalashnikov and aimed the butt at the soldier's forehead.

Paul opened the door a crack and made the nonsense noise again. Nothing happened. He took a deep breath and peeked outside: nothing but a nurse, her back to him, pushing a cart down the far end of the hall. He looked left and right, saw a hand-painted sign that said exit, and did.

Paul ran track in high school and the thing he hated most was running stairs. There's nothing like climbing up or down after a good five-miler to put the fear of God into you. No wonder the coaches used stairs for punishment. But Paul was not in high school, hadn't run five miles in more than six months, and after being used as a punching bag by Rane for most of the afternoon, felt like each flight, if not each step, might kill him.

He closed his eyes, hung on to the rail, and pushed on. One more. One more. One more. At the fourth floor he saw a cluster of signs hand-painted in blue in English and in Hindi, but one word caught his eye: laundry. Inside was a dark, damp space taking up half the fourth floor but divided, by wooden partitions, into smaller cubicles. Along one wall were closets and Paul kicked one door open, and then another, before the pain in his ribs and back forced him to his knees. A wave of darkness passed over him. The closets contained plastic jugs Paul presumed were cleaning supplies. He spied a hamper by what looked like the world's longest ironing board. He struggled to his feet and limped to the hamper—it was full of dirty clothes. He pulled out a white shirt and found the front saturated with blood.

Someone shouted and Paul looked up, saw a puzzled worker in a tan laborer's uniform. Paul shouted back, held up the bloody shirt. The worker gestured that Paul should follow him. Around a corner, the worker pointed to a room where hundreds of garments lay folded and stacked, sorted like mail onto shelves along the wall. The worker watched while Paul rummaged through the boxes until he found the largest shirt and pants there. They were white, but that was okay. On his way out, he grabbed a large red rag and a thin white towel. He left. The worker said nothing. Out of sight by the stairway, Paul changed clothes, fashioned the rag around his head like a bandana, and wrapped the gun in the towel.

He gimped downstairs to the ground floor where he found a crowd of frightened staff and workers barricading the main entry with desks and tables and chairs and couches. He turned down a hall lined with identical doors. Paul presumed the hall housed administrators: accountants and purchasing agents and the like. He tried handles until he found an unlocked door. Inside, a heavy-lidded young man behind a desk stared at a computer. The blinds were drawn and the light was out, but the room was lit by the glow from the monitor. The man seemed indignant at the interruption and shouted something short and sharp to Paul, which Paul countered by uncovering the sten gun and pointing it at the man. He walked around the desk and saw that the man was surfing porn.

The man rose and began to shake his fist at Paul.

Paul asked, "Do you speak English?"

The man said nothing.

"Sit down and shut up," Paul said.

The man did not move, but he did shut up. Paul looked at the porn, a busty blond astride a black man, and made a clucking sound with his tongue. He yanked the blinds up and saw that the window faced a small paved lot with a loading bay on the back side of the building. There was a cluster of blue-uniformed private security guards huddled against the wall by the gate, but no one near the window. The window was solid—there was no way to open it—but the butt of the sten gun made short work of the glass. Paul wrapped the gun back in the towel and climbed painfully through the window and dropped to the ground.

The security guards looked at Paul but said nothing. He walked past them to the gate and out into the alley. At the end of the alley a police line faced the protestors. The crowd was loud but preoccupied with looting the stores across the street and not with the hospital. Paul tapped a policeman on the shoulder and pointed out. The cop eyed him suspiciously, but then

Paul pointed to the stitches in his lip and eye. The cop waved him past, and Paul blended into the southbound crowd and disappeared.

# Chapter 55

W hen the adrenaline wore off, Paul swerved out of the crowd and hid from the rain under the shelter of some trees in a Jewish Cemetery that rose from nowhere in front of him like something from a bad dream. He felt like all the blood had run out of him. He lay his head on his knees and tried to muster something. Anything. He'd figured out where he was—Joshi Marg—one of the main north-south roads in Bombay, and he knew if he could make it just a few kilometers south, he'd be back in what he called his 'Bombay stomping grounds'—his home territory. He leaned against the tree and blacked out, and when he awoke he was sitting in three inches of water and shivering uncontrollably. The mob was gone, but traffic was backed up in either direction as for as far as he could see. It was so bad that many drivers simply got out, abandoned their cars, and walked home—and that didn't help traffic any. Even the busses and cabs sat empty—it was faster to walk.

Paul knew he should call somebody, but who? He had not memorized his friends' ten digit Indian telephone numbers. Even if he had, since the cops took his phone, there was a rock-solid chance they'd be monitoring those numbers. Especially when they found out that he flew the coop. He needed to see someone in person. He backtracked to Jacob's Circle and turned down Nair Road. He bought *chai* and some biscuits. That helped his blood sugar, at least temporarily, though he was so hungry he could, as they say in America, eat a horse. He continued south towards Mumbai Central Station.

He passed the station, which was in utter chaos, with cops and soldiers in the street, everywhere searching people, and everywhere angry mobs chanting and shaking fists and swords at one another. And in amongst the rioters were half-a-gazillion ordinary working stiffs trying to make it home in the rain. He wondered what was up with the searches. India, he thought. Who knows?

He made it to Nana Chowk, by Grant Road Station, where an architect he knew had an office above the market. The office was locked. He stood in the doorway and watched the evening shoppers haggling over the price of vegetables with the vendors. On days like today, Paul guessed, prices, like tempers, went up. Everyone was frightened and in a bad mood. It was going to be one of those disaster days that everyone in Bombay would talk about for years, like the time a meter of rain fell in twenty-four hours.

In the lane Paul found a vendor who had set up a gas skillet under an umbrella and was selling *pav baji*. Paul bought a plate and two rolls even though he hated *pav baji*. He ate voraciously, squatting on his haunches and using the gun wrapped in the towel for a table. When he finished, he tossed his plate and bought a bottle of water. He spotted a shopper who looked like a student and asked him what the stir was about. The kid shook his head and launched into a tirade about politics tearing India apart. In the end he got to the point—a couple of LeT terrorists tried to blow up a commuter train. The cops were out chasing them and then some angry Muslims defaced a statue of Bal Thackaray's mother. Now the Shiv Sena was protesting the Muslims who were protesting the cops who were looking for the terrorists. And heaven help us all if the mobs got together. In Gujarat, mobs killed thousands of Muslims a few years back after a rail car full of Hindu pilgrims caught fire and burned in a Muslim slum.

Paul wondered who Bal Thackaray was, and why defacing a statue was such a big deal. Wash it off and move on. It's only a statue.

"Who would do such a thing?" the student asked.

Paul shrugged his shoulders. Who knows? He walked away. And then he stopped, in the middle of the lane, a thousand people moving in streams around him, and thought, Christ, if it wasn't for all this shit-storm going on, the cops would probably be out in force looking for *me*. And he thought, She couldn't have. But he knew that she did. Her house was not far. If she wasn't there now, he thought, she would be soon.

Along the way Paul threw up all the *pav baji* and bread, and after that, he shit blood. It was embarrassing, huddling in an alley with his pants around his knees, but what else could he do? The cramps clamped him almost in two. He could not stand. Eventually a passerby—alarmed perhaps, at seeing a foreigner in distress—helped Paul to his feet. The man gestured down the road and jabbered at Paul in Hindi. Paul caught the word "hospital," pushed the man away, and stumbled on. He didn't mean to be rude, and he knew he must have looked crazy, but he was in no state of mind to explain. It was all he could do to walk. And he sure as hell wasn't going to a hospital. He found a bootblack, a poor Dalit boy walking disconsolately in the rain. Nobody getting their shoes shined in this shitstorm. Paul bought a rag from the boy and tin of brown polish. The boy was so ecstatic he ran straight across the street to a liquor store.

Paul passed the Girgaon Police station. Standing in an alley just south of that he rubbed polish onto his arms and hands and face. The smell was pungent, alcoholy. It stung his eyes. It felt greasy. The rain beaded up on his skin, but the stain held. There was probably a warning on the can to avoid contact with skin, but what of it? Paul remembered to rub the stain into his eyelids and behind his ears, caught the edges of his beard, covered the bald spot on the back of his head. He kicked off his shoes and stained his bare feet and his legs up to his knees. They're looking for a white man, he thought. Let them look. He left his shoes on a trash pile where someone would find them.

He approached the alley from Lamington Road, the same spot where only two nights before he had kissed Zara goodbye. The alley was too quiet for his tastes, but he walked down the middle of the road. Not a soul stirred. Even the windows in the surrounding buildings were dark.

Krishna the pimp materialized out of the shadows and blocked Paul's way. The recognition dawned slowly. He pushed Paul against the wall of the building opposite the whorehouse. In the shadows he said, "Police come, you go."

Paul was glad for ever cent he'd given Krishna, every beer he'd bought since the last time they almost fought. "Zara?" he asked.

Krishna shook his head. He was clearly agitated. "You go," he hissed. "Police come."

Paul dug in his pocket and pulled out a sodden wad of hundred rupee notes. He pressed five into Krishna's hand. "Bring me whiskey," he said. "Big bottle. And one for you."

Krishna looked at the money, then at Paul. Paul slid the sten gun from the folds of the towel and Krishna's eyes bulged. He took the money and returned with the whiskey.

# Chapter 56

Sometimes on slow nights, sitting in the confessional, Father Greepa closed his eyes and pictured himself writing a book about his experiences. It would be a series of monologues between an aging, cynical priest and the endless line of parishioners who peered at him through the grating and whispered their confessions. He wondered if it were possible to tell a story entirely from the confines of a 3 x 3 x 8 box? Why not? It had probably never been done. It might make him famous. He imagined the protagonist, weary, balding, with sagging jowls, a pot belly, scoliosis, varicose veins, and a nagging prostate problem. Not exactly an action hero, but cerebral, likeable. Someone you can warm up to because they understand your suffering. And true, while not very interesting in and of himself—oh what a cast of characters to work with: the supplicants whose eyes he knew so well, peering back at him through the embroidered screen that separated parishioner from priest, good from evil, so to speak. In their eyes he read the fear, pain, sorrow, the vacant slack-jawed stare of the alcoholic or drug abuser, the red-rimmed jumpiness of the sociopath as he or she wove a web of lies. Why, he wondered, seek absolution, while adding to one's sins? In his book he would tell why—because he had the power to save souls.

Father Greepa sighed. In real life he feared that he could not save souls. Even, he thought, his own. He was seventy-one. He had asked for a replacement three years ago, but so far, there had been no response. He would probably die in Bombay, sitting in his confessional at the Gloria Church in Byculla. He might be dead for a week before anyone noticed. Would God absolve you of sins if you confessed them to dead priest?

It was hot in the confessional. A few years ago Father Greepa had a small fan installed, but it broke after only two weeks, and he did not have the heart to ask the electrician, a parishioner, to return to repair it. Instead, he pretended every time he saw the man that the fan was fine and he was grateful. It didn't matter. Add to his ills that his hearing was failing. He could barely hear his parishioners over the fan's hum when it *had* worked. He twirled the blade with his finger. Tonight it was more the humidity than the heat. The church, almost 100 years old, was designed like an English cathedral, and was not built to move air in the way the local mosques did. The roof leaked. The stones sweated moisture even when it wasn't raining, and everything mildewed. In heavy rains like today, the sewers backed up and flooded. What to do? There were so many things about India that the British never saw, or never accepted if they did.

Father Greepa had said the 8:00 PM mass and heard confession— not that a small crowd of mostly octogenarian widows had much to confess. A jealous episode over another's recipe for gingered bananas, lustful dreams in an afternoon nap, Mrs. D'Souza's weekly anguish that she did not kiss her husband goodbye the morning he rode off to work on his bicycle, as he had ridden off every morning for forty-five years, the day he was killed by a runaway truck at the bottom of the hill where Pedder Road intersects with Warden Road.

"No matter," Father Greepa said. "Your husband knew that you loved him. And God knew that you loved him. Your actions over the years spoke louder than words." What Father Greepa wanted to say, but didn't, was this: So what? You'll be dead in a year and then you can kiss him all you want in hell for all I care. You were a frigid old scold who hated his guts and made his life miserable. You think he didn't confess his sins to me, too? That girl and the bastard kids he kept in a flat in Cotton Green? That time he caught you with his brother? His *brother*? And now you want to pose as a devoted, grieving widow? He bit his tongue, closed his eyes, and thought, Sorry. He sighed. Perhaps people change. It had been a difficult week.

He listened for the scrape of feet across the stone floor, for the creak of the confessional door to open and the snick of the latch when it closed, but no one came. He was sometimes so lonely that he prayed for parishioners to sin so they would come to confession. Alone in the dark he said, "God, have I done anything in my life deserving of a miracle?" And then the door to the confessional opened and a voice said, "Hello."
Through the veil he saw the eyes and his face reddened. "What do you want?" he asked.

"I came to tell you I'm sorry," Zara said.

"But you're not even Catholic."

"I can still be sorry, can't I?"

The priest nodded, twirled the fan absentmindedly. "You're right," he said. "The fault was mine."

"No," she said. "What I did was wrong. I know that now."

"No greater than what wrong was done to you."

"No," she said. "It was one thing to try to change my fate. It was another to do something that affected others. I should have found another way."

"I believe that God will consider that, though you might take into account the opportunity to avail yourself of his mercy while you still can. You did the best you could with what you had. The question now is, What will you do tomorrow?" When she didn't reply he asked, "What do you want?"

"Did you get the phone?"

"I did."

"I want two things."

"What's that?"

"I need a ride home."

"And the second?"

"If you don't hear from me by tomorrow night, destroy it. If you do hear from me, then I need you to bring it to me. I'll tell you where."

"Is that all?"

"Yes. Well, one more thing?"

"What?"

"Can you say a prayer for me?"

"I have prayed for you every night for a long time."

"I'll wait for you out front."

The old priest remembered the night they met. It was his ring that gave him away. He had meant to take it off but he forgot. He realized in a panic, alone with the girl in the room, and slipped it off when he undressed and hid it in his pocket. Later, as he was getting dressed, the ring fell out and rolled under the bed. He had not heard, but Zara picked it up and handed it to him. It impressed him that she was honest. After that, he came to see her regularly, sometimes for sex, sometimes just for companionship. And then one morning he saw her in church. He almost died from shame. What were the odds in a city of thirty million people? He swore he would never see her again, but then, there she was, sitting in the confessional one morning, and she said to him, "Don't worry, your secret is safe." There is, he thought, more than one kind of confessional. That was before the phone call. He should have known. Nothing is done in the dark but that it should be brought out into the light.

He changed in his room, started his reliable old Ambassador in the garage behind the high school. Around the front of the church he found two women, Zara and a stranger, lurking under the eave of the front entry. They climbed into the front seat and sat beside him. He was taken slightly aback. They were dressed in jeans and *salwar* shirts, expensive ones, with garish embroidery, and their wrists shimmered with bangles and their

216

fingers glittered with rings. They wore high heels and carried designer purses. They had their hair made up. He smelled perfume. He nodded meekly at the second girl, a blush rising in his cheeks. He drove to Lamington Road. The traffic had eased.

Sharmilla climbed out but Zara lingered. She laid her hand on the priest's left arm. He looked at her, his face haggard, his eyes hollow. "Before I was a priest," he says, "I had several girlfriends. There was one I wanted to marry, but she . . . I wish. . . I thought that if—"

"No one will know. If I don't call by tomorrow night," she said, "then thank you for helping me." Father Greepa grasped her hand. "I am sorry that I did not do more," he said. "You did more for me than you know. My friendship—"

"It's okay," she said.

After they got, the old priest drove for hours. Alone in the car he said, "Anyone can sin of the flesh. I sinned of pride."

# Chapter 57

Zara watched the priest drive away, then turned and walked down the alley towards the brothel. Sharmilla followed, sticking close to Zara's shoulder. It was more than the usual late-night dark and quiet. The *paan*-seller had rebuilt his little stall—the one the cops ran over when they raided the brothel—but he was gone and the shack padlocked. No point in staying open on a night like tonight. On nights like tonight, when the gods conspired to make the city a nightmare, everybody went home. The house would be quiet, the girls watching TV. There would be few customers, if any. It was a good night to do nothing. Zara looked up and down the alley. The intuition remained that it was too quiet, but at least now she listened.

She heard a sound across the alley, stared into the space between two garbage cans, saw a beggar sprawled on the wet ground. He had spread a scrap of blue plastic tarp over the cans and made a crude shelter. She saw the man fumbling with a bottle, heard the chink of glass, and then it was quiet again.

Sharmilla tugged on Zara's arm. The rain was coming on again, fat drops pattering on the wet stones. They turned into the dark stairway and climbed the steps carefully.

At the head of the stairs they found the gate crudely repaired. There was a chain and padlock, but the door was open. Malika sat in her customary spot on the bench under the statue of Ganesh, her *lathee* in hand. She nodded as if expecting Zara, then eyed Sharmilla curiously.

"This is my friend," Zara said. "She took me into her house. Now I want to take her into mine."

Malika nodded and gestured for them to come in.

Sharmilla looked around the room.

"It's okay," Zara said. "No one will hurt you here."

"Right," Sharmilla whispered, "Like they wouldn't hurt you, either."

Beyond Malika, the girls sat in a semicircle watching television on what was left of the benches encircling the room. The lockers were broken open and most of the drawers missing, the mirrors on the walls were shattered, and the bedroom doors down the hallway had been torn from their hinges, but the statue of Ganesh was not disturbed, and the TV hadn't been touched. Even in a whorehouse, Zara thought, some things were sacred. At least someone had swept up the debris.

The girls looked from Zara to Sharmilla and offered subdued greetings, then drifted back into the program—a silly movie about an accident victim with amnesia who fell in love with a poor girl only to discover that he was not really the poor transport driver everyone thought, but a rich man who had only been in the truck because his car had broken down and he was desperate to make it home to see his rich fiancée. Now he had to choose between the two. It was an old movie and they all knew how it ended. There was only one kind of ending for that kind of movie, but they watched it anyway.

Abishek came in from the kitchen. "Are you hungry?" he asked. He offered them plates of rice and *dal*. Zara ate. Sharmilla declined.

"It won't kill you," Zara said. "I ate your food."

"My kitchen is clean," Sharmilla said. "I've seen roaches in here."

Zara wobbled her head. What to do. "If you don't eat it, they will."

After a while, a couple of merchant seamen came in and the girls lined up for them to choose. Sharmilla clung to Zara's arm and wouldn't get off the bench.

"It's okay," Zara said. "Just look mean. They'll pick someone else."

"I'm not getting up," Sharmilla said.

While they were arguing, one of the seamen chose Lakshmi. No surprise there, but the other seemed set on Sharmilla. The more she argued with Zara, the more he focused his gaze on her. He was from the south, Tamil Nadu, perhaps, or Sri Lanka, where there were also many Tamils. He was tall and dark, with a thick mane of long black hair.

He pointed to Sharmilla, who, suddenly terrified, shook her head frantically. A squabble ensued. Malika swore at the seaman but he became even more insistent.Krishna appeared, and Abishek. The sailor lunged at Sharmilla, but Zara got in between them. She put her hands on his chest and whispered something in his ear. He smiled. Then he took Zara by the hand and led her down the hall to the A/C room.

When they were gone, Malika herded Sharmilla up the stairs to the loft. "Stay here," she said. Alone in the room, Sharmilla crossed to the window and looked down into the alley below. The room had an evil feel. There was a single mattress against one wall, some trunks and boxes stacked along the other. Sharmilla returned to the door and looked down the stairs. She thought of Zara with the sailor, pictured her naked and on a grimy bed with the man on top of her. She cringed. How could she? But then she thought, She's doing it so I won't have to. She closed her eyes, but in the dark she smelled Uncle Wet Eyes, felt his hands on the nubs of her breasts, between her thighs. She wanted to vomit. What would have happened to me, she wondered, if my family had not had money?

She returned to the window and looked down into the alley. There was a man there beside the *paanwala*'s stall, looking up. While she watched, he turned and disappeared into a doorway on the opposite side of the street. And then, a minute later, another man appeared.

Sharmilla felt a chill. She went to the boxes, none of which were locked, and opened them one at time, feeling in the dark for something heavy or something sharp.

# Chapter 58

T he sound of rain on plastic brought back memories of Vietnam even when Paul was home in America. The heat and smell of Bombay only made the feeling stronger. You're huddled under a pup tent with a machine gun in your hand. But it's 2008, not 1966. And you thought you had left your past behind. There were so many things Paul thought he left behind—wanted to leave behind—when his freedom bird touched down in San Diego. He thought he left the army and he thought he left the war. He thought he left drugs and booze and killing. When he met Anne he thought he'd left his wild ways behind. It had been more than twenty years since Paul had a drink, a toke, or a shot of morphine that wasn't administered in an ER. Almost forty years since he held a gun. Now it felt like yesterday. His hands had not forgotten, even if his mind tried to black it all out. He'd never expected to be in a whorehouse again, either. But some things follow you sure as your shadow. And now he was shitting and shaking, and the only thing he could keep down was whiskey, and it was not the burn in the gut he wanted, but the old anger—the bravado with which nineteen-year-olds block out fear—block out the incomprehensible act of ending another human being's life. Maybe, he thought, fate worked in reverse. It wasn't newly minted by the universe. You thought you left your past behind, but really, everything you did came back to you. He remembered a line from *The Teachings of Don Juan*, "Sometimes death just turns off his headlights." It was just like old times. He was hunting in the dark.

The rains slacked off. Paul knew that Zara knew he was there. She saw him when she passed. He didn't know the other woman, but that didn't worry him. Rane worried him. If Rane knew he was here—well, what's the use in an ambush if they expect you? That's when you really get fucked.

And they had to know he had the sten gun. They wouldn't underestimate him twice. Rane, Paul thought, wouldn't come in a uniform, and he wouldn't come alone. As for the rest, he'd just have to take his chances.

He took another hit from the bottle, and squinted into headlights as a car turned into the alley. A cab. It stopped and a couple of drunken sailors got out and headed up the stairs. He sipped and waited. It would be easy to lie down and sleep. Lie down and something. Die even. This was a young man's game. He rubbed his palms into his eyes and then ground his knuckles into the gravel by his feet and looked at the blood that oozed from the cuts. On the other hand, he thought, young men make mistakes, too; only theirs were more fundamental—like pride. And then he heard footsteps coming from the other end of the alley.

In the dark, a shadowy figure. A click and a flair of light, then the glow of a cigarette sucked in the dark. The man was tall. He turned away from Paul and Paul couldn't make out the face. He gripped the gun and checked the safety. Old habits die hard. But he was not nineteen, and he felt the wrenching in his gut, the broken ribs stabbing his side with the beating of his heart, the way the bones in his shoulder grated when he twisted or turned.

The man in the alley threw down the cigarette and entered a doorway opposite the brothel. Paul relaxed, then listened. He heard footsteps again, this time approaching from Lamington Road. He held his breath. The man walked by on the opposite side of the alley, almost touching the south-facing wall as he passed. He paused by the *paan* seller's shop, looked up and down the alley, then turned up the stairs to the brothel.

Paul waited five seconds, then ten. From where he crouched he had not seen the man clearly. Had he not come so quickly, Paul would have shifted to where he could have seen better, caught a view of him passing under the streetlight. It might be Rane. It might not. Ten seconds, twenty. He uncoiled from under the tent and stretched painfully in the alley, looked left and right. He listened, then looked carefully at the doorway where the first man disappeared. There was no light, no smoke, no glow, no nothing. He eased along the wall to the stairwell by the *paan* seller's shop. Far above he heard the hollow thud of footsteps and the creak of a metal door on rusty hinges.

# Chapter 59

Sharmilla stood at the door trying to remember everything Zara said in describing the brothel. In the boxes she'd felt only clothes and knick-knacks, cosmetics and jewelry. Nothing useful. She knew they had a cook and a kitchen. They ought to have a knife. She opened the door and crept down the stairs.

In the hallway she froze. Rane beckoned from the main room. He was standing with a .45 in each hand. He gestured with one that she should come closer. Sharmilla came to the end of the hall. Malika and the girls huddled on the bench on the far side of the room beneath the TV. You have no gun and you face one man who has two. What do you do?

"Where is she?" Rane asked.

"I'm . . . looking for her, too," Sharmilla said.

"So I heard. Where is she?"

Sharmilla took a step towards Rane.

He narrowed his eyes. "She has to be here. The two of you have become inseparable."

She took another half-step.

Before I shoot you," Rane said. "There's something I always wanted to know."

"What's that?"

"What you look like naked."

She took another step and he drew back the hammers with his thumbs. "Easy," he said. "I'm in no hurry."

She took another step.

"Easy," he said.

She took another.

And then he kicked her, fast and hard, driving her back into the hallway where she crumpled into a gasping heap on the floor. "The *salwar*," he said. "Take it off."

Sharmilla wanted to throw up. Breathing was painful. But then, in the broken glass on the wall behind Rane, she saw the reflection of a shadowy figure at the top of the stairs. She got to her knees.

"Off," Rane said.

She pulled the *salwar* over her head.

"Now the shoes."

She slipped them off, one at a time, tossing them on the floor in front of Rane.

"And the bra."

She unclasped it, hesitating a moment before letting it fall.

Rane whistled through his teeth. "Pretty bitch for a cop. Too bad I never had the chance to fuck you. We all wanted to, you know. All of us. You were the subject of much conversation."

The figure, Sharmilla saw, had passed the iron gate and gathered in the doorway. She stood slowly, placed one hand on the wall to steady herself. She unfastened the snap on her jeans.

"Shaved?" Rane asked.

Sharmilla looked him in the eye, thought, on me, on me, on me, worked the buttons, one by one, until the jeans parted like a flower. She shimmied and they slid off her hips. She wore black panties.

"And—" Rane said.

There was a solid metallic click as Paul chambered a shell.

Rane froze, open-mouthed.

Paul pressed the gun to the back of Rane's head and pulled the trigger. The gun didn't fire.

Three things happened simultaneously. Paul dove at Rane's back while Sharmilla lunged at his feet. Rane ducked, but fired both guns as he fell. One bullet ricocheted off the marble wall and careened back and forth across the room until it found the bench between Shilpa's legs and left a hole in the wood the size of a two-rupee coin. The other killed the tall merchant marine who had just stepped out into the hall behind Sharmilla.

Paul latched on to Rane's wrists, putting all his weight into keeping the guns pointed down the hall. Rane lay on top of Sharmilla and struggled to stand without letting go of either gun. Sharmilla lay face down under Rane trying to push or twist her way free while keeping Rane from gaining his balance. The girls, except for Malika, huddled screaming on the far wall. Malika leapt to her feet and rained blows at Rane with her *lathee*, but as many found Paul as struck the cop.

Paul knew on a good day he could break Rane like a stick man, guns or no guns. But it wasn't a good day. Paul had two broken ribs and a broken shoulder, he had been shitting blood all night and he hadn't kept down a meal in twenty-four hours. It was all he could do hold on, but he held on with all he had. Still, slowly, Rane pulled himself up to his knees.

Sharmilla clawed at his face.

Malika knocked the gun from Rane's right hand, but Paul and Sharmilla together couldn't stop him from raising his left, pointing it down the hall to where Zara stood, revolver in her hand, pointing uncertainly at the pile of people on the floor.

Zara saw only the face of a man lying on a near-naked woman sandwiched beneath another man, brown and wrinkled like a raisin. She closed her eyes and pulled the trigger. When she opened them Rane was dead. She dropped the gun, sank to her knees, and covered her face with her hands.

Sharmilla scrambled out from under Rane—a feat made less easy because her pants had worked themselves down around her knees. She was drenched with his blood, a pool widening across the floor, running out from the hole in Rane's forehead. She pulled up her jeans and tried to fasten them, while kicking away the other pistol. She fumbled with the buttons until she gave up and sank to the floor, as well.

Paul lay on his back in the blood and thought about the pain in his broken shoulder.

Zara crawled through the muck to his side.

This was what Ashok saw when he came in: three men on their backs in pools of blood, two women sitting by two of the men, a fat woman with a stick standing in the middle of the floor, and bunch of terrified girls huddled under the TV. One of the girls on the floor had a great set of tits. "Which one of you is Zara?" he asked.

Zara got up slowly. Out of habit she pushed back her bangs with the back of her hand and smoothed the front of her *salwar*. Her hands left bloodstains on the shirt. She noticed the blood and wiped her hands on her jeans.

Ashok carried a Glock 9mm in his right hand, a camera phone in his left. He pointed the phone at Zara and said, "Smile." He snapped a photo. "Before and after," he said. "That was before."

Sharmilla stood and moved to Zara's side. She covered her breasts with one hand and held the jeans closed as best she could with the other. "I'm Zara," she said.

Ashok said, "Put your hands in the air, darling, I know who you are." When she did, he took a photo of her, too. "How does it feel?" he asked.

She grunted.

"That's not an answer," he said. "If I heard correctly, I believe Rane's last words were, Are you shaved?' In honor of our friend, I'd like to know the answer to that question. Drop your jeans, darling." He smiled.

Sharmilla shook her jeans down to her ankles and kicked out of them slipped her thumbs into the elastic of her panties. They were bikini style, neither brief nor thong. Black lace, not quite sheer. She looked into his eyes, rolled the top edge forward and down an inch. "Like this?" she asked. And then another inch, and half-inch more.

A look of disappointment crossed Ashok's face. He held the camera at arm's length, aimed at Sharmilla. And then Sachin bashed him in the head with his tire iron. The Glock clattered to the floor, Ashok's eyes rolled up and he fell face first, landing with a solid crack.

Sachin looked around the room, the bodies, the pools of blood, the damaged drawers and mirrors, the girls huddled by the TV.

Paul stood up slowly, looking dazed.

Zara watched slack-jawed.

Sharmilla scrambled back into into her jeans.

Paul picked up the .45 Malika had swatted away from Rane. He ejected a shell, looked carefully at the gun—a Colt, American made. He knew it well. He rolled Ashok over and studied the face. Then he emptied the remaining five rounds into Ashok's chest; a nice tight group, where the heart, if Ashok had one, ought to have been. He tucked the pistol into the waistband of his pants and sat down by Zara on the bench.

Zara rested her head on his shoulder.

Sharmilla picked up the *salwar* blouse. It was soaked in blood. Shilpa got up and went into a back room and returned a minute later with another blouse—pale yellow and serviceable. Sharmilla put it on and sat down beside Zara.

Sachin went out into the entry and came back with his camera case.

The movie had ended. On the TV, a news anchorwoman railed about the day's riots. One of the girls shut it off.

There was a shriek in the hallway. It was Laskshmi and the other merchant marine. They emerged from a bedroom and tiptoed gingerly around the lake of blood spreading across the floor. The merchant marine bolted for the door. Lakshmi stood transfixed.

Sachin shot a dozen photos, working carefully around the room and noting all the details. When he was done, he said, "Do you want me to call the police?"

"I am the police," Sharmilla said.

He nodded. "Do you mind if—" he cocked his head towards the door. "Go ahead."

Zara stood up and looked at the girls still huddled on the bench on the far wall. "Who was it?" she asked. "Who sold us out?" She looked from face to face. What was it Rane had said in the interrogation room? When I look someone in the eyes and they look away, then I know they know.

Lakshmi, Shilpa, Riya, Neera, Geeta, Montaj. Montaj looked away.

"It would have worked," Zara said. "If we'd stuck together. What did they promise you? Money? Your thirty pieces of silver? And after what they did to us, you believed them? It would've worked. We could have got a little flat of our own, an honest job, had a life. None of this would have happened."

Abishek and Krishna appeared, creeping down the hall, past the bodies, through the blood. They carried tattered suitcases. Behind them, the houseboys, Rahim and Ravi, followed—owning nothing and carrying nothing. They picked up speed as they neared the door. When they turned the corner, they bounded down the stairs, taking them two at a time.

Malika followed. Then Montaj. And Shilpa, Riya and the rest, until no one remained but Paul, Zara, and Sharmilla. When the room was empty, Ashok's phone began to ring. Sharmilla picked it up and took a photo of the bodies, Ashok and Rane, face-up on the floor, and waited for the ringing to end. She hit the call back button and sent the photo SMS.

She turned to Paul and said, "You must be Paul. I don't think we've been introduced." But Paul was staring into space and made no answer.

And then Zara stood up. Another man at the door. "Sanjay," she said. "This is not a good time."

# Chapter 60

Sanjay looked at the blood and the bodies on the floor, and at Paul, Sharmilla, and Zara. "You double-crossed me," he said.

"What did you expect? I paid you to do a job and you quit in the middle."

Sanjay looked at the sten gun and the glock on the floor.

Paul, back in the present, rested his hand on the butt of the .45. "Go ahead," he said. "One more won't make any difference."

"We'll settle this later," Zara said.

Sharmilla picked up the Glock. "We don't have time for this," she said. "We gotta go."

"Where?" Zara asked.

"I don't know, but we have to get Paul to a hospital. Look at him."

Paul said, "I'm not going to any damn hospital."

Zara said. "Hospital going."

"Who is this?" Sanjay asked.

"Take me home," Paul said. "It isn't in my name and the cops can't know about it. We'll be okay there."

"You doctor," Zara said.

"Who is he?" Sanjay asked again, pointing at Paul.

"Maneshka will come," Paul said.

"Not now," Zara hissed at Sanjay.

"Do you have another boyfriend?"

Paul looked at Sanjay, then at Zara. "Who the hell is he?"

She looked at Paul and said, "Him thief. He helping." She looked at Sanjay and snapped, "Shut up. Do you have your cab?"

They drove, crossing the Grant Road Flyover before turning down Warden Road, past Breach Candy and then up Napean Sea Road to Paul's apartment. They called Maneshka. He came. "Dear God!" he exclaimed when he saw Paul on the bed. "What have you done?"

"I had a police problem."

Maneshka had saline solution and a pain killer, antibiotics and bandages which at least made it harder for Paul to move. He fretted about x-rays and damaged organs, a possible ruptured spleen, a stroke that might be brought on by a concussion. "You need to be in an ER."

"That's not going to happen," Paul said. "If I die, I die at home, not with some cop beating on me." He remembered another old joke. When I die, I want to go peacefully in my sleep like my grandpa, not screaming in terror like everybody else in his car.

Paul slept, Zara beside him. Maneshka slept on a chair beside the bed. Sanjay slept on the floor. Sharmilla stood watch by the window until dawn.

In the morning when Zara awoke, Sanjay was gone. She sat up in a panic but Sharmilla said, "I sent him to fetch some coffee and snacks."

Zara groaned and checked her purse. It was empty. She threw up her hands and said, "Stupid cop!"

Sharmilla sat down. "He said he would bring coffee. I was trying to be nice."

"He's a thief from Delhi," Zara said. "That's what they do."

Paul woke up, and Mansheka. "What's she talking about?" Paul asked.

"We lost our ride."

"I have a car," Maneshka said.

"I don't think you want to be seen with us," Zara said. "They might kill us."

"She's right," Sharmilla said. "This isn't going to be pretty."

Maneshka shrugged. "I'm eighty-nine years old. If they kill me, so what?" He looked at Paul, Zara, and Sharmilla and shook his head. "If you're serious, and I think you are, then you should take me along. They wouldn't kill you in front of me, would they?"

They thought about this for a moment, then Zara said, "I can make a few more calls."

# Chapter 61

They met at the Girgaon Police Station, arriving one by one, and taking their seats at the table in the big conference room. There was Inspector Yadav, Utam Ganesh, Gabi Fernandez, Ram Pachauri, Prashant Dashpante, Commissioner Parwar, and Romesh Mistry. And there was Kumar Singh from the *Express of India*, with Sachin Bal, and Dr. Maneshka. Charlie Nostrandt came from the consulate, grumbling, with three lawyers whose names nobody knew. And a man named Mayawati came representing the CPI. He and Kumar Singh glared at each other. Lurking in the back of the room were a few other police and two men from Delhi representing the ISI Indian Intelligence. They were there because of the terrorist charges.

Last of all came Sharmilla, Paul, Zara, and Father Greepa. Zara and Sharmilla had bathed, though they hadn't a clean change of clothes. Paul had changed clothes but had only a sponge bath, since he was heavily bandaged. He was still almond brown from the shoe polish, and shaky on his feet. They had to help him up the stairs, but he wasn't going to a hospital until all this was behind him.

Dashpante clapped his hands and said, "Do you have it?"

Zara nodded.

"How do we know?" Pawar asked.

"One of us," Yadav said, "should see."

That started an argument, but Father Greepa said, "I hear confessions in confidence every day. I should look."

"No," Ganesh said, "You're too close to her."

"And what," the priest bristled, "is that supposed to mean?"

"You know exactly what I mean."

The argument raged until Zara said, "I can fix this." The room fell silent. She took the phone and called up a photo, got up and walked around the table. She bent close to Ganesh and showed him the screen, her hand shielding the image from the others' eyes. He nodded. She moved on to Dashpante, then to Yadav and Mayawati.

"Okay," Dashpante said. "I think we get the picture. No pun

intended."

Pawar asked, "So what do you propose we do with it?"

The question set them to arguing again, with the Congress people asserting that the phone should be saved for use later on if there were any incriminating photos of BJP politicians in it. But there was another faction led by Kumar Singh who countered that the phone should be destroyed, precisely to make certain that it did *not* fall into the wrong hands. "You had your shot at it," Singh said. "And you blew it." The ISI men wanted to examine it to consider the terrorist angle but that was shouted down by both sides.

"There is no terrorist angle," Yadav said. "We made that up." Kumar Singh raised his eyebrows and Yadav added, "That was off the record so keep your mouth shut."

"Hey," Zara said, standing up again. "Until I get what I want, nobody gets the phone."

"And what do you want?" Dashpante asked.

She pointed at Paul. "I want him safe and out of the country." She pointed at Sharmilla. "I want her to get a raise and a promotion." And then, her voice fading, she said, "And I want immunity. And I want my wages." She sat down.

Yadav began counting on his fingers. "Let's see," he said, "we have five dead bodies; twenty cases of blackmail; two million angry Muslims; five million angry Saniks; thirty million angry Mumbaikars; charges of sedition, inciting a riot, destruction of property, making terroristic threats, assaulting an officer, escaping from judicial custody, and burglary. We can probably come up with a dozen more. These are chargeable and nonbailable. You set off an international incident. And you want immunity? Are you crazy? We have the whole nation to answer to. Sonia Gandhi is on her way from Delhi as we speak. Someone," he said, "has to pay."

"Sonia Gandhi?" Zara asked.

"Well, two out of three ain't bad," Nostrandt said. "I say you take the envelope."

The room fell silent. All eyes were on Zara. She said, "*The* Sonia Gandhi?"

Kumar Singh cleared his throat. "There is always," he said, "another option."

"And what's that?" Dashpante asked.

Singh opened his briefcase and took out a copy of the *Express of India*. "Has anyone bothered to read the paper today?"

No one had.

Singh opened the paper to page two. "It says here that an unnamed female police officer killed one of Mumbai's most notorious gangsters in an encounter last night in a guest house off Lamington Road." He paused and looked around the table for effect. "The police laid a trap for the man identified as the killer of Inspector Godbodle and the CPI agitator from Kerala. Unfortunately, one officer and a bystander were killed in the exchange of gunfire. I believe," he said, "that this takes into account all the bodies."

A nervous silence settled in the room.

"Page one, of course, is devoted entirely to the alert officers who foiled a potential suicide bombing on the train. The fanatics may have gotten away, but the city—including the Muslim community—is eternally grateful for the prevention of bloodshed. I can, of course, provide names in tomorrow's paper, when the department releases more details about the investigation and the officers involved. Any volunteers?" He looked at Yadav and Parwar.

Nostrandt nodded. "Impressive," he said. "Have you guys got any coffee? Good coffee—not that Nescafe shit."

"What about Mrs. Godbodle?" Mistry asked.

"What about her?" Sharmilla replied.

"She lost a husband and the contents of her safe. She's going to rail about that."

"She's got insurance on the valuables. No doubt she'll claim ten times the value of her loss. And as for Godbodle, he's a hero now." She looked at Dashpante. "The government ought to be able to do something for him. If nothing else, at least the police could report in her favor, if there is an investigation."

Mistry glared at Sharmilla.

Dashpante said, "Well, it would seem that we have something to satisfy everybody." He looked around the table. "Do we have a deal?"

Zara set the phone on the table.

"And now," Ganesh said, "we are back to the question of what to do with it."

The room re-erupted in pandemonium until Paul took the .45 from inside his coat and hammered the phone with the butt. They stared at the pieces. Yadav reached for the remains, but Paul brought the pistol down again, almost catching the inspector's fingers, and then again, and again, and again. "Like it never happened," he said. "Which it shouldn't have to begin with. And if that doesn't satisfy you, you can burn what's left."

Fernandez, who had just lit another cigarette, offered his lighter.

They melted the memory board and then got up to go.

"Not so fast," Sharmilla said. She turned to Zara. "You took care of everything but one thing. What about the gangsters?" She looked around the room. "Nobody made a deal with them."

"That's not our problem now," Dashpante said.

"Not our problem," Yadav agreed.

"But you have to," Sharmilla said. "It isn't fair."

Zara shook her head. "You can't protect me from them."

"We can hide you," Sharmilla said. "We can give you a new name and a job in another city. You have to do something." She looked at Parwar. "You can't just leave her to die."

"She's right," Mayawati said. "Zara's become something of a hero. We have to protect her. We owe her that. Besides, if she's killed there'll be more protests, and we don't need more protests right now."

"Mayawati's right," Kumar Singh said.

"I can take her to America," Paul said. He turned to Charlie. "You can fix that up, can't you?"

"I'm not doing anything for anybody until I get a cup of coffee. And none of that Nescafe shit, either. Jesus, what's wrong with you people?"

"No," Zara said. "No America. No hide." Speaking in Hindi she continued, "There's no place I can run. I'm through with running. Let them come, if they dare."

"Will you come?" Paul asked.

She shook her head. "You fine, me fine. You going, my heart good." She touched her breastbone with her right hand. There was a time, only a few days ago, when Zara would have jumped at the chance to go to America. But so much had happened since then. One door closed but another seemed to open. An idea had formed. It was outrageous, of course, audacious, but no worse than the idea that a few whores could knit their way to freedom. "I want to meet Sonia Gandhi," Zara said.

"What?" Dashpante gasped.

"I want to stand for office in the next election."

"What did she say?" Paul asked. He got the Sonia Gandhi part, but not the rest of the sentence. But it was obvious from the silence that what she had said had stunned everyone.

"The only place to hide is in the open. If I make myself that visible, they might leave me alone. They might have to."

Dashpante sputtered, "You've got to be kidding!"

Kumar Singh said, "It's been done before—Phoolan Devi, the Bandit Queen."

Ram Pachari asked, "How popular do you think she's become?"

"We could do a survey and find out. It would only take a couple of days," Ganesh said.

Fernandez said, "It would certainly make Congress look like we care."

Mayawati stood up and slapped the table, "I propose to run her as a communist. She started the agitation, you know. She's a worker among workers. She belongs in a worker's party!"

"She came to us first," Dashpante said.

"And you refused her."

The argument broke out again. For five minutes they shouted. Then, as if something had been decided, one by one they got up and left the room. Charlie left in search of his coffee. The ISI men and the rest of the cops followed. The lawyers left to draw up papers—the immunity would be in writing. Kumar Singh and Sachin left with Yadav and Pawar to discuss the details of the police investigation. Mayawati stormed out in protest, but not until he promised to call Zara with an offer from the CPI. Dashpante and Ganesh and Fernandez left to arrange the meeting with Sonia Gandhi. And then there was only Father Greepa, Maneshka, Sharmilla, Zara, Paul, and Mistry.

Mistry stood up. At the door he turned to Sharmilla and said, "I underestimated you."

"Which you?" Sharmilla asked.

"All of you. You don't suppose—"

Sharmilla shook her head. "Goodbye, Romesh," she said.

Outside, the world had congealed into a soggy, exhausted morning.

Tiny shreds of monsoon clouds tore by overhead, flowing swiftly up from the south. For the moment there was a splash of sun. The paperboys on the sidewalk chattered about the TERRORISTS TURNED BACK and the MASSACRE ON LAMINGTON ROAD. There were some sensational photos of the corpses. The papers flew off the stacks.

Father Greepa drove away slowly in his old Ambassador.

Dr. Maneshka took Paul and Zara and Sharmilla to Jaslok Hospital. While Paul was being x-rayed, Sharmilla and Zara waited in the lobby. "There's one thing you didn't say," Sharmilla said.

"There's lots of things I didn't say," Zara replied.

"That wasn't the phone."

Zara looked at Sharmilla in mock surprise. "But you saw the pictures." She grinned.

Sharmilla shook her head. "For some reason, I don't trust you."

"You don't trust *me*? After all we've been through? How can I run for office if people don't trust me?"

"*Especially* if you run for office."

Zara smiled. "Can you keep a secret?"

234

Sharmilla nodded.

"There never was a phone—not like you thought. We knew the cops would come for it, so we stored the pictures in somebody else's account."

"Let me guess," Sharmilla said, "Ratni?"

"Ratni? Why would say Ratni?"

"Who would suspect a dead girl?"

"Very good! You should trust your instincts more often. Besides, if I gave up the phone—or at least, the photos—what leverage would I have with the gangsters?"

"You think you can cut a deal on the side?"

"With the pictures," Zara said, "I might be more useful to them alive than dead. At least, for today. I think they'll wait and see. Anyway, I wouldn't be the first politician with ties to the mob."

"Does that mean I'm going to be investigating you again?"

"I hope not," Zara said.

"It's going to feel a little weird," Sharmilla said, "not having you around."

"I could use a place to stay for a night or two. I need a bath and some breakfast if your mother doesn't mind having a girl like me in the house."

"A girl like you? A future MP? We'd be honored. In the mean time, if you're going to meet Sonia Gandhi, we should go shopping. You need a change of clothes."

"When English gets out."

"Of course. When English gets out."

But Paul wasn't getting out. They kept him overnight for observation. "Go," he said, waving his hand towards the door. "Tell Sonia I said hello."

Outside they hailed a cab. On the way to Sharmilla's house Zara said, "You know, if I get elected, I'll need a good secretary. Somebody who can teach me to read and write. And to drive. And swim."

"I don't know much about politics," Sharmilla said.

"You don't know much about police work either, but you did okay."

"You bitch," Sharmilla said. "You ungrateful bitch."

**Melvin Sterne** grew up in Georgia and West Texas. He worked in union construction for 24 years, primarily with the boilermakers' union but also with the ironworkers' and pipe-fitters' unions, before becoming a serious university student. He earned his BA (Magna Cum Laude) from the University of Washington, his MA from the University of California at Davis, and his PhD in Creative Writing from Florida State University.

He has published twenty short stories in national and international magazines, winning several awards for his fiction. He has taught at the American University of Afghanistan, the American University of Bosnia and Herzegovina, and currently directs the Passport to Excellence Program at the S P Jain School of Global Management in Singapore.

The novel, *Zara*, came from a story he heard from a victim of human trafficking he met while traveling in India. Though the novel is fiction, most of the biographical details of Zara's life are true.